MY BEST FRIEND'S SECRET

MEN OF FAIRLAKE

ROMEO ALEXANDER

ROMEO ALEXANDER

Editing by Jo Bird
Beta reading by Melissa R

ADAM

Squirming in my seat, I attempted to ease the ache in my lower back. I'd been driving for hours, and my back steadily grew louder in protest. Sitting like a bent shrimp while I drove certainly hadn't helped.

My trip was nearly done, but now I was paying attention to the growing ache I knew would drive me crazy before long. With a sigh, I eased my truck onto the narrow grass shoulder of the two-lane road. I opened the door and stepped out into the afternoon sunlight, breathing in the fresh, clean scent. It wasn't until then I was reminded of just how much I'd missed the mountain air.

Groaning, I stood up straight and arched my back, begging the muscles to ease their death grip. Then, shaking my shoulders a bit to try to loosen them, my eyes fell to the backdrop lining each side of the road. The Rockies rose against the horizon, blue-gray mountain peaks topped by peaceful caps of white. It was an unusually warm spring, but it looked like it hadn't reached the mountaintops yet.

Turning, I felt a slight tug in my chest as I laid eyes on the sign on the side of the road only a few yards ahead. When I'd left just under a decade ago, the sign had been small, dangling from chains attached to a post. Now it was three times the size, constructed of what looked like two wooden beams stuck into posts made of rocks.

Despite the change, the words printed on the sign were the same as all those years ago, albeit with nicer printing.

"Welcome to Fairlake, the best place in all of Colorado."

I remembered leaving down the same road I now stood on when I was only nineteen and eager to get as far from Fairlake as possible. I'd had my whole life ahead of me and was ready to live it to the fullest. Back then, I had a head full of dreams and all the determination and confidence that comes with being nineteen. Of course, back then, I didn't know what the world had in store for me or just how treacherous living could be.

"You're getting morbid in your old age, Adam," I chided myself, and the thought brought a smile to my face. Serious had always come easy to me, or as my soon-to-be ex-wife liked to call it, depressing. Then again, in the past couple of years, there hadn't been a whole lot about me that she hadn't found depressing, irritating, or downright worthy of loathing.

With a grimace, I pushed the thought away, back to the recesses of my mind where it wouldn't bother me for a while. The past couple of years had been miserable, and despite my return to Fairlake being more of a retreat than a grand return, it was the first good thing to happen to me in months.

The town would be a respite from the chaotic and busy world I'd lived in for years. I looked forward to seeing familiar faces, hearing familiar voices, and perhaps finding some peace in a town that had once seemed so quiet and boring that I thought I'd lose my mind. There were, of course, my parents, who I hadn't been able to see for a few years, and I found the prospect of my mom's home cooking, conversations with my dad over the TV, and a couple of beers to be some of the high points of my return.

Then, of course, there was Bennett. He and his parents had moved to Fairlake when I was only three, but we wouldn't meet until the first grade. At first glance, it was a strange friendship, combining an already quiet and somewhat serious child with a boy who was all energy and laughter. Bennett had been the first person, other than my parents, who hadn't expected me to talk or smile all the time, who had been content to be around me and be happy about it.

The pleasant memories fizzled away, and I was left with guilt while I stared at the new yet somehow still familiar sign. My friendship with Bennett had been so strong, from that first day when I laughed at some stupid comment he'd blurted out to the teacher right up until about five years ago. From the moment I met Bri, so many other things in my life stopped mattering as much.

Sadly, my friendship with Bennett had been one of those things. It had started slowly, but little by little I found less time for him. There was always something that took my attention, some event Bri wanted to drag me to, some work assignment I had to focus on. Over the years, our twice-weekly phone calls became once a week, then once every couple of weeks, maybe once every couple of months. Right up until the past year, where I'd barely had more than a brief text conversation with him.

My back wasn't hurting nearly as much, and I walked back to my truck, hefting myself up into the cab. Glancing in the rearview mirror, I was reminded quickly that the bed of the truck was stuffed with the things of my life that I'd accrued over the past ten years, thinned down to what I thought I would need when I eventually managed to get back on my feet.

I reached for my phone, which I'd tossed onto the passenger seat a few hours before. My brow raised when I realized I had service and a text from my mom.

Hi sweetie. Hope you're being safe! If you're not going to get in too late. Could you pick up a whole chicken from the store? And a gallon of milk?

She and my father were taking me back into their home, and I knew what kind of imposition that was. No matter how much they professed that they were more than happy to help and how nice it would be to see me again, I was still moving back. The lives they had built for the past decade would be interrupted, right along with their habits and living conditions.

So yeah, I was pretty sure I could spare time to grab whatever my mother needed from the store.

It was another ten minutes before I caught sight of Fairlake as I crested a hill. The town had expanded since the last time I saw it, but it still looked as though it were nestled on all sides by forest and mountains, just as it had years ago. From a distance, the symmetrical layout of the town was obvious, including the patch of green in the middle which served as both town square and public park. If there were events, festivals, or even sometimes birthday parties, they would happen there.

Unless the town had changed since my last visit five years before, I knew the town hall sat on the outskirts of the park. The police station and firehouse were nearby, central to the rest of the town. I had never realized before, but clearly whoever designed Fairlake had been one hell of a perfectionist.

Descending into the town, I wasn't surprised to get curious stares from a few people on the sidewalks. Fairlake had never been a huge, bustling tourist town, but strangers weren't unknown. For those seeking a peaceful vacation for a week or two, it was the perfect place. It wasn't so far off the main highways that backroad drivers didn't occasionally pass through, both charmed and befuddled by the slice of small-town Americana that had existed in Fairlake for as long as it had been here.

I was relieved to see that Greene's Market was still there, though its parking lot had grown since I'd last seen it. Finding a spot near the front, I pulled into a parking space and headed inside. The sign was cleaner and new, but nothing else seemed to have changed.

I earned another few curious glances as I entered but hurried toward the back. Only my parents knew I was coming back to town, and I didn't want to have too much interaction with anyone who might recognize me after all these years. There would be too many polite but invasive questions, and if anyone picked up on the fact that I was back due to hardship, there would also be barely contained sympathy.

For the first few days back in Fairlake, I didn't want to deal with anyone, let alone their sympathy.

I managed to find a whole chicken in the frozen section and grabbed a gallon of milk. Habit from the past five years almost had me grab the skim milk, but then I remembered I was shopping for my mother and got the whole milk instead. My family firmly believed that fat was important in all food. It was only my exceedingly health-conscious ex-wife that had me seek out "safer" options.

Making it to the front, I put both things onto the belt and smiled at the cashier. She was young, probably far too young to recognize me. That detail seemed important when trying to buy groceries without being noticed.

"Will that be all?" she asked brightly, looking me over.

"That it will," I replied, pulling my wallet out to grab my card.

"Alrighty then," she said, her eyes lingering on me before moving to the screen beside her. "That'll be—"

"Well, as I live and breathe!" a loud voice called, piercing through the relative quiet of the store.

I twitched and turned, knowing that voice. Mr. Canticle had grown thicker in the middle since the last time I'd seen him, but his face had remarkably remained the same. Narrow and sharp, yet somehow warm and inviting every time he smiled.

"Hey, Mr. Canticle," I greeted warmly, both happy to see a familiar face and uncomfortable for the same reason.

"I almost didn't recognize ya," he said with a chuckle, leaning on the counter. "Adam Jensen, what brings you back to town?"

"That's...well, I'm just back for now," I said with what I hoped was an understanding smile.

"Well, I know your mama and daddy have missed ya," he said, a twinkle in his eyes. "And we all know Bennett has missed you sorely."

"Has he?" I asked vaguely, handing my card to the girl who was now watching me with more interest.

"O' course," he chuckled. "You two were thicker n' thieves once upon a time."

"We were," I agreed with a slight sense of unease.

"And now he's a deputy."

Which I sort of knew. Bennett had joined the police force in Fairlake shortly after I left. He'd sent me a picture of him in his uniform, positively beaming at the camera. It had been so strange seeing him in a new uniform. His once shaggy sandy hair buzzed short, hazel eyes brimming with the familiar glitter of mischief and happiness that he seemed to exude. As proud as he was, I'd teased him that he looked like a little boy playing dress-up.

"Oh, well, that's...good, good for him," I said, feeling

6

another twinge of guilt. Bennett hadn't told me about that, but then again, I hadn't exactly made myself available for him.

"Surprised you didn't know," he chuckled, waving a hand at the cashier. "Don't worry about it, Annie. I think we can afford to let Adam here take a chicken and a gallon of milk. Gettin' it for your ma?"

"Yeah," I said, not wanting to argue with the man. I had already failed at not being recognized. I didn't need to draw more attention to myself.

"How long you stayin' in town?" Mr. Canticle asked, bagging up the groceries for me.

"Not sure at this point," I hedged. In a town this small, there was no chance people wouldn't start talking. I gave it a few days, if that, before everyone knew Adam Jensen had come crawling back home, tail between his legs, the last of his worldly goods stuffed into his truck. The longer I could put off the inevitable sympathy and probing questions, the better. "Haven't made up my mind yet."

"Oh, well, hopefully you can make it to the Flower Festival," he said brightly, looking me over. "Lord, you been driving the whole way here?"

"Uh, yeah."

"From Boston?"

"Thereabout, yeah."

"Good lord, I hope it wasn't a straight drive."

"No, I stopped a couple of times."

"Well, ya look like something the cat dragged in."

"Thanks, Mr. Canticle," I said dryly with a shake of my head. Honestly, I probably didn't want to know what I looked like right now. I had been stuffed in my truck for hours at a time for the past three days.

He chuckled. "Well, might wanna put yourself together

before your ma sees you. Otherwise, she's gonna hem and haw over you constantly."

"She's already going to do that," I told him, taking my groceries. "I expect to be fussed over for at least the next couple of days, if not longer."

"Well, you let her. It's been ages since she's got to see you. Let her have her fun," he told me with a chuckle.

"You got it," I said, raising my free hand in farewell. "You take it easy, both of you."

I nearly cringed when I watched his eyes dart to my hand and linger for a moment. Unthinkingly, I'd raised my left hand, and I was no longer wearing my ring. I had no doubt anyone and everyone knew I'd gotten married four years ago.

"You take care of yourself," Mr. Canticle said with a warm smile that betrayed nothing. I wasn't fooled, though. The Canticles were probably the nosiest and best-informed members of the community. Sure they were kind and incredibly generous, but if you didn't want everyone to know your business, you made sure the Canticles didn't hear about it.

"Sure thing," I said, backing out of the grocery store. I had just earned myself even less time before the whole town found out about me, especially with this juicy little tidbit in the man's gossip list. I could only count myself lucky that I hadn't been pestered with probing questions, even if the young girl at the register had been watching me intently.

Scurrying to my truck, I threw myself in before anyone passing by could recognize me. I set the chicken and milk on the passenger seat and pulled down the visor to flip open the mirror.

"Christ," I muttered, rubbing at my face. There were rings dark enough to make me look like a raccoon under my eyes, which were dark enough as it was. I had been putting off a haircut for too long, and now it was positively shaggy as it drooped down to the top of my ears…when the black strands weren't sticking out like I'd been wearing a hat for days. Coarse, black stubble peppered my cheek because I hadn't been near a razor in days. Then again, I couldn't complain about the stubble since at least it added the illusion of volume to my thin face.

"Fuck it," I muttered, flipping the visor up and turning on my truck. There was a slight hitch as it turned over, but the engine roared and then purred. I would have to see if my dad would let me use the garage to look my car over and see where the issue was.

For any strangers driving into town, it would seem eerie how quiet Fairlake was as I made my way around the central square. However, anyone who lived here knew it was just the quiet hour. Midafternoon was when most people finished their lunches at work, took the first steps toward preparing dinner at home, or enjoyed some quiet time in front of the TV before the peak of the day started.

I knew I had another hour, maybe two at the most, before people flocked onto the streets. Kids let out of school would move in packs, either toward their homes or the edge of town. The central park was too full of adults for most kids and teenagers, and they preferred to play or get into trouble where there weren't any sharp adult eyes around who could whisper their doings to their parents.

What little shopping and entertainment there was in Fairlake was in the center of town, and if you blinked you could easily miss it as you moved into the quiet neighborhoods to the north. It was a little noisier on the west side of town, where the lower-income families lived, and a whole lot more run-down as well. My mother had always warned me away from that part of town, but the kids from the area had always seemed alright for the most part.

I pulled onto my street and felt my shoulders begin to

relax. Very little had changed about the small houses with their spread-out lawns. There were a few with children's toys littering the yard that I was pretty sure had been childless the last time I'd been here, and the thought brought a smile to my face.

Bri and I hadn't decided one way or the other about children. It seemed like there was always something to pull our attention away, or an expense that made us put off having kids. So, she'd kept up with birth control, and I'd even toyed with the idea of getting a vasectomy. I suppose with everything else that happened, choosing not to have kids was probably one of the best decisions we made together.

Pulling into my parents' driveway, I noticed they'd replaced their old Range Rover with a Jeep but still had the old Monte Carlo my mom loved nearly as much as she loved my father and me. They were parked in a line, so I pulled in beside them, turned the truck off, and leaned back in my seat. I mentally braced myself for what was essentially going to be my life for who knew how long.

I would always be grateful that my parents were happy to pick me up and help me when I desperately needed it. However, that didn't change the sting of my pride or the ache of my shame. I'd left Fairlake with an eye full of stars and a head full of dreams, and now I was limping back with an abysmally miserable failed marriage, a business in tatters, and nothing to my name but what I'd managed to stuff in the back of my truck.

I sat up straighter when I saw the front door open, the glass pane catching the afternoon sunlight before my mother stepped out onto the porch. There were smears of dirt on her jeans and stray pieces of plants on the cuffs of her long-sleeved shirt. No doubt I would see more dirt under her nails when I got closer, courtesy of the backyard garden she had maintained for as long as I could remember.

Pushing open the driver's side door, I grabbed the groceries and hopped down onto the driveway. Walking around the truck, I weaved between their vehicles and walked up the narrow path that was, as usual, lined with flowers.

My mother looked me over before wiping her hands on the plain apron around her waist. She put on a broad smile, but I saw the look of alarm and concern on her face before she covered it up.

"Hey, Mom," I said, resisting the urge to shuffle my feet awkwardly. Even while I stood on the ground and she was on the front porch, she still only managed to come up to my chin. Yet now that I was right in front of her, I felt like an awkward ten-year-old boy who couldn't quite find it in himself to admit what he'd broken.

"Hello, sweetheart," she said warmly, stepping forward and wrapping her arms around me.

As every one of my previous girlfriends could attest, I wasn't big on physical affection. Not unless I was extremely comfortable with the other person, and even then there were limits to how much I would accept before growing uncomfortable. The discomfort was even worse when I was feeling down or upset. It had driven many of my ex-girlfriends crazy, Bri in particular, that my reaction to being upset was to retreat into myself and dislike too much physical contact.

My mother, however, was one of the rare exceptions. Touch was one of the ways she showed her love for other people, and I would never deny her, no matter how vulnerable and fragile I felt. If my mother wanted to pull me into a surprisingly tight hug for a woman her size, then I would give it to her gladly.

"I don't know how, but you got bigger and thinner at the same time," she said, pulling back to hold me steady by my

11

shoulders as she looked me over. "And please tell me you didn't sleep in your truck."

"I didn't," I promised. I wasn't so far in the hole financially that I couldn't afford a few nights in cheap motels. On the other hand, I wasn't neck-deep in money either, so it wouldn't be long before I needed to start looking for work.

She continued to look me over, scrutinizing me. "If you say so."

"I didn't, Mom," I said with a roll of my eyes. "I just look like shit because my life is shit at the moment…well, and I spent most of the past three days locked in my truck."

Her eyes drifted toward the truck, her brow quirking. "I thought you'd have a trailer."

"Didn't need one," I said, gesturing toward the truck. "I didn't have much I needed to bring with me."

A shadow passed over her face, and I knew she wasn't taking me at my word. The truth was, most of what I once considered to be mine was still in the spacious apartment I'd shared with Bri. It had been easier to leave her with most of our things if only to avoid another argument in court. It felt like the closer we got to the final steps of our divorce, the more vicious and aggressive Bri and her lawyers became.

At this point, it was easier for me to let her have what she wanted. Anything else would just be another knock-down, drag-out fight, and I was sick and tired of fighting. I just wanted to have time to lick my wounds and try to put the pieces of my life back together.

"Well, all that isn't gonna fit, even if we clean up the basement," she said with a snort. "Which no one's done since we moved in."

"That's fine. I planned on using one of the storage units Mr. Hopkins owns," I said with a shrug.

"It's not Bert anymore. His son took over a few years back," my mother told me, grabbing the groceries. Before I could manage more than a sound of protest, she waved me off. "I think I can manage to carry a tiny chicken and some milk, Adam."

"It's not that tiny," I grumbled, mounting the stairs and following her into the house. "It was the only one they had."

"I doubt it. You and your father wouldn't know your way around the grocery store if you were given a map and compass."

"Mom, no one uses either of those things anymore unless they're out in the woods. Phones take care of everything now."

"Well, it would be handy to learn. You never know when you might find yourself stranded without your phone!"

"Mom," I complained, pulling off my boots and sighing in relief as the cool air hit my socks, "I was in the scouts. I learned how to do all of that, remember?"

She continued down the hallway, straight toward the kitchen. "The real question is whether or not you remember anything."

"I remember enough," I said with a shake of my head. "If I promise to stay away from the woods until I brush up on my navigation skills, can we drop this?"

She stopped in the open doorway, light streaming in to cast a glow about her. "Of course, sweetheart. I'm sure you've had a long enough trip without showing up and having me nag you."

"That's not…" I began and then sighed, letting it go. My mom wasn't often willing to let go of a point she was trying to make. My father and I had learned long ago that you either headed her off at the pass or made yourself comfortable for a lengthy diatribe.

"I'm just so glad you're here," she said, raising her voice as she entered the kitchen to put things away. I wandered to the living room, finding it hadn't changed, still a mix between

Better Homes and Gardens' front page and a hunting lodge. A perfect merger of two, from the soft leather furniture with hand-knit blankets thrown over it to the potted plants in the window and the deer head perched over the fireplace mantle. "And I know your father is just as excited. Honestly, you'd think it was a holiday."

"Yeah, not what I would call it," I muttered, eyes drifting over the pictures on the mantle. There was a younger version of me, barely six years old, grinning from my father's shoulders as we stood on a mountain path overlooking the forest. Me at twelve, a small smile on my face as I held up the badges I'd earned over the summer. My parents, one of them beaming as they stood over the pumpkin that had won them first prize at the harvest festival, and then again looking content together as they stood, their toes digging into a white sandy beach.

"What was that?" she called back to me.

"Just talking to myself," I replied, tapping the frame of the photo from the last Christmas I'd seen them three years ago. Things between Bri and I hadn't quite deteriorated, and the business had been going strong. I had flown my parents out to stay with us, so they could experience Boston with a knowledgeable guide and celebrate with my wife and her family. It was the last time I had a clear and definable memory of being happy and optimistic.

"Oh!" My mother reappeared, wiping her hands dry with a dishcloth. "I didn't want to ask him the last time I saw him, but does Bennett know you're in town?"

"I didn't tell him when I was supposed to show up. I kinda…wanted to get settled in, maybe get on my feet for a bit before I tried socializing," I explained.

"Well, you might not want to put it off for too long."

"Look, I know I should have spoken to him a lot sooner than this, but—"

My mother snorted, waving at me with the towel. "I'm not sticking my nose in all *that*. I meant that Bennett comes around here every so often, and I never know when he's going to stop by."

"Wait, he comes here?" I asked with a raised brow.

"Just because you're not around doesn't mean I can't appreciate seeing Bennett now and again," she told me with a tone that brooked no argument. "Plus, he's friends with that nice Everett man who moved in down the street a few years back."

"Everett?" I asked. The name rang a bell, and after a few seconds I recalled the image of a surly loner, standing apart from the rest of the class whenever possible. Well, except for his friend, whose name I couldn't remember. Bennett would probably remember, considering he knew anyone and everyone, even if they were a couple of years older. "As in, Chase Everett?"

"That's the one," she said brightly. "Nice man, quiet, keeps to himself. I don't know when it happened, but he and Bennett became good friends a little while back. Chase got himself a job at the garage downtown, takes good care of himself."

"Uh, when you say friends," I said slowly, thinking back to Chase and examining what I remembered. He came from the western part of town, and it was widely rumored that he lived with his grandparents because his parents were drug addicts, until his mother had stabbed his father in a rage. He carried himself like someone who didn't want to be bothered with other people, though other than a couple of fights he never made a problem of himself. More importantly for my dear friend Bennett, the Chase I remembered had been tall and built strong, and his broodiness only made him more attractive.

15

My mother turned to look at me curiously. "Unless the meaning of the word has changed since I last knew, yes."

I rolled my eyes. "So, he just started being friends with the guy out of the blue? Like, no rhyme or reason."

She arched a brow. "Bennett could make a dozen friends at a grouch party, so I don't think it's all that weird. Now, if you're asking if they were dating, I don't think so. If you're asking if I think they're doing other things, I'll tell you what I've told others, that it's none of my business and none of theirs either."

I could tell from her tone that she wouldn't tolerate me asking more, so I kept quiet. I didn't know why I was all that interested anyway. Chase had never made too much trouble, but there had always been something unsettling about him that I'd never been able to shake. I had no right to question Bennett's decisions, whether romantic or sexual, especially after I'd pretty much been out of his life for years now.

"Don't you go worrying about what Bennett is or isn't doing or who he is or isn't doing," she scolded, waving the damp towel at me in warning. "That boy might not be able to sit still to save his life, but he's got a good head on his shoulders. And I'll point out that he's an officer of the law and can take care of himself."

"Yes," I agreed, knowing it was the only thing that would spare me the coming rant. I was already feeling worn down and ready to give up. The conversation about Bennett just brought up the guilt I already felt and the shame that made me want to avoid ever looking my old friend in the eye again. "You're right, I know."

"Good," she said. "Now you look about ready to drop. Why don't you get a shower to help you relax and then take a nap? I can wake you up when your father gets home. Or for dinner, whichever you want."

"Dinner's fine," I said with what I hoped was a passable

smile. "I'll probably take, like, today and tomorrow to get back on my feet. Maybe get out of the house, find some work, you know."

"That's a good idea," she said with a wink. "I aired out your old room and changed all the linens. It probably is going to be a little weird staying in a room that hasn't changed, but—"

"I appreciate it, trust me," I told her, retreating to the hallway and taking the old wooden stairs up.

"I love you," she called down the hallway.

"I love you too," I called back, waiting a few heartbeats to see if she would say anything else before continuing up to the second floor.

Once out of sight, I let my shoulders sag and a heavy sigh escaped my lips. I knew my mother was trying her best to help me feel comfortable and not push me too hard, but I knew the questions and the concerns were coming. It would come from a good place, but all I wanted to do was pretend like I was here on vacation for a little while, ignore the reality that had been my life for over two years.

Maybe after that, I could try to make things better...maybe.

BENNETT

"Livington!"

At the sound of my last name, barked out by my apparently irritated-as-hell chief, I jerked hard enough to spill my coffee all over the table in front of me. My partner jumped back, but not fast enough to prevent the steaming hot liquid from dripping into his lap.

"Jesus Christ, Bennett," Jesse hissed, swatting at his lap only to groan when he struck a little too hard.

"Sorry," I muttered, glancing around to find where my chief was. Fairlake wasn't a large town, and our only police station was appropriately sized. That was the theory anyway, but I swore someone had purposefully built it to be like a maze once you got past the lobby and into the heart of the building. "Shit, where is he?"

"Can you go," Jesse grumbled, dabbing at his wet crotch with the tiny napkins that came with our coffees, "one week without getting yelled at for something?"

"I don't know what I did," I insisted, scowling when Jesse rolled his eyes. "I don't!"

"That's literally half the problem, bud," he told me with a

18

sigh. "I'm going to see if I can manage not to cause myself any more scrotal injuries and clean this up in the bathroom. If the chief kills you, please do it away from our paperwork. I don't want to clean up blood."

"You are my *partner*," I hissed, trying to catch him by the sleeve. "You're supposed to back me up, to save me!"

"I can save you from an angry drunk with a baseball bat wrapped in barbed wire, but I can't save you from your own stupidity," he told me with a dark look and made for the bathroom.

Thankfully, our chief wasn't exactly known for being light on his feet, and along with the heavy stomping, I would swear he was growling like an injured grizzly. Seeing a distinctly angry-looking shadow coming down the nearby hallway, I darted in the opposite direction.

"'Scuse me," I whispered hurriedly as I slipped between two other officers talking in the middle of the walkway between cubicles. I barely managed not to cause another coffee massacre.

"What'd you do this time?" Jane asked me, twisting so I wouldn't bump into her cup.

"I'm being framed!" I hissed, darting out of sight.

I managed to turn the corner just in time to hear Chief Price snarl at the two officers, "Where is he?"

I pleaded with Jane with my eyes, hoping she'd take pity on me. She rolled her eyes and shrugged. "Haven't seen him, Chief. Did you try the break room?"

"If I had, I would have saved myself the need to find and strangle him," the chief growled.

Oh shit, so *that's* what this was about. I hadn't expected him to be so angry about a few new decorations in the break room. I mean, god, the place was so depressing, with barely any color among the brown and beige that made up most of the station. A little splash of color and some nice-smelling flowers were exactly what was needed.

Wait, was he allergic to certain flowers?

Crap.

I almost missed the small gesture from Jane's partner, Dick, shooing me away. I didn't miss the approach of heavy footsteps, however, and continued on my way. If I could avoid the chief for the rest of my shift, which was only half an hour, I might be in the clear. He would, of course, find me the minute I came in the next day, but hopefully he'd be calmer by then.

"Fine, then where's Holowitz?" Chief Price growled at them. I swear the man only communicated in grunts, growls, and the occasional snarl. Even when he was being nice, he sounded like a testy bull.

"Haven't seen Jesse," Dick said lightly. "But if either of them heard you coming, you can bet they're hiding."

Jane snorted. "Especially Jesse. He'll want to be as far out of the fallout zone as possible."

I wished I could argue with her assessment, but it was so spot-on I could only feel I should hang my head in shame instead. After six years of partnership, Jesse and I agreed it was better he distance himself from whatever trouble I might find myself in, especially regarding our chief. Jesse had a profound respect for the older man and a deep terror. I only had the former, though when I was being hunted by the small-town, human equivalent of a Xenomorph in uniform, I felt more than just a twinge of fear for my well-being.

Taking the opportunity while I had it, I slowly edged away, making for the next corner. The safest place I could theoretically hide was in the break room, where he'd already checked, or somewhere he wouldn't think of looking for me.

I was busy trying to think of something that would tick that particular box and didn't notice the metal cart in my path. Turning, I smacked my forehead into it, barely stopping myself from making a noise as pain radiated through my skull and down my neck.

"What the hell was that?" the chief asked, still quite annoyed and now suspicious.

"Probably the fax," Jane said, sounding more casual than anyone had a right to be with Chief Price growling in their face. "I keep telling you that thing is older than you are and needs to be priced."

"I'm not that old, and that fax machine didn't come out of the sixties," the chief huffed, and I wondered if Jane was fearless or somehow got a thrill out of poking the already grumpy dragon in the eye.

"Wait, what?" Jane asked.

"The first modern fax machines came out in the sixties, mid-sixties," the chief told her.

"Why do you know that?"

"Because some of us read more than those trashy romance novels."

"They are not trash!"

"They are kinda smutty," Dick offered up as I finally recovered and moved around the cart.

"Smutty isn't the same thing as trashy," Jane protested. "Just because the two of you are as romantic as boiled dirt doesn't mean the rest of us have to be."

"What does that even mean?" Chief Price demanded, and I knew he was talking to Dick. It wasn't so much that Jane didn't make sense than she tended to say things that were just slightly...off. Poor Dick, everyone always turned to him whenever something off-kilter came out of Jane's mouth, and he was always left to shake his head in confusion.

I didn't need to linger to know how the conversation would go, and I sent the pair a silent thanks as I shuffled down the hallway. Now I no longer had to stay ducked down,

I was able to stand up straight and power walk toward the end of the hall. I knew full well I could thank Jane for her sacrifice by ordering the new book in the romance series she was reading, but Dick would be a little tougher. I could probably buy the man a nice steak and he would be pleased, even more so if I gave it to him raw and let him cook it up in the peace of his home.

Once at the end of the hall, I considered the door ahead of me which led to the break room. It would undoubtedly be one of the last places he would think of looking, but it would also take him a lot less than the time I had for my shift to end before he circled back to the beginning. Worse yet, if I was in the break room, I wouldn't have anywhere to hide or escape if he walked in. There was only one entrance, no windows, and not even a closet to stuff myself into.

I considered the evidence room, but the damn thing had a keypad and electric lock system so loud it would alert everyone within a mile radius. It would be simpler to just step into the main room, wave my hands around and shout while painting a target on my forehead.

My next idea was, well, quite brilliant, if a little insane. On the one hand, it looked like the chief had left his office unlocked with the door cracked open, so I had access. I'd never tried to hide in there before, so he wouldn't think to look. On the other hand, if he caught me in his office I would probably have to endure a lot longer chew out than the one he already had planned.

"Livington!" I heard him bark from the main room. "Quit hiding. Come out here and face the music."

"Yeah, not gonna happen, Cap," I muttered, deciding that a good idea, no matter how insane, was still a good idea. Hoping he wasn't closer than he sounded, I pushed open the door and slipped inside.

The inside of the chief's office wasn't new to me. Lord

knew I'd been pulled in there to get chewed out many times in the past ten years. When I'd started on the force, it had been under Chief Price's predecessor, and the former Chief Luce had been even scarier. Strangely, the former chief had become the town's local friendly old man who liked to dress up as Santa during Christmas and live out the rest of his life quietly with his wife of forty years.

Sometimes I wondered if the power of love and retirement would be enough to take the edge off Chief Price.

It was always cluttered in his office, no matter how much he grumbled about the mess or how often he seemed to be organizing things. Books dominated one of the three chairs, two in front of his desk, and the tall chair he used whenever he was working. Partially used notebooks were scattered about his desk, along with folders, because he avoided using technology when he could, which was why his computer looked like it had been new at the turn of the century.

I ran my hand along the small set of shelves he'd hung up after taking over the role of chief. One was dominated by pictures. Chief Price before he took the job and the former Chief Luce, shaking hands and smirking at the camera. Pictures of him working with a group of young kids for the work fair the local school had hosted, and one of the few where he was genuinely smiling. There was also one of all of us in front of the station, most of us grinning at the camera, but one could be forgiven for thinking there was a twinkle in his eye.

Not for the first time, I wondered where the pictures of his life outside work were. Everyone else in the station kept at least a couple of pictures of friends, family, or partners if they had them. I had a picture with my parents and another of me standing with Adam and his parents shortly after we'd graduated.

The reminder made me sigh, and I pulled my hand away

from the shelf. Adam was supposed to be coming back to Fairlake at some point, but he'd been as vague as ever about the details. Once upon a time I'd thought nothing could get between Adam and me, that our friendship would be as strong as ever. Even when he was planning to move out east, I still held to that belief. Now though, I was left with the barest fragment of that belief, and I could only hope that whatever brought him back to Fairlake would give me a chance to reconnect with him.

"A woman, it's always a woman with you straight boys," I muttered, drumming my fingers on the edge of the chief's desk.

I winced, silently chastising myself for the thought because that wasn't fair. Maybe Adam's wife was part of the problem, but Adam had made his own choices. I had long ago told myself I needed to be wary of being irritated when Adam's girlfriends wanted more of his time. It was, after all, a perfectly normal desire, and jealousy of his time and attention came all too easy for me.

"Probably safer to accuse myself of being a cliché," I muttered as I dropped into the chief's seat and grunted in appreciation. The man might be old-fashioned about many things, but he apparently wasn't against comfort. "Imagine being such a clichéd homo that you fall in love with your straight best friend."

My words hung in the air, going unanswered. Not that it bothered me, I had talked to myself when I thought I was alone for as long as I could remember. Even as far back as my toddler years, I had apparently liked to babble to myself. It helped me center my thoughts and make sense of them when they were trying to bounce all over the place.

At a distant thump, I froze, cocking my head and listening closely to see if the sounds grew any closer. After nearly a minute of silence, I let my breath out in relief and glanced down. One of the bottom drawers of the desk was open, and I could see something catching the overhead light, glinting faintly in the dark.

Despite my common sense, which went ignored more often than was probably wise, telling me to mind my own business, I opened the drawer. I almost felt disappointed when I saw it was only a framed picture, albeit a frame that was older and more worn than the ones on the shelves. The picture encased safely inside was older too and showed two men grinning at the camera, their arms wrapped around one another's shoulders.

It wasn't until I stared at it longer that I realized I was staring at a much younger Chief Price. He couldn't have been much older than eighteen at the time, and I don't think I'd ever seen him look so happy and relaxed. I'd never thought about it before, but my chief was a pretty good-looking man for someone approaching fifty, and he'd been impossibly handsome at that age. The guy next to him was just as cute, though his head was a stark contrast to the chief's, with a bright shock of blond hair instead of the pitch black the chief had once possessed.

"Why are you hidden away in here?" I asked the picture, looking down at the drawer.

Before I could come up with an answer, I heard another thump, this one louder and closer. Jumping, I stuffed the picture back in the drawer and closed it. Standing up, I moved toward the door and froze when I heard Chief Price's voice grumbling to himself.

"Turning my goddamn break room into a florist shop. And streamers covered in glitter. Glitter in my damn coffee, on my goddamn uniform," he complained, getting closer and closer.

I had to resist the urge to groan as more of the mystery was being solved right before me. I had seen the streamers in the party shop and had snatched them up without looking. I hadn't realized they were covered in glitter until I'd removed them from the packaging and started stretching them over the ceiling of the break room.

I probably should've paid closer attention, and now I was going to die because my chief looked like he'd gone to a strip club.

Holding my breath, I only let it out when I was sure he'd stomped past the office door, heading toward the break room again. Pulling my phone out, my heart leaped with joy when I realized it was time to clock out.

Taking another deep breath, I opened the door and peered out, finding the hallway empty. It was probably the only chance I would get, and I darted out, heading for the next hallway and hurrying toward the front. Ira sat at the front desk, bent over in her chair and staring at her tablet. She had been working the front desk for longer than I'd been alive and was as much a fixture of the station in the minds of the townspeople as the large brass bell hanging over the nearby fire station.

"Heya, Ira," I said, leaning over to take control of her computer and bring up the system so I could clock out. "Good book? Good movie?"

She peered at me from over her half-moon glasses. "Trying to make a break for it, are you?"

"Ira, I don't know what you mean," I said, hurriedly typing in my identification number and password. I probably should have chosen a computer that wasn't nearly as ancient as the chief's, but I would have been more exposed. "I'm just happy to have ended another productive day."

"Bennett, I might be old, but that doesn't mean I'm deaf and blind. I saw Trevor on the prowl, and there's no question who he's been looking for," she said, sounding amused. Then again, I suspected the chief could have publicly executed me and she would have still found it amusing.

She had a weird sense of humor.

"Oh, nothing to worry yourself over," I said, drawing up the time clock. "Just a little—"

"Ira!" Chief Price barked from the back of the building. "Is that him up there with you?"

"Just might be," Ira called back, and I cursed her as I hit the clock-out button.

"Livington! Get your ass back here!"

"Sorry, Cap!" I called, knowing there was no point in pretending I wasn't there, backpedaling toward the door. "Union rules state I can't discuss anything work-related unless I'm clocked in."

"The only thing we're discussing is removing my foot from your ass and the dry-cleaning bill you owe me!"

"Gotta go!"

I practically burst through the double front doors, ignoring the stone steps leading toward the sidewalk and leaping down. I didn't quite run, but I managed to get myself moving, trying to get as much distance between him and myself as possible. To my dismay, a few guys at the fire station were outside, cleaning one of the trucks.

Normally, that would be a sight worth admiring, as even the least attractive guy on the squad still had a stellar body. Sometimes they liked to wash their equipment without shirts, and sometimes they wore the tightest cotton shirts in existence while doing so. Sometimes they even let me watch, chuckling to themselves as I pretended I wasn't, and they pretended they weren't enjoying the ego boost.

"Heya, Bennett," one of them called out, and I spared a wave as I tried to speed past. Isaiah was the firefighter I knew best, being one of the only other guys in Fairlake who lived as an openly gay man. There were a couple more as well, and probably some hiding away. Sometimes I wondered just what was in the air for there to be so many in such a small town. "Are you speed walking?"

"Fleeing," I called out to him, waving to the other guys. Most of them waved back, but the brooding redhead who'd recently joined the fire station only stared back at me, expressionless. I could barely remember the guy's name, let alone his personality. "I'll ogle you guys some other time."

Isaiah opened his mouth and stopped when we both spotted Chief Price barreling out onto the sidewalk outside the station. His expression turned knowing, and he shook his head. "Have you managed to go a week without getting your ass chewed out?"

"Hold on to that obvious daddy joke for the next time I see you!" I called out to him, and finally broke into a run as I heard Chief Price shout after me.

Up ahead, I spotted a familiar car coming to a stop at a nearby intersection. Grinning, I darted toward it, yanking open the passenger door and sliding inside. Chase Everett glanced at me in surprise, his normally dour expression looking almost comical with shock.

"Bennett?" he asked, glancing around. "What the fuck are you doing?"

"Why, hitching a ride! Why don't we hang out?" I said cheerily. "And while we're at it, why don't you hit the gas before the chief commits a felony in full view of half the town?"

Chase looked over and rolled his eyes. "Christ, Bennett. Do you know how to stay out of trouble?"

"I do try my best," I said, relieved when he finally started driving, heading toward his house. "But good intentions, the road to hell, you know how it goes."

"It only works that way with you," he grumbled, glancing

over at me. "You look fine, so I'm guessing you got off scot-free."

"Aw, aren't you sweet?" I asked with a chuckle. "Since when did you start trying to flatter other people? I'm not sure it suits you."

He sighed, leaning against the driver's door and steering with one hand. "You're still running on the adrenaline from your great escape, aren't you?"

"Probably," I said brightly, drumming my hand on my knees. "If it makes you feel better, you're not an accomplice to a crime."

"Yeah, well, I'm not too worried about what your chief is going to do to me," Chase grumbled, rolling down the window to light a cigarette. It was my turn to roll my eyes as I rolled down my window as well.

"Those'll kill you," I said.

"Not immediately," he said, uninterested in the conversation about his cancerous habit, just like always.

"So," I said, "should we continue talking about your bad habits or the fact that despite your grumpy attitude, you're actually kind of fond of Chief Price?"

"Silence always works," he huffed.

His sour attitude didn't fool me. Despite how good he was at coming off surly and scary, I knew Chase had a good heart. He often went out of his way to repair people's cars outside the shop when he knew they were struggling financially. He thought I didn't know he'd volunteered to be the representative for the garage at the elementary school's job fair the year before.

He was also a dedicated cuddler, not that I would tell anyone that. Chase had been struggling with his sexuality for as long as I could remember. We'd never been serious, but he'd grown more comfortable sleeping with me, until we'd decided to put a stop to things a year before. I just hoped the couple of years we'd been slightly more than friends had helped him get more comfortable in his skin and might one day show some lucky guy more than I'd ever seen.

"Actually, why haven't you been over?" Chase asked, blowing a cloud out the window.

I snorted, leaning back in the seat. "You know you can ask me to come over any time, Chase. I can still kick your ass at Smash Bros, insult your sense of decoration, or just shoot the shit."

Chase snorted. "I meant because your boy toy has been back for a few days."

"Boy toy? I haven't had anything resembling a boy toy since last year," I said slowly. A few hookups outside town, but nothing that resembled a relationship. As a matter of fact, I hadn't had a real relationship since the first year I was a cop. I'd tried, but it just hadn't worked out, and I wasn't all that anxious to change that fact while I was content with how my life was going.

"Fine, not boy toy. I guess he's strictly into pussy," Chase said, as well-mannered and classy as ever. "That one guy you were always spending so much time with. I live, like, two houses down from his parents now, remember? You always used to go over there."

"Wait, Adam is *here*?" I yelped, twisting around to stare at him.

"Yeah, he showed up, like, three days ago, with a truck full of shit. I've seen him, like, twice since then."

"When was the last time?"

"I dunno, this morning I think. Looked like shit, probably hungover. In their backyard, in some shitty-looking pants," Chase said with a shrug. "You really didn't know?"

"No, I sure the fuck did not!" I said. "He was supposed to tell me when he was coming!"

"I don't know why you're surprised," Chase said as he

pulled into his driveway. "The guy hasn't spoken to you in, like, what, months? A couple of years now?"

"He texted me about coming back," I said, immediately feeling a sense of disquiet. Nothing he'd said would have led me to believe he'd show up with a truck full of stuff and under the radar.

"Right, because that really told you a lot, apparently," Chase snorted, putting his car in park. "Guy's an asshole who left you holding the bag for years. You really surprised he's doing the same shit just because he's come crawling back home to Mommy and Daddy?"

"I'm sorry, what was that?"

Chase rolled his eyes. "That one girl who works at the store, uhh—"

"Annie."

"Right. I guess the guy who owns the store—"

"Alan Canticle, you've been here your whole life, Chase, c'mon."

"Whatever. Anyway, I guess she saw him roll into town a few days ago. Looked like shit but was 'kinda cute' according to her. Alan noticed the guy wasn't wearing his wedding ring either."

"That—" I began and then frowned. "Wait, why was Annie gossiping to you?"

"Fuck, man, I don't know. She talks to me like that all the time."

"Probably because she noticed your biceps are as big as her head," I chuckled, patting the arms in question. "Now, if only she knew what you were hiding in your—"

"Shut the fuck up," Chase grumbled, shoving open the driver's door. "Ya fucking degenerate."

I cackled, troubled by what I'd heard. "Fine, I'll leave you be."

Chase eyed me over the roof of the car. "You're going to be an idiot, aren't you?"

"By that, do you mean going over to see Adam?"

"Yeah, that's what I mean."

"Then I guess, yeah."

Chase shook his head, jamming a finger toward his house. "You cannot be an idiot. Come in, have a couple of beers, tell me what you did that pissed your boss off, and I can call you an idiot."

"Rain check?" I asked, shoving my hands in my pockets.

Chase shook his head. "Fine. Whatever. Don't say I didn't tell you this was a bad idea."

"You always tell me that about my bad ideas," I called after him as he walked toward his front door.

"Probably because they fucking are," he grumbled, and I laughed.

I didn't bother taking the sidewalk and jogged across a couple of lawns, leaping lightly onto the Jensen's front porch. I didn't hesitate to open the front door and step inside, utilizing the open invitation I'd had since I was sixteen, which was reaffirmed a year after Adam left Fairlake.

"Yo!" I called, my voice echoing down the hallway and up the stairs.

Mrs. Jensen appeared, leaning out from the kitchen. "Oh, I should've known it would be you."

"Well, hiya," I called brightly, walking down to meet her. Mr. Jensen was sitting at the kitchen table, a magazine in one hand and a coffee cup in the other. "Well, hiya to both of you."

"Hi, sweetheart," she said, wrapping me up in a one-armed hug. "Surprised it took you this long to show up."

Mr. Jensen snorted, laying the magazine down. "Adam didn't tell you, did he?"

"He did not," I said brightly, trying to conceal how much

it bothered me. Had my friend really gone through a divorce and a forced move back to his parents' house and said nothing?

"Told you we should've messaged him," Mr. Jensen scoffed, which pleased me. Erik Jensen had always been a no-nonsense man and wasn't easily impressed by other people's excuses. Diane Jensen was no less no-nonsense, but she was generally more empathetic and understanding.

"I know," she said to her husband, shooting him a dirty look. It was one of those looks I associated with married couples, laden with meaning and messages only the two could understand. "But Adam said—"

"What did Adam say?" I asked, curious.

"He said he was going to message you himself," she said quietly. "Of course, that was when he also said he was going to rest a little bit and then start reaching out to people."

"And instead, spent the past three days lying in bed, barely looking at either of us," Erik finished with a scowl. "Found our alcohol just fine, though."

I glanced at Diane, who looked troubled. "Uh…that true?"

"A little," she said, looking uncomfortable. I didn't blame her. Even I felt uncomfortable at the revelation. I didn't think I'd ever known Adam to be so down in the dumps before, and I was quickly growing concerned. "Where is he?"

"Upstairs, sleeping," she said.

"Passed out more like," Erik grumbled.

"Erik," I said, eyeing him, "you're not helping. I get it. He's living a miserable existence and drinking your booze. Can we bring this back around to new information?"

Erik huffed. "Married that harpy of a woman, things went to shit, she took most of everything, and now he's here."

"So…this is probably the first time he's dealt with anything?"

"You call this dealing?"

33

No, but unless Adam had gone through a drastic personality change, he definitely hadn't been dealing with things before. Adam was one of the most steady and tough people I knew, a product of his mother's patient understanding and his father's stern but fair co-parenting. Yet he was more like his father in some ways, which included ignoring his emotions and being frustratingly stubborn sometimes.

But yeah, this sounded less like dealing and more like the dam had burst, and Adam was quickly drowning.

"He's up in his room, sweetheart," Diane said, reaching out to put a hand on my arm. "Maybe you can get something out of him. Maybe an old, friendly face will do the trick."

"Anything's better than this bullshit," Erik grumbled, but I caught the well-hidden but not completely buried worry in his eyes.

"Language," Diane chided, pointing at him. "We're not at the shop. Watch it."

"I'll go see what I can do," I told her, hoping it would make her feel a little better.

Flashing them both a smile, I made my way upstairs. Despite having visited the Jensens almost weekly for the past several years, I'd rarely had a reason to go to the second floor. It had only been during the occasional visit from Adam that I'd ever needed to go upstairs. Before he'd left Fairlake, I'd used his bedroom almost as much as my own, and he had done the same with mine.

Gently, I opened the door, letting the light spill into the space that was still familiar. The dark-blue fringed rug still sat in the middle of the floor, and the wide dresser was still close to the door. Various athletes were still plastered on the wall, though they'd curled with age, the tape holding them up growing brittle and weak.

It looked like Adam had grown a bit since the last time I'd seen him, sprawled out in the middle of his bed. He had managed to wrap his blanket around him, an arm thrown over his eyes and soft snoring coming from him. His shirt had ridden up, and I could see a patch of dark hair that trailed from beneath the waistband of his lounge pants toward his chest.

Despite my concern and annoyance, I felt a familiar pang jolt to life in my chest. I was sure he probably didn't look the best at the moment, but just seeing him brought back a familiar longing that I hadn't felt in years. Even disheveled, practically passed out, and in sore need of some sunlight and water, Adam Jensen somehow managed to get even more attractive with age.

Because of course the bastard had, and of course I still wanted to reach out and run my hand down his—

"Oh no," I muttered, shaking my head. "No, no. That's… no, not what we're here for. Focus, Bennett, focus."

Now I just had to wake him up, and I thought perhaps doing it in a very…Bennett Livington style would do the trick.

ADAM

In the darkness of sleep, I was comfortable, almost at peace. The alcohol might have helped dull some of my thoughts and helped me cling to others, but I didn't need any of that while I was asleep. With the help of alcohol, though, I didn't dream. I drifted through the welcome darkness and not—

Bright light pierced my eyelids just as the most god-awful noise filled the air. I flailed, cursing when my hand slammed into the thick bedpost at the head of my bed. Trying to roll away from the offending assault on my senses, I found myself wrapped up tight in a cocoon of fabric before hitting the ground in a horrific crash.

Hey, I just met you, and this is crazy! But here's my number, so call me maybe?

This song, oh god, this song!

"What the *fuck!*" I bellowed, squirming in sheer desperation to free myself and find the source of the accursed song and end it quickly.

Your stare was holding, ripped jeans, skin was showing, hot night wind was blowing, where you think you're going, baby?

I twisted around to find a small Bluetooth speaker on the

edge of my dresser, blasting the hellish song into the atmosphere. It was bright pink and practically vibrating from the bass it somehow managed to put out. And there, standing next to it, leaning on the doorway with a shit-eating grin—

"Bennett!" I barked. Somehow I managed to feel a flush of pleasure at the sheer familiarity of that grin and the desire to throw the speaker directly at his face. "What the fuck is wrong with you?"

"Well, hiya, Adam," Bennett said, reaching over to tap his phone and, thankfully, spare me the rest of the song. "I thought you might enjoy a little blast from the past to help bring you back to the world of the living."

"That song was crafted by Satan himself," I growled, now fighting with the blanket until it released me from its death grip. "I hate that song, and you know it!"

I had hated "Call Me Maybe" from the first moment I heard it on the radio. To my absolute dismay, not only had Bennett liked it, but he'd been beyond delighted at how much I despised it. In no time at all, he'd managed to get his hands on it, making sure to play it at the most inopportune times imaginable.

Taking a shower? Of course he would open the door and blast it into the bathroom from somewhere in the hall, where I would have to scramble for a towel to stomp out and turn it off. Under my mom's car, trying to help my dad fix something? You bet Bennett would blast the damn thing while I was wrist-deep in the guts of the car.

"Well, I suppose that while you're still having a little BDSM session with your blankets," Bennett said, and my eyes widened in horror as his finger moved toward his phone.

"Don't. You. Dare," I hissed, glaring at him.

"Oops," he said lightly, tapping his screen.

So here's my number—

"You son of a bitch!" I barked, flopping onto my back to unwind myself with hurried shoves and flailing limbs. "Your ass is mine."

"Promises, promises," he said, grabbing his phone and speaker in one hand and backing into the hallway.

It took another couple of shoves to get the blanket off. Finally, with a grunt, I shoved my hands against the ground and launched myself toward him. However, Bennett had been watching me and was prepared, darting away faster than I thought I'd ever seen him move.

"Close!" he called, hoofing it for the stairs. "But not close enough!"

"You little," I growled and took off after him.

I was as close on his heels as I could manage, but he clearly hadn't been lax in working out like I had over the past couple of years. He all but flew down the stairs, swinging himself around at the bottom to land in the hallway nimbly. Even though I had to take the stairs a little more carefully as I tried to keep my breathing even, it wasn't hard to follow where he was going; his cackling preceded him.

"'Scuse me!" Bennett called as he barreled through the kitchen toward the double doors that led to the back patio. I heard a clatter as I hurried after him, watching him yank open the door and toss his phone and speaker onto the table next to my father. My mother stood by the fridge, her eyes wide, while my father barely moved except to push the two devices away without looking up from his magazine.

"Bennett!" I barked as he hauled ass onto the patio and toward the yard.

Even with his speed, he'd been delayed by opening the doors and getting rid of the phone and speaker. I had a feeling he was going to head toward the tall fence shared with the neighbors, and I cut to the left. Sure enough, he careened left as he attempted his escape, and I knew I had him. Hopping onto the low wall surrounding the patio, I launched myself at him, catching him in the middle and dragging him down into the damp grass with me.

We hit the ground roughly, shoulders first, and slid. Bennett was still quick and was already working hard to get out of my grip. Sadly for him, it didn't matter how fast he was or how much better in shape he technically was, I was still bigger, and I was still strong. I tightly wrapped my arms around him as we rolled across the grass. He was slippery, though, and I had to work to keep him from wiggling out of my grasp.

"Don't you two break anything!" I heard my mother shout from the house. "Or you're gonna take yourselves to the hospital!"

"Lemme go, you ox!" Bennett growled as he pushed against the ground and nearly managed to escape.

"Like hell I will," I grumbled back at him, finally rolling over to pin him to the ground with my superior bulk. I had to give him credit, he had more stamina than I would've predicted because he was still managing to thrash and wiggle, making it an uphill battle to get a good grip on him and keep it.

After another minute, I finally managed to pin one of his arms against his side with my leg. I inevitably had to hold onto the other with one hand and pin it to the ground. That left me a little off-balance and having to deal with even more of his wiggling, but it was the best position I could manage.

"You're an *ass*," I informed him, glaring down. "You're a full-grown man, for god's sake."

I saw something flicker in Bennett's eyes, and not for the first time since I'd known him, I wondered what really went on in his head. It was usually just a moment of...something I couldn't quite put my finger on. Even when I couldn't name what I'd barely glimpsed, sometimes I felt almost guilty, and other times I felt an uneasy twist in my gut. More often than not, I had the distinct feeling Bennett was hiding something from me.

"Maybe you should look at the cleanliness of your own hands before you start pointing fingers," he told me with a smirk. "You've been here for three days, you absolute dick, and I didn't even know you were arriving this week, to begin with. Maybe getting woken up to horrible pop songs is the kindest punishment you could have expected."

My annoyance faltered in the face of him being completely right, and I loosened my grip on him. Despite fully intending to do what I'd told my mother I planned to, I had done the complete opposite. I had woken up from my nap on the first day, and the full weight of everything had come crashing down upon me.

I cleared my throat. "Look, I…hey!"

The little bastard took advantage of my distraction and freed his arms with two sharp movements. Before I could recover, he rocked his hips, shoving into my side and sending me spilling onto the grass. With far more grace than the goofy bastard deserved to display, Bennett somehow managed to roll smoothly with me, perching himself on top of me. He didn't bother trying to pin my arms to my side as I had. Instead, he simply straddled my waist, his hands resting on my chest as he looked down at me triumphantly.

"You absolutely should have seen the look on your face after you hit the ground," he crowed. "I thought you were going to have a stroke."

"God, I wonder why," I grumbled, finally looking him over.

He had grown a little bigger in the arms and chest, but he was still the same old Bennett. Light sandy hair had grown a little longer than close-shaven, just enough to fall loosely around his forehead, and he had the same bright hazel eyes that perpetually sparkled with mischief. His face had lost some of its roundness, but there was still a softness to him and those caterpillar eyebrows that were always moving, no matter his expression. The only real difference was a patch of pink near the back of his head.

It was only then I realized just how much I'd missed the little gremlin.

"Did my parents put you up to this?" I asked.

Bennett snorted heavily, easing himself off me in a way that felt almost reluctant. "As if I needed them to give me any ideas. They just told me where you were, and I did the rest."

"That sounds about right," I said, absentmindedly noticing the absence of his weight as I sat up.

"Thing is, I think they moved some things in the kitchen before we got downstairs."

"That also sounds about right."

Bennett fell back onto his butt in the grass, and I continued looking him over. It was only now that I realized he was in his uniform, now smeared with stains and grass. A sense of ease hung around him, which I also deeply envied, as he sat there idly picking the grass off his pants with an easy smile.

"What's uh"—I pointed toward the almost perfectly circular patch of pink near the back of his head—"with that?"

He frowned, reaching back to tap the back of his head lightly. After a moment, his eyes widened and he let out a laugh. "I forgot about that! Yeah, so, if you're picking up temporary hair color, the stuff in a spray can, make sure it's not actually spray paint."

I had so many questions, and I'm sure most of the answers would boil down to the fact that that was just how things worked with Bennett.

"Why were you trying to color your hair pink?"

"Oh. We were doing this 'first day of spring' thing with the pre-k kids. I wanted to, like, paint flowers in my hair."

"And you ended up with spray paint?"

"Well, someone put a can of it near the hair spray. I wasn't paying attention and didn't realize until I did the first petal that it wasn't actually for coloring hair. Trust me, the smell is totally different. But I managed to go back and get the actual hair spray, and my hair turned out great!"

Yep, that was just how things worked with Bennett.

"Do I wanna know why you didn't bother to…check the can to make sure? Or notice they might look different?" I asked wearily.

"Eh." Bennett shrugged. "They all looked kind of alike. It's not like I was supposed to know someone would be that big of an ass…or that lazy."

I reached out, running my finger over the pink spot. "You never change, do you?"

Bennett laughed. "Probably not, even if I insist that things do. Chase laughed his ass off at me when he saw me with this stupid pink spot in my hair and then called me a dumbass."

"Sounds nice," I rumbled, not really appreciative of someone I didn't know insulting Bennett. "Does he usually call you a dumbass?"

Bennett smirked. "What, like everyone else in my life hasn't called me that before? I'm pretty sure you did at least once a day back in high school."

"I guess he's taken over the job," I said, telling myself I had no right to be annoyed at the idea. It wasn't like Bennett hadn't made an effort trying to keep in contact with me over the years. I was the one who'd been too stubborn and "busy" to see what was slipping away.

"Eh." Bennett shrugged. "He's grumpier than you could ever hope to be."

"That…doesn't surprise me," I said, thinking of the sour-faced teenager he'd been when I last saw him. "I wasn't sure he could talk, if I'm honest."

Bennett rolled his eyes. "He talks. Not to most people, but he talks. He's, well—"

I eyed him. "What?"

He shook his head. "He's got his own stories, his own reasons. They're not mine to tell, so I'm not getting into it. Trust me, though, he's not the grumpy jerk he acts like."

I wondered if the suspicion I'd voiced to my mom the other day was right. Bennett spoke of Chase with a fondness I didn't hear very often from him. Bennett was just a friendly person, and his goofy nature had always been a magnet for other people. Yet Bennett rarely got close to other people, despite how gregarious he could be.

My former high school girlfriend had been the one to point that fact out to me. Bennett could joke, laugh, and talk to people all day and night if given a chance, but few people got to know him.

"It's just," she had said with a frown, shaking her head, "it's like there's this secret part of him no one ever sees. Way down deep inside him. I don't think most of us have a clue what's down there except you."

The subject changed after that, but her words had stuck with me for quite a while. It made me think of all those times I'd seen something in the back of Bennett's eyes, though I could never quite identify what it was. There was something or things hidden within Bennett, and while she had probably been right that I had a clue or two, that didn't mean I knew precisely what was there.

So, I knew that tone of voice from him. I'd heard it only a few times before. It proved nothing, but I had to ask. "You two, uh…a thing?"

Bennett looked up, stark surprise on his face. "Wait, what?"

I snorted. "I'll take that as a yes."

"We're not together," he said quickly, frowning at me. "What made you think we were?"

"I don't know," I said, quick to cover up the discomfort in my stomach at the thought and from what I thought was my understanding of how he was. I had no right to assume anything or have an issue with anyone in his life.

"Right," he said, arching a brow.

"So, *are* you seeing anyone?" I asked, in a hurry to change the subject before he started probing for more information.

If *I know what you're doing and you can't fool me* was a facial expression, it was the one Bennett had on his face. "No. It's been a little while since I've dated anyone."

"Dry spell?"

"Nah. Sometimes I wanna get laid, so I get laid. Dating though? Eh."

Once again, I wondered what he kept locked away inside. For as long as I'd known Bennett, I had never known him to date anyone seriously. In our senior year, he'd dated a boy from another town over, which lasted just over three months. Bennett hadn't seemed all that interested in the other boy and hadn't been all that bothered when it ended.

"So, just living the horny single man's life?" I asked lightly.

Bennett scoffed. "It's not like I'm getting laid all the time. Most of the time, my boyfriend works just fine for me."

"Your...you said you weren't—"

Bennett held up his left hand. "My boyfriend. Never tells me I can't go out at night, doesn't tell me to turn the subtitles on a movie off, and hasn't strayed."

I ripped some grass up and threw it at him, creating green confetti. "You're ridiculous."

Bennett laughed, brushing off the few strands that landed on him. "No, Adam, I'm not a ho. Sometimes I wanna see another guy naked, so I go and see another guy naked. My boyfriend doesn't mind."

"Dumbass," I muttered without thinking.

Bennett grinned. "See? You're still doing it years later."

I sighed. "You make it too easy."

"Probably," he said, wagging his brow. "But it's part of my charm, and you love it."

"Not the word I was going to use."

"Well, after my charm, there's only my ass. And I *know* you haven't been appreciating that."

The comment made me smile a little. He had come out to me at fourteen before telling anyone else. I'd wondered before he ever said the words and hadn't cared in the slightest when he finally told me. It had been a defining point in our friendship, and he had grown more comfortable with me afterward.

Which meant he was perfectly comfortable making jokes that were, well, quite gay and usually at my expense. There had been the occasional rumor about the two of us after he'd come out to everyone, but I hadn't cared, and Bennett had found it hilarious. I was comfortable enough to admit he was a good-looking man and considered it a compliment that people thought he'd want to date me in the first place. But just the return of the old joking style warmed me, and I felt it pool in my stomach.

"Can't say I have," I said dryly. "Admittedly, I didn't get a good look at it while you ran through my parents' house like a maniac."

Bennett snickered. "Fine, but don't ogle it too much when I get up. Because I want a beer and need to get off this lawn."

He hooked his leg around the other and pushed himself up. I had to laugh at the absurdity of the entire movement as it did indeed push his ass toward me and accentuate it as he stood up. Whether it was because he had been working at squats or because of the uniform pants, it looked like it had gotten a bit bigger. Then again, I didn't remember ever paying that much attention to his ass in the past, so I didn't know how the comparison could be made.

"Ah, my laundry bill is going to be so painful," he sighed, looking down at himself. With a shrug, he held out his hand. "Come with me?"

"Sure," I said, pulled out of my thoughts and accepting his hand. "I probably won't have that beer with you, though."

"Oh, well, your dad will be happy to hear that," he said, pulling me up with an ease that surprised me. He hadn't looked like he'd bulked up all that much, but he'd clearly been building strength. Even with my assistance, he helped me get up with surprising ease.

I was distracted, however, by his words and immediately winced. "Okay, I guess they mentioned a lot more than where I was sleeping."

"They might have," he said lightly, finding another stray piece of grass and tossing it away. His tone suggested he was talking about the weather or his schedule for the next day, but the glance spoke volumes. "Feel like talking about it?"

"I feel like I talked about it enough with that ridiculous couples therapist Bri insisted on us going to," I grumbled, the first stirrings of the good mood I'd been feeling starting to wilt.

"Well, you guys pulled out all the stops before ending it."

"I didn't—"

"You're not wearing your ring, Adam. You weren't wearing it when you rolled into town a few days ago. Your truck still has a bunch of your shit in it, and you've spent three days in a half-drunken stupor. Don't talk about it right now if you don't want, but c'mon, don't act like I can't see what's going on."

I groaned. "Dammit, I *knew* Mr. Canticle had spotted it and was going to spread it—"

"Divorced or divorcing?"

"I…divorcing, almost divorced. Just another couple of months, and it'll be finalized."

"She get all the shit?"

"Most…most of it. I just—"

Bennett shrugged. "That's all I really wanted to know for the moment. That way, I know what I'm trying to help you with."

"Bennett, I don't need—"

"Adam?"

"What?"

"Shut up. You don't have to go into details. And yeah, you're an ass for basically leaving me on the top shelf to collect dust for years. But you can explain that later, and you can talk about what's been going on with you when you're ready to talk about it. Right now, though? I'm just happy to see you out of bed, and I'm going to help you because, whatever happened or didn't happen, we're friends, alright? Alright, now let's get me a beer."

His speech didn't alleviate my frustration and guilt, but I didn't have the energy to argue. Trying to get into a debate with Bennett about anything required a full meal and slamming a couple of cups of coffee beforehand. The man could run circles around people and never relent until his opponent simply gave up or somehow hit him with a counterargument strong enough to knock him out of his rhythm.

"You can't bully people into feeling better," I told him wryly as we climbed onto the patio.

"Not trying to bully you, and I'm not going to try to 'force' you to feel better," Bennett said with a shrug. "But I can at least try to help surround you with better shit than cheap liquor and oversleeping."

47

I rolled my eyes when I heard my father's irate voice. "It wasn't cheap!"

"Quit eavesdropping!" Bennett and I both called back, which only earned us more grumbling about how we were loud, this was his house, and a host of other things I couldn't quite make out.

"Also, you still planning on looking for work?" Bennett asked, raising a brow.

"I, uh, figured I'd see what was available," I said with a shrug, feeling awkward. I knew Bennett was preparing to help me with that, and I didn't know whether to be grateful or ashamed.

"Cool. Feel like fixing up a couple of things at my house? My back deck needs some boards and a railing replaced, and I'm pretty sure my front door is about to fall off," he said with a grin. "And last I checked, I'm still not allowed power tools or anything sharp."

"Well, I'd need to look at things and then get whatever materials," I said slowly, showing a reluctance I didn't feel. Since I'd closed my business over six months before, I hadn't done any work. The idea of once more sitting down, evaluating a problem that *could* be solved, putting it all together, and working with my hands again sounded like a godsend.

"Sure, what's your going rate these days?"

I jerked in surprise. "Rate? Christ, Bennett, I'm not going to—"

"Yes, you are," he said, arching a brow. "If you wanna push some sort of discount on it, be my guest, but I'm paying you for your work. Don't argue with me, alright? Trust me, I'm not hurting for money."

It wasn't about the money, and he damn well knew it. I didn't want to have Bennett pay me when I owed him more than a few days' worth of repairs around his house. Not to mention he could have also just called someone else to do the work, rather than an out-of-work professional, but was asking me to do me a favor.

"We'll argue about this later," I grumbled at him instead. At least then I would have time to generate whatever counterarguments I'd need to win.

"Hey, Diane?" Bennett called into the house innocently.

My eyes widened. "Don't you dare!"

"Yes, sweetheart?" she asked, appearing in the doorway.

"I'm going to have Adam come by my place this weekend to fix some things."

"Oh! Well, that'll be nice. I'm sure he'd like to get to work on something."

"He's also trying to do it for free."

She rolled her eyes, gesturing behind her. "He gets that much honest, along with the stubbornness. Adam Richard Jensen, do not take a page out of your father's book. Accept payment for a job well done. Bennett?"

"Yes, ma'am?"

"You make sure he doesn't get one over on you, either. Maybe let him give you a discount if you get a six-pack and a pizza to split."

"I can do that," Bennett said with a grin.

"Good," she said. "Are you staying for dinner?"

"I might be persuaded," Bennett said, all smiles and charm now he'd all but won this little dispute…by *cheating*.

"I'll take that as a yes," she said, disappearing inside.

"You are awful," I growled at him when I thought she was safely out of earshot.

He beamed. "I forgot your middle name was Dick. Always seemed so unfair that the straight man had a dick in his name."

Groaning, I put my face in my hands. "Why are you like this?"

"Because God loves you but wants to see you tormented

as well," he said, reaching up and hooking an arm around my neck. I had to lean over so he wasn't on his tiptoes, but he didn't seem to mind. "Now let's go eat some of your mom's cooking, and if I survive running into my chief tomorrow, we can see each other again on Saturday so you can be Mr. Fix It."

I was momentarily distracted by the familiarity of our position, his arm around my neck, and me walking a little lopsidedly to allow him to. His grip was firmer than I remembered, but the warmth and comfort of his skin against mine was a welcome familiarity.

"Wait," I said as we reached the door, "why might your chief kill you?"

BENNETT

The spring might have been unseasonably warm for how early it was, but the mornings were still cool. With a light mist in the air and the sun having just risen above the horizon, I did what I usually did on Saturday mornings and went for a run. I never stuck to a specific route, though I always tried to stop downtown to say hello to the other early birds.

I took my time today, pacing myself as I alternated between pushing myself and slowing down to a moderate jog. Even then, by the time I reached downtown after weaving randomly through the neighborhoods, I could feel how much sweat had accrued. The air felt good against my warm skin, though, so I didn't pay much attention.

I only slowed when I reached the fire station and found the large doors to the garage open. Isaiah was standing just inside, talking to a couple of the other firefighters. Well, one of them anyway, the other one was the surly-looking redhead whose name I couldn't remember, and he looked like he wasn't talking at all.

I pulled one of my earbuds free and waved as I came

closer. "Morning, gentleman. Pulled the morning shift, did ya?"

"Sure did," Isaiah said, looking me over. "Looks like we're your last stop. Trying to give the people something to gossip about?"

I snorted, looking myself over. I was wearing my jogging shoes and a pair of comfortably loose shorts that were tight enough near the top not to feel like they'd fall off as I ran. Other than that, there was only my tank top, which hung loosely off me. "Everyone knows the firefighters get all the stares in town."

Isaiah rolled his eyes. "Right, because some people haven't been not so quietly demanding a 'Men in Uniform' calendar. All to raise funds for the city, of course."

"I'll point out that they brought it up to *you*, not anyone else," I pointed out with a smirk.

The other firefighter only rolled his eyes, well used to the fact that Isaiah and I spent a fair amount of time flirting. At this point, everyone figured we were either not interested in each other or had gotten it out of our systems. In all fairness, we had gone on a single date just to see what it was like. The end result had been us going to a club a few towns over and picking up different guys. We simply worked better as friends, but that didn't mean we couldn't hype each other up at the same time.

Interestingly, this was the first time the redheaded firefighter paid me any attention. His expression always looked sour to me, but if I wasn't mistaken, he somehow looked more annoyed as the conversation continued. He didn't say a word or even look at either of us, but he was winning the angry staring contest he was having with the ground.

Huh, interesting.

"Well, you can tell them they can take it up with Chief

Price," I said with a chuckle. "And I'm sure we'll see how quickly that idea stops being mentioned."

"Probably," Isaiah chuckled. "Heading home after this?"

"Yeah," I said, wiping my brow. "Adam is supposed to be heading that way soon. I've got him coming over to play Mr. Fix It for me and get my back deck in better shape."

"Oh, that's right! I totally forgot he went through, like...a bunch of trade skills."

"I'm pretty sure he could build a house," I said with a snort. "So yeah, giving him some money, a few beers, and dinner, so he'll fix that and a couple of other things."

"Nice," Isaiah grunted. "And I know you're probably gonna wanna keep him to yourself."

"Isaiah," I said with a roll of my eyes. He was the only person in town who knew how I felt about Adam. I had been drunk and got a little lost in my feelings, spilling the beans. I hadn't mentioned that the feelings were still there, but apparently he'd managed to figure that part out on his own. "I'm not going to hog my best friend from the world. Now, what do you want?"

"Hey, I've got things that need fixing, and if he's going to offer fair rates, I'd rather have him over. Otherwise, I'm probably going to have to order from over in Fovel, and you know we prefer to ask our own first," Isaiah said with a shrug. It was one of the unspoken rules of living in Fairlake. You helped your own. Of course, you were also told to mind your own business, so trying to figure out the line between giving and respecting boundaries was blurred, and people often didn't bother with it in the first place. "And hey, his rates can't be any worse than that grumpy bastard over in Fovel."

I laughed. "Alright, you got me there. Had him and his sons come out last year to help me get my shed put up, and they were pretty freaking rude."

Isaiah smirked, eyes glittering with amusement. "And they wouldn't be anywhere near as fun to watch work, unlike Adam."

"I'll be sure to let him know, both that you're interested and that you're going to stare at his ass," I said with a roll of my eyes. I knew he was trying to get a rise out of me, but I wasn't going to give him what he wanted. Adam was comfortable in his sexuality, but he wasn't going to touch another man sexually with a ten-foot pole. "And uh...pass the word along if he does a good job?"

"You got it," he said, cocking his head.

"You guys have fun," I said, waving at them and placing my earbud back in my ear.

I veered away from the road that would take me home and stopped by the grocery store instead. I only grabbed a bottle of water from the cooler and slipped a couple of dollars to the cashier. The conversation with Isaiah had left me feeling a little off-kilter, and I hoped the jog home would shake the residual unhappiness away.

It had been years since I'd first realized I had feelings for Adam that were beyond platonic. At first, I tried to tell myself it was strictly sexual and was nothing to be worried about. Even as a teen, Adam had been handsome and strong, and god, he had grown even more so with age. However, that had only been the delusion of a teenage boy, terrified he would scare his best friend away.

Truth was, I had been completely, utterly, madly in love with him for years.

Time and distance had done a lot to ease the worst, but I had felt the old jealousy flare up when Isaiah made his admittedly innocent comment about Adam. I knew even if, in some absurd universe, Adam showed interest in Isaiah, something told me Isaiah would never let anything happen.

It was more the resurgence of the old and once-thought-dead jealousy that bothered me more than anything.

"Have a good one, Annie," I told the young clerk with a smile. "Make sure these old goats don't work you too hard."

"I can hear you!" I heard Mrs. Canticle call from the front office.

I winked at Annie and headed for the door. Draining half the bottle before I took two steps, I put the cap on and resumed the pace I'd been managing before. Using the holster on my arm, I tapped my phone to change the song to something with a better beat and started pushing myself as I reached the corner that would take me back to my house.

My pace was good, and I was starting to feel the familiar and welcome ache in my legs as I pushed my way uphill. Sweat broke out on me again, and I savored the morning breeze over my heated skin. By the time I made it to the little two-bedroom house I'd bought a few years ago, my mood had lifted considerably, and the usual spring in my step was back.

I needed to get the siding replaced. The gray that had come with the house was starting to get dark enough that it looked like dirt. I'd replaced the concrete walkway leading up to the front porch with stones and kept them clean. The concrete steps and porch I had paid to have ripped out and replaced with a wooden one that looked a lot better, especially with the potted plants I doted on dangling from the roof and standing on the steps.

It wasn't a grand house, but it was mine, and I loved it. There were a few things I wanted to do with the yard, namely to rip out the trimmed shrubs out front and put in something with more color. Also, the roof shingles needed to be redone, and I thought maybe I could convince Adam to help me with that. The inside was all hardwood flooring except the bathroom and the exceptionally hideous bright green tiling in the kitchen.

Jogging up to the porch, I paused when I saw a familiar truck coming up the road. It took me a moment to recognize it without all the stuff jammed into the bed. When I heard country music that would have been perfect a generation before our parents blasting from the speakers, I snorted hard enough to wonder if I might cough up the water I drank earlier.

Adam pulled in next to my car, hopping out after turning the music off. Rounding the truck, he stopped when he saw me, blinking.

"Well, hi there, stranger," I said, cocking my head. "I see we're in a music mood today."

Adam turned to look at his truck, pointing at it and then back at me. "Uh, yeah. What…what are you doing?"

"Why hoping to get a shower and change before you showed up after my morning jog," I said with a laugh. "Clearly, I mistimed things a bit."

He cleared his throat. "Just how hard do you run? You're covered in sweat."

I snorted. "Well, that's what happens when you discover running is an excellent use of all the pent-up energy you used to keep locked up inside. Hasn't made me normal, but it's taken the edge off."

The bewildered look on his face disappeared, and he frowned at me. "You're normal."

"I think that's the first time anyone other than my mom has said that to me," I chuckled. "And even then, I knew she was lying through her teeth. It was for love, but still a lie."

Adam sighed heavily, shaking his head. "I'm going to grab my stuff."

"Cool," I said, undoing my bottle of water. "I'm going to

hop in the shower real quick before all this sweat starts to smell…well, not like me, and more like sweat."

Adam hesitated again, turning to raise a brow. "Uh, sweat doesn't always smell like sweat?"

"Straight men," I teased.

"What? I bathe!"

I laughed, shaking my head. "Nah, I'm sure you do. But yes, sweat and BO are two very different things. For example, some people think pheromones in sweat make you more attractive to certain…other people."

"Think?"

"Science can't make up its mind. Some say we don't have the equipment that lets us detect them in the first place. Other people point out studies that show otherwise. And hey, some people do smell better than others, even if they have fresh sweat."

Adam was one, or at least had been, but the torturers of hell couldn't drag that little nugget of information from me.

"Oh, I guess…I didn't know that," he said, and for one horrifying moment, I thought he was going to ask me if he smelled good when he was sweating. There had only been a few times in our friendship that he'd ever asked me an uncomfortable question, and every time I was eternally grateful for my ability to make a joke of just about anything.

"Knowledge is power," I said, jabbing a thumb over my shoulder. "Going to go take that shower now before the bacteria find me."

"Yeah, alright," he said with a shrug, though his brow was still stitched together in confusion.

I left him to his puzzlement and happily retreated into the house. There was only a small entryway, enough room for two people to squeeze in, but mostly a place for me to drop my shoes on the rack behind the door. I stepped through the small archway into the living room, running my hand along the couch that faced the rest of the room, namely the large TV where I binged shows and video games in equal measure.

Pulling my shirt and socks off, I stopped at the doorway in the far right-hand corner of the living room and tossed them into the hamper at the foot of my bed. Snatching up the towel I'd used the day before for my shower, I went to the other doorway and into the dining room. Which I didn't use as a dining room since living alone meant I was perfectly content to eat on my couch. The table was used to put puzzles together when I was in the mood, the shelves to store the figurines I liked to build and paint, and other assorted crap to keep me busy.

Ignoring the closed door that led to the small guest room, I walked into the bathroom and flipped the shower on. Closing the door behind me, I stripped my shorts off and dropped them onto the floor behind the door. Usually, everything went into the hamper when I remembered, but I was conscious that Adam could walk in any minute and I'd kept my shorts on.

The shower was brief but utterly relaxing as I let cool water run down my heated skin, only to warm it up and leave a nice glow about me. My mind ran from the day, glad Adam was back despite my heart hurting a little for his situation. I didn't know what the story was, but there was no question it weighed heavily on my friend's heart.

I wasn't in the least bit surprised when my mind trickled back to the brief conversation outside. When we'd been younger, I'd always loved the smell of him after he had been working hard or just working up a sweat helping his dad fix up the house or their cars. It was a smell I could never quite explain, but I'd always associated it with Adam. Thankfully I had never been so intent on the smell as to steal a piece of his clothing, but it had been hard to keep myself from sniffing him at times.

The thought stirred in my groin, and I reached down, wrapping my fingers around my shaft. It was hard, and just the idea of getting hard over Adam again made it pulse against my palm. The last time I'd taken care of myself had been a few days before, and if I was willing to dredge up an old fantasy, because there were dozens upon dozens, I was sure I could get myself off in no time.

A thump from somewhere in the house made me jerk and feel a twinge of guilt. "Adam, that you?"

"Yeah, sorry, dropped my bag," he called back.

There was no way in hell he knew what I was doing or why I was doing it, but the guilt had already ruined the mood. In all fairness, it was probably better that way. No need to poke at old wounds and risk falling into bad habits.

"Alright, I'll be right out," I said, looking down and scowling when I saw I was still rock-hard.

I flipped the hot water off and fought the urge to hiss when cold water cascaded down my body, but it took care of my problem in no time. Shivering and trying to shake the chill off my skin, I hopped out of the shower and hurriedly dried myself off. I glanced around, realizing I hadn't grabbed clothes.

Wrapping my towel around my waist, I stepped out of the bathroom. Adam was bent over the small card table where a half-finished puzzle sat, a toolbox and a large thick fabric bag at his feet.

"I've been meaning to finish that damn thing for six months," I chuckled.

"I forgot you used to do puzzles," he murmured, almost to himself.

I wondered if I'd wandered into something almost private. "You okay?"

He twitched but stood up straight and smiled. His expression flickered for a moment, and he shrugged. "Sorry, getting lost in my thoughts, I guess."

"Well, just so long as they're not a bad place to be," I said as he looked me over. "What?"

"I just…" he said, sounding almost embarrassed. "I guess I just haven't seen you for so long. It's just…"

I looked down. "I mean, I know we weren't exactly the comfortable with nudity kind of best friends, but—"

He gave the barest flinch, and I wondered what I'd said wrong. "No, it's not that. Actually, I was thinking the other day, wondering where the hell you'd got all that strength from. It didn't look like you got *that* much bigger, but without your uniform or…much of anything, I guess I can see I was wrong."

"You guess," I snorted, taking up a small pose. "You were *definitely* wrong, you mean."

"Oh god, don't let it go to your head," he groaned. "And don't lose your towel in the process either. There are some things I don't need to see."

"It, along with my ass, are gifts I can bestow upon mankind," I told him proudly, even as I reached down and made sure I wasn't going to lose my towel. The most of Adam I'd ever seen was the one time one of his teammates in high school yanked his shorts down as a joke. Adam had been facing away from me, but I'd gotten an eye full of his ass.

Again, no torturer would ever force me to admit the fantasies that had rolled off that one memory.

Adam shook his head, looking down at the floor. "How about you put some clothes on, and I'll take a look at your porch?"

"Yeah, you do that," I told him with a chuckle and squeezed by him to get to my room.

After throwing on a pair of jeans and a shirt I wouldn't mind getting dirty, I left and headed through my narrow kitchen. Taking the few stairs down to the landing before the stairs that led into the basement, I opened the back door. Adam crouched near the part of the small deck that ran along the outer wall of the house, knocking on boards.

"What's the diagnosis?" I asked him.

"Well, they definitely need to be replaced. And the whole thing could afford to be power washed to clean it off. After it dries, you're going to want to put some treatment on it and probably stain it," he said, eyeing the railing. He stood up, and I had to admit it was fun to watch him take his time, quietly analyzing everything. "When was the last time you did anything with it?"

"I didn't," I said with a shrug. "It came with the house when I bought it a few years ago. I knew I needed to do something, but I just uh—"

"Kept forgetting," Adam supplied for me as he looked over the railing. "Honestly, it's amazing this thing hasn't collapsed with you on it."

I looked around, eyes wide. "The whole thing? Jesus Christ."

He looked askance at me, a little smile on his face that made my heart beat a little harder. "No, not the whole thing. But those boards are so rotten it's a miracle they didn't crumble during a hard storm, and the railing is only a little better. At this point, getting these things repaired is a safety requirement."

"Alright, I've been living on the edge and didn't even know it," I said with a chuckle. "What's that going to cost me?"

"That would require me to know what the cost of lumber is like out here, which I don't," he chuckled. "And there's no lumber store in town, is there?"

"Nope," I said with a chuckle. "Funnily enough, there's no real handyman around here either. You know, like the stuff you're doing now."

"There's plenty of them," Adam said with a frown.

"Nah, not as many as there were, and I'm sure none of them are as licensed as you," I said with a shrug.

Adam shook his head, standing up. "I know what you're trying to do, so just stop. We'll need to make a run. I can probably get this done today, depending on how bad the rest of it is."

"Alright, I'll grab my wallet. We can head over to Fovel, they've got a Home Depot," I said, with a tone that insinuated how important that was.

He laughed a little at that. "Is that stupid rivalry still going on?"

"You bet your ass!" I exclaimed. "Mrs. Dovey is still fuming because I beat her cookies in the bake-off last fall!"

He arched a brow. "You...bake?"

"Look, when you're not living with your parents, and there's not a lot of options other than the diner and one McDonalds, you learn to fend for yourself."

It had actually been a lot harder than I was making it sound. I was easily distracted by nature, which did not work out all that well with baking. As a result, there had been more burned cookies, pies, and cakes those first few months than I would admit to anyone. Frustration had nearly driven me to tears until I got mad at the entire thing and determined that my inattention and a damned oven would not beat me.

"What'd you make that beat her cookies?"

"Chocolate banana bread," I told him smugly. "It was moist without falling apart, chocolatey without overwhelming the banana, and vice versa. It was delicious."

"And I can tell you're very modest about it." He chuckled,

walking toward me. "Maybe you should take the opportunity to put your money where your mouth is."

"If you want me to bake something for your sugar-addicted ass, just say so," I said with a knowing look. "And as I recall, strawberry rhubarb season is only a few months away. Maybe I can be convinced."

"I get the feeling you're already convinced," he said.

"You finish your investigation so we know what we need from the store, alright?" I said, reaching out and gripping his forearm, giving it a light squeeze.

"It won't take me long," he murmured, and I could tell he was only half paying attention to me as he squatted to look over the railing. "Just lemme write down what we'll need."

"Sure," I said with a little smile, slipping into the house. Seeing him absorbed in work was many times better than finding him in a half-drunken funk in his childhood bedroom. Maybe it would only be a day's worth of work, but I hoped it proved the first step on a gradual road to getting back on his feet.

ADAM

I lay back, a low noise of pleasure rolling out of my chest. Strong hands gripped my thighs, and my heart fluttered as I felt lips press against sensitive skin. Their touch was loving and heated, and the sensation was better than anything I could ever recall.

Reaching down, I shoved my hands into thick hair, curling into a fist to tug gently. That earned me a soft groan, and I felt warm breath gust against my thighs. I hadn't quite been trying to hint at anything, but the mouth moved anyway, working upward with patience and precision that threatened to drive me crazy.

I knew I was somewhere comfortable, somewhere I would be safe to bask in the moment. That was until I looked up and saw a door in the middle of the room. It was covered in filthy streaks of dirt and cobwebs, cracks formed along the door's edge, some small and spidery, others thick and gaping.

The door was cracked open and I could see darkness swarming, somehow both a force and a presence. The light from the room I was in bled into it, but instead of bringing warmth it faded and disappeared. Whatever was past that door was eating the light, taking its warmth, and giving nothing in return.

"You okay?" a soft voice asked beside me, and I turned to find kind eyes staring back at me. "I know you have to go soon."

"I don't want to go," I said, curling to press myself against a warm chest and smiling. "It's good here. It's perfect."

"Things only seem perfect because you can't see the cracks."

"The door has cracks. A lot of them."

"So do you."

"I see them all the time."

"Of course you do. You stare into them all the time. But that's no way to fix them."

I shook my head. "I don't want to leave. Not again."

"You did it once. You can do it again."

The light in the room was dimming, and I could feel a chill settling into the air. So long as I could lay against this chest, listen to this voice, however, I would be fine. There was a pleasant scent here, one I couldn't think of the words for, but I wanted to breathe it in deeper.

"Please," I begged. "I don't want to go."

"I'm sorry, but maybe one last thrill before you go?"

It wasn't what I wanted, but I would take it if that was the only thing I'd get. Reaching down, I cupped him in my hand, smiling as I heard his next breath come out as a sigh of relief. There was so much I wanted to say, so much that I had to do, and god knew I still had to make up for it. But maybe, just maybe, this would be something I could still give, something to help balance the scales.

"Bennett," I breathed, drawing closer to his lips. "I need to—"

* * *

THE FIRST THING I became aware of as my eyes flew open was the screeching of pop music from my bedside table. With a growl of annoyance, I reached over and flipped it off. I had no idea how the hell Bennett had managed to get into my phone, download a song, and set it as my alarm without me noticing. I also wasn't sure if I should curse him for making me wake up to Britney Spears or be impressed at his sneakiness.

The second thing I became aware of was when I rolled over, pressing my previously unnoticed erection into the bed. A tingle of pleasure from the contact was enough to freeze me in my tracks as my dream floated back into my consciousness.

"Um," I managed, staring at my pillow as I lay there, frozen in shock.

Had I...had a dream about Bennett? A *sex dream*?

I felt my face warm as I looked at my phone, my heart beginning to thump harder. It wasn't often that I remembered my dreams, save for the occasional bits and pieces I usually ignored once awake. Didn't help that most of my dreams were just boring or weird, and I didn't have to think too much about them.

But *that*? I couldn't recall having ever had a sex dream before, especially not about another man, let alone about *Bennett*. The thought was downright unnerving, and I quickly rolled over so every little movement I made didn't push my erection against the bed. The last thing I needed was my already confused brain to start associating the little tingles of pleasure from simple friction with the dream.

"Weird dream," I told myself, pushing out of bed and trying not to notice how hard I was. Morning wood wasn't a strange phenomenon, and I wasn't going to allow my mind to apply more significance to a natural biological function than was necessary. "Really, really weird dream."

Plus, there had been other aspects to the dream that didn't involve an exceptionally naked Bennett...doing things with me. The whole thing had been bizarre and felt disjointed, and I couldn't even say where it had taken place. I could safely walk away from the dream, glad I didn't find out what was behind the door.

And most certainly not wondering what would have happened with Bennett if my alarm hadn't gone off.

Before I'd managed to take two steps away from the bed, my phone started buzzing. Turning, I felt a flash of guilt as I saw Bennett's name on the caller ID. Grimacing, I reached down, my thumb hovering over the button before I finally swiped to answer it.

"Good morning," he greeted cheerily.

"Morning," I said, sitting on the edge of the bed.

"Thought you might be up at this hour."

"Would that have anything to do with the nasty little surprise you left for me?"

Bennett's laugh rolled through the phone line, and I felt a strange swooping sensation in my stomach. "I don't know what you're talking about, Adam. Did you have a weird morning wake-up or something?"

Immediately my eyes fell to my lap, where I was *still* hard. "Right. I'm sure you don't know anything. Not a damn thing. Your timing is impeccable. That's just a coincidence."

"Of course," he said with a chuckle. "Now, if you're done falsely accusing me, I was wondering when you were planning on coming over."

Ignoring my predicament, I shrugged. "I don't know, planned on getting in a shower and some food before I did anything."

I hadn't finished the job in the time frame I'd predicted. With a bit of help from Bennett, we'd managed to tear up the ruined boards and the railing, but there hadn't been much progress otherwise. In truth, I had forgotten just how distracting Bennett could be and kept finding myself lost in conversation with him while he caught me up to date on current events in Fairlake.

Births and deaths, marriages and divorces, new arrivals and those who decided to leave the town. Bennett had been in Fairlake since I'd left, and he'd kept up on all the comings and goings. Fairlake was still too big for him to know *everything*, but he'd been there when a new bakery popped up, and everyone found out that it was apparently famous. He'd been around to see the fire that broke out at the Baptist church on the edge of town and to watch people come together to help make it whole again.

While I had been caught up in the little details, the petty dramas, and the upheavals of my own life, Bennett had been in the thick of everyone else's lives. Not that I found it all that surprising, Bennett had always been the more outgoing of the two of us and possessed a fair amount of nosiness. And though I hadn't said it to him yesterday, I noticed he talked and talked but never asked about my life or what I was starting over from.

"Alright, well, I'm going to go for my morning run then," he said, sounding as cheery as ever. "If you get to my house before I get back, just let yourself in the back."

The thought made me close my eyes as I remembered coming across him yesterday, fresh from his run. Without the layers of his uniform, I could see just how strong he'd become in recent years. All his muscles had become compact and toned around his arms and chest. He had been covered in sweat, but there was only a slight redness in his face, and he looked like he'd been having a grand time. I had found myself taken aback by the sight, almost impressed with the work he'd put in, and hadn't thought of it again.

That is, until now, as I desperately tried to get my morning wood to go away so I wouldn't continue getting strange and mixed signals.

"Sure, yeah," I said roughly, standing up. "I'm going to hop in the shower."

"Sure," he said, and I could picture a small crease forming in his brow. "You alright? You sound…rough."

"Not all of us roll out of bed ready to cause mischief and mayhem from the moment we're awake," I told him gruffly. "Especially when they get woken up to 'Baby One More Time' as their fucking alarm."

Bennett cackled. "Alright, get yourself washed and fed, I'll see you soon."

I ended the phone call, staring at the screen before tossing it back on the bed. No way in hell I would let a weird dream, no matter how…well, I wasn't going to let the dream interfere. I was going to get ready to go, and that was going to start with a shower.

Possibly a cold one.

* * *

"HEY!" Bennett called as I hopped out of the truck.

I waved back, hoping my relief didn't show on my face. From the dampness of his hair and the fact that he was wearing jeans, I had to guess that I hadn't caught him immediately after his run. If I were a little more honest with myself, I had purposefully spent time with my mom in the kitchen before I decided to head out to Bennett's. At least with her, I wouldn't be left alone with my thoughts or the uncomfortable feeling I'd been left with in my gut since waking up.

I'd left all but one bag of tools at Bennett's, retrieving it from the truck. "You know, most people aren't usually perky after having to run."

Bennett chuckled. "That's because those people haven't been doing it long enough. After a while, you start to miss it if you go too long, and I always feel great afterward. I don't even need coffee anymore, just a good healthy jog and I'm set for the day."

He certainly looked perky, but then again, that was just Bennett. I rarely saw him in anything but a good mood, and usually an exuberantly good one at that. Running had never been my thing, so I had to take his word for it.

"I think we can settle on the idea that you're just strange," I said with a snort, mounting the steps to greet him at the door.

"Yeah, probably. You shoulda heard Chase when he found me doing yoga in his backyard one time," Bennett said, opening the door to let me in, my work boots thumping against the floor.

The house was pretty cramped, and Bennett certainly hadn't avoided filling it with his things. He had been like that when we were younger too, his bedroom stuffed to the gills with whatever he liked or wanted to keep on display. I had to admit, though, he had mostly done a good job of keeping the house in good shape, even down to cleaning and waxing the wooden floors to protect them from damage. It was cluttered, and things clashed, but it was vibrant and well taken care of.

"You know," I said as I followed him into the dining space that looked more like the hobby room of a squirrel on crack, "I don't think I ever came over to this neighborhood before. How'd you find this house?"

"Oh, uh, you remember Mrs. Crem?"

"Little old lady, lived by herself. Quiet, but always helped at the church."

"Right, well, she got a little weak in her later years. I guess her kids convinced her to move to some group home or something."

His tone caught my attention, and I glanced at him. "You don't sound very happy about that."

"Eh, it is what it is," he said with a shrug. However, his expression told a different story, and I could see it bothered him. Bennett wore his emotions on his face for everyone to see, or at least it had always felt that way. More than once, I'd wondered if that was really true after the conversation with my ex.

I pulled out my notebook from the day before, opening the back door to review the supplies we'd bought to ensure we had everything.

I looked over at him, cocking my head and smiling. "You were upset because your friend moved away."

It was only when I saw his expression fall briefly that the full implication of what I'd just said struck me.

"Yeah, I guess you could say that," he said with a humorless smile.

"Bennett," I began, unsure what to say to make up for it. Whether to make up for drawing attention to the elephant in the room before we were ready to talk about it, or because the elephant was there in the first place because of my own choices.

He shook his head. "She still calls me about once a week. She wasn't all that happy about going at first, but she was happy I bought the place from her. A few years later and, well, she's actually really liking her time there. I'm also pretty sure she's got a boyfriend, even if she won't admit it."

The scrunched-up look on his face made me forget my guilt for a moment, and I laughed. "Well, good for her."

"Did you know the fastest growing demographic of people infected with STIs is our elderly population in care and group homes?"

"Jesus Christ, Bennett, I'm torn between wondering how you know that and why you thought you should share."

"It's a perfectly reasonable subject jump!"

"And a perfectly disturbing one!"

Bennett let out a huff. "I tried to tell her to be safe with… whatever she was doing. And either she knew what I was trying to say and was playing dumb, or she genuinely didn't get it."

"Bennett," I said, trying to sound patient and understanding, "I've heard how you try to drop hints to other people. There's a ridiculously high chance she didn't know what you were talking about."

"That's because you don't know how wily that woman can be," he said, pointing at me as though in warning. "Trust me, she's tricky. And hey, I'm pretty good at dropping hints."

"You thought leaving ads around the house was a good way to tell your parents what you wanted for Christmas."

"They were all open to the same thing! And I mentioned wanting it!"

"Oh yes, the picture of subtlety. And let's not forget Calvin."

"What about…oh *god*."

"The guy you *swore* up and down was not into guys but was into you specifically. And how did you go about trying to get him to admit it and show you were interested in him?"

"Adam, please, let's not go over—"

"By constantly asking if he liked your *shorts*. Or your pants."

Bennett buried his face in his hands. "It seemed like a perfectly reasonable question to ask at the time!"

"No, it didn't." I snorted, putting my notebook back in my pocket. "You just wanted him to look at your ass and say something like, 'With that ass, yeah, they look good.'"

Smooth operator? Not Bennett Livington.

"I'm not awkward like that anymore," Bennett groaned, rubbing his face. "I swear."

"Well, I'd hope your idea of flirting with someone wasn't asking if they like your new shorts," I said with a raised brow.

Admittedly, he *did* look better than he had at seventeen. He might not have grown as tall as me, but he had still grown, and quickly in his sixteenth year. The result had been a gangly mess of limbs that tripped over themselves. At that age, Bennett had been equally accident- and mischief-prone. There simply hadn't been a lot to him.

Now though? Well, I suppose I had to admit that he'd probably have a lot easier time reeling in people. Then again, I wasn't sure how his scene worked. I knew from casual comments made by other gay men I'd met that things were a lot easier, at least when it came to hooking up. Relationships weren't all that different, it seemed, just as likely to crash and burn as any other.

Bennett frowned at me. "Please tell me you are not evaluating whether or not you think I'm hot enough to pick someone up. I really do not need my straight friends doing that as well as my gay ones."

I tried not to show my surprise. "You have gay friends?"

"Believe it or not, there's a few here."

"Really? Huh. Fairlake isn't all that big."

"Yeah, well, maybe the water is filled with secret gay hormones. We had some issues with frogs turning gay a few years back."

I leaned back, raising a brow. "S-seriously?"

Bennett rolled his eyes. "No, Adam, I'm not serious. It's a reference, one I'm not going to explain."

"Why not?"

"Because you'll look at me like I'm a lunatic when the dumbass who said it is the real lunatic. Now, why don't you go back to manhandling that wood and put on a show for my neighbors? The lady next door is a widow and would love to watch you work."

It was my turn to scoff and roll my eyes, though I decided he was probably right. As nice as it was to feel like I was falling back into a familiar rhythm with Bennett, there was something just as nice about focusing on a problem I could fix with relative ease. I knew Bennett was doing this to get my mind to focus on something other than my problems, and I was privately grateful.

It had been months since I'd even picked up a hammer or measuring tape, and the feel of the hammer's grip in my hand and the weight of my tool belt was welcome. Over the next few hours, I worked my way through the repairs. I had to take a minute to make myself a couple of new sawhorses, but they proved useful as I filled in the holes in the deck's floor.

The railing had kept us at the store the longest the day before. Unfortunately, I didn't have the necessary equipment to spindle the wood into balusters and needed to use the store's tools instead. However, I managed to get them to look like the original but fresher and cleaner. Affixing them took me well into the evening, but by the time I was finished, the deck was repaired.

Smiling to myself faintly, I looked over my work, confident everything was exactly like it was supposed to be but refusing not to check. I had helped to build rooms, decks, furniture, and whole houses, and not one went without at least a double check, if not triple. People relied on the things I made, and I needed to ensure they were safe.

"Here," I heard Bennett say and felt something cold pressing against my shoulder. I looked over, smiling and grabbing the beer.

"Thanks," I murmured, brushing my hand along the boards on the deck one more time to make sure they were even. "If you wanna do it yourself, I can give you my power washer. You can strip most of the gunk off the rest of the deck. Then, give it a few days of dry weather, and you can treat and stain it. Do that once every year or two, and you won't have issues for a while."

Bennett chuckled, dropping into one of the deck chairs. "I kind of forgot what it was like to watch you work."

I took a sip of the beer, remembering how my father had always told me that beer tasted better after a hard day of work. This hadn't exactly been hard, but there was something gratifying about it all the same. "When did you see me work? I didn't take my apprenticeship until I hit Boston."

"You did stuff with your dad all the time. Sometimes I'd come over and interrupt you, sometimes I'd help, but most of the time I just sat with your mom and drank coffee while we talked shit about how serious you both looked and how you only seemed to communicate in grunts," Bennett said with a lazy smile.

I snorted, plopping down into one of the deck chairs. "You don't need to talk a lot when you both know what you're trying to say."

"I guess no one knows what I'm trying to say, considering how much I talk," Bennett said in amusement.

"Or you just don't trust other people to understand what you're trying to say."

"Well, look at you! Getting all insightful and thoughtful. Are you saying I have trust issues?"

"Clearly not," I said dryly, considering he was already making me feel like I'd never left. "Otherwise, I wouldn't be sitting here."

"I guess that's true," he said, his eyes drifting away from me and growing thoughtful. Although there was nothing in his tone or expression, it left me wondering if perhaps things weren't *quite* as easygoing and comfortable for him as I was making them out to be.

"I've thought it before," I said before thinking.

"What, that I don't trust other people?"

"Well, sometimes. I don't know. Something always told me you were keeping a few things close to your chest."

Just like that, the strange foreign thing I could never name flashed across his face. And just as before, it was gone before I could give it a name. Quickly, it was replaced by a vague smile as he leaned back in his seat, turning his eyes up toward the darkening sky.

"Since when have you ever known me to keep a secret?" he asked me with a chuckle.

"Never said you were being secretive. It's not exactly a surprise that people will have a secret or three they don't tell."

"You asking if I'm keeping any secrets from you, Adam?"

"Yeah, no, definitely not doing that. I've already stepped my foot in one thing too many by opening my big mouth."

His eyes glittered, though I couldn't tell if it was amusement or curiosity. "I guess you have, and more than you know."

"Uh, is this where I say I'm feeling a chill go down my spine because I'm feeling like I should have a chill down my spine," I admitted.

"Well, for one, you already have another client," he said, reaching into his pocket, drawing out a stack of bills, and laying them on my thigh.

"Bennett," I complained, gathering up the money and holding it out to him. "I told you—"

"And I told *you* that I'm paying you," he said, raising a brow and pushing my hand away with one finger. "Don't try to argue with me over it either. You're not going to win. Because even if you win the battle of words, you're not going to win the war. I'll find a way to get that money to you one way or another, so save both of us the trouble and accept it already."

"I just, I already enjoyed—"

"Good, because Isaiah has a couple of things that he wondered if you could look at for him."

"I-Isaiah? Like, that weird kid we knew in high school? A couple of years below us?"

Bennett scowled at me. "He wasn't…okay, he was a little strange at times, but be *nice*. He's a good guy, one of the firefighters."

I stared at him. "Isaiah? Isaiah Bently, that scrawny little…nothing."

"I said be nice."

"That's just the truth. He looked like someone could blow him over if they breathed hard enough."

"And if you remember, I didn't get my growth spurt until later. He was a sophomore when we graduated and was a late bloomer. Be. Nice."

I held up my hands at his annoyed growl. "Alright, alright, I'm just…I didn't see that one coming, is all. He was like four feet tall and weighed eighty soaking wet."

"He wasn't that bad," Bennett chided, but I could see the way his lip twitched. "Anyway, he wanted a couple of handyman things done around his place. He said if you did a good job to send you his way."

"I get you asking, but—"

"You're local."

I opened my mouth to protest but decided it was probably better to keep my mouth shut. I knew how the rules of towns like ours worked, and although I was less "local" than Bennett, I was from here, I had grown up here, and my family was still here. Sure, no one knew how long I was planning to stay in Fairlake, including myself, but by that simple measure, I was still local.

"Do you have any idea what he wants done?" I asked with a sigh, tucking the money away. Perhaps when I wasn't dealing with Bennett directly I could devise a plan to give back the money without him knowing. That would be particularly tricky because despite how flaky and forgetful he might seem to some people, I knew he paid too much attention to a lot of things.

Come to think of it, that's probably what made him such a good cop.

"Not a clue," he said, taking a drink. "I think he just wants to have someone we can trust do it, and for a fair price. Also pretty sure he wants to stare at your ass."

"Oh, so Isaiah and Chase are—"

"Chase isn't gay," he pointed out to me. "Isaiah is, though. Only one at the station, but the guys there treat him good for the most part."

"For the most part?"

"There's a new guy…not sure what to say about him. Isaiah hasn't talked much about him and usually finds a sneaky way to change the subject if I bring it up. So either they're not getting along, or something weird is going on."

I sighed, flopping my free hand into my lap. "Alright, I suppose I can give him a call. Or he can call me, whatever works."

"Cool, I'll text him your number."

I had a sneaking suspicion this was part of some grand plan on Bennett's part, but I knew better than to ask. If Bennett wanted to share his plan, if there was one, he would have already been proudly breaking it down for me in incredible detail. If there was a plan in motion, he would keep it to himself and let me figure out what was happening while he snickered in the background. I knew better than anyone, except his parents, just how much chaos and mischief really lay behind that bright smile and easy laugh.

"People still think you're sweet and not in the least diabolical, don't they?" I asked dryly, taking another sip of my beer.

"Because I am," he said brightly. "Oh, one more thing."

"Oh, lord."

"Shush, I was thinking—"

"Oh, *lord.*"

"Funny, man. Anyway, I was thinking, since you could do with a little night of fun, something that isn't sitting at home and staring at the walls or being crammed into my house—"

I eyed him. "Really? You think I don't like being over here again?"

Bennett shrugged. "I'm not going to pretend to live inside your head."

It was a slight reminder, and I tried not to let it sting nearly as much as it wanted to. "Probably should finish the rest of your idea."

He snorted. "And since you also seemed interested in homosexual mating habits, I figured…ew! Gross!"

The spray of beer couldn't have been better aimed if I'd tried, but I couldn't help it as it spewed from my mouth. I coughed hard, feeling my face warm as I bent over and tried to catch my breath. Meanwhile, Bennett was wiping himself furiously, trying to get what I'm sure was a disgusting combination of spit and beer off his face.

"Seriously, dude? That's nasty," he complained, picking up his shirt to wipe his face.

"What is *wrong* with you?" I wheezed, picking my head up to glare at him once I managed to get my lungs working correctly.

"Me? What's wrong with you? You just puked all over me!"

"That wasn't puke. That was beer and some spit because there's something seriously wrong with you!"

"It was a joke, you drama queen," he grumbled, still wiping his face.

I couldn't explain to him that I was feeling a little sensitive about the topic considering the dream I'd had that morning. That would have led to a bunch of questions I wasn't prepared to ask myself, let alone try to answer for him.

"I was not interested in…whatever the fuck you just said," I grumbled, wiping my mouth. "Get to the point, Bennett."

Bennett grunted, wiping his cheek with the back of his hand. "Sometimes I go to this bar a couple of towns over when I'm feeling like socializing with people who aren't in Fairlake and have a couple of drinks. If you're interested, you can join me next weekend."

"A bar?"

"I can see the question on your face. Yes, a gay bar, Adam. I promise to protect you from the big scary men who might hit on you."

"I don't need you to protect me," I protested with a scowl. "That's not—"

"What, are you going to be the one to suck them off in the bathroom to assuage their overwhelming need for sex?"

"Their—" I huffed, suddenly finding the conversation even more ridiculous and annoying. "Jesus Christ, you know damn well I don't think gay men are a bunch of horndogs who can't go more than a day without sex, right?"

Bennett grinned wickedly. "Oh, I know, but I can't help seeing if I can get that interesting shade of red on your face."

"And if someone gets handsy, I don't need you to deal with it," I said, my stomach unsettled at the thought.

Bennett rolled his eyes. "Everyone there knows I'm a cop. They're going to behave themselves. And I'm not going to try to suck someone off to calm them down, sheesh, Adam."

"I really don't like this conversation anymore," I grumbled because I didn't.

"Alright, then wanna cut it short and just agree to go with me next Friday?"

"I think I can manage that much."

"Cool, pick me up, or I pick you up?"

"I'll drive. I'm not really...probably better I don't have more than a few drinks."

Bennett smiled, and I could sense something inside him relaxing. "Cool, we'll make a night of it, just the two of us."

It was nice to see him at ease again, and I too, settled in. I wasn't quite sure how I felt about going to a gay bar with him, but there was no point questioning the decision now I'd made it. I'd been to them before and had never felt uncomfortable, so I just had to chalk it up to the strange day I'd had, the strange week, and the even stranger past couple of years.

Things would be fine. There was no need to worry.

BENNETT

With a groan, I stretched out, pushing against the floorboards of Adam's truck and arching my back so I could stretch my arms behind me. Eventually, my hands thumped gently against the glass of his rear window, and I let out a contented sigh as I felt the muscles in my body finally ease their death grip on one another.

"We've been driving for half an hour. You can't be cramping up yet," Adam told me dryly from the driver's seat.

"No," I groaned, leaning over to get another angle and relieve another set of muscles. "But I've been sitting at a desk all day, and I feel like one big cramp. I probably should have gone for a short run after my shift."

"Have you ever considered the possibility that you have an unhealthy obsession with running?"

"Have you ever considered that maybe you're just making fun of my enjoyment of running because you get winded climbing the stairs to my front porch?"

It wasn't strictly true, but it was still fun to poke at him a little. I actually didn't know what kind of runner he was, though from his aversion I'd guess he wasn't a very good one.

Adam was still in good shape, which his outfit tonight only emphasized.

I was trying not to notice how his dark jeans managed to hug his thighs perfectly, enough to show them off but not enough to make me wonder just how he put them on. The light blue plaid button-up hugged him, and he'd rolled the sleeves just past his elbows. Which meant his forearms were on display in a way that normally drove me a little crazy, but there were even more layers considering it was him.

"Running is for rabbits," he grumbled, gently passing someone going ten under the speed limit with ease.

"I thought that was supposed to be leafy green food," I said, remembering someone once telling me that they found the sight of a man driving erotic. At the time, I'd been confused about how something so mundane could be sexy. Yet, watching Adam navigate the road without a hint of annoyance and with complete confidence was appealing.

My brain was a weird place, and I would never be able to explain it.

"I like salads...and vegetables," Adam said with a frown, easing the car back into place and readjusting his grip on the wheel.

"Probably because your parents can actually cook," I said, laughing. "Remember when my mom tried to make a vege-tarian lasagna?"

"It looked like it had grown out of mold...growth," Adam said, wrinkling his nose at the memory. "And tasted like... nothing. Salt and nothing."

I chuckled, glancing out the window so I wouldn't stare at him while he drove. Our friendship had only started rebuilding about a week and a half ago, but I was already struggling to deal with the emergence of old feelings. I had hoped I might be better, but it turned out Adam was...still Adam. A little too serious at times, a little too easily flustered, but generally calm and even, steady and thoughtful as he moved through the world. His confidence might have taken a hit recently, but to me he still seemed like a man who could cope with any situation without doubting himself. Perhaps I'd thought there would be a change with all the time we'd spent apart or simply because we'd been pushed apart because of him.

I didn't know whether to be disappointed or relieved that he hadn't changed.

"She hasn't got much better," I informed him. "Thankfully, since she and Dad decided Arizona was the place to live, of all places, I haven't been subjected to her cooking."

"He says as if he doesn't miss his parents," Adam said, taking the exit I pointed at.

"Yeah," I admitted with a shrug. "But I talk to them at least once a week, and they make it up here for Christmas most of the time. My birthday a couple of times."

I missed them dearly, but my parents were happy where they were. Personally, I didn't think I'd know what to do being surrounded by a brown desert, where the only green came in the form of cacti. Give me colder winters, lush forests, and towering mountains any day. Hell, for all I knew, I would change my mind when I reached retirement age.

"It's been…pretty nice, seeing my parents more often," he said slowly, and I had to hide a smile.

There had never been a question in my mind as to whether or not Adam loved his parents because he did. I also knew his parents tended to drive him up the wall a little. It probably didn't help that he'd been forced to retreat to his parents' house to try to put his life back together. Adam had always been so self-sufficient and independent that I was sure it stung his pride more than a little.

In the past, I'd wondered whether that self-sufficiency and independence were precisely why we'd always gotten along so well when we were younger and perhaps had been the driving factor of Adam pushing away from me. Neither of us liked being dependent on other people and had always been fond of doing things our way. When those values were violated too heavily, I tended to get restless and a little wild, prone to impulse and whim, while Adam usually withdrew, a brooding, grumpy, stubborn man who balked at being moved further.

"Here it is!" I proclaimed happily, pointing at the building, a squat thing with fresh siding, a clean parking lot, and a well-lit sign.

"Stop n' Glow?" Adam asked as he pulled into the parking lot.

"Yeah, like a glow up?"

"Really?"

"Well, glow up is like—"

"I know what it means, Bennett. I haven't been living under a rock, and if that's some sort of gay term, you're not the only gay man I've been friends with."

I wish I could say that thought made me happy and not annoyed, but the flash of irritation was there all the same. "Well, the old building burned down and was left sitting there like an eyesore. Guy who bought it a handful of years ago came from Denver, had a butt ton of money, poured it into the lot, and revitalized it. So, it got a glow up."

"That seems like a name that will lose any relatability in a few years."

"I never said it was a good name. Makes me laugh, though."

"Yes, making you laugh, a difficult feat indeed."

I chuckled, shoving open the passenger door and hopping out. "I love life and laughter. What can I say?"

"Knowing you? A lot of things."

"You're so clever. That's what I like about you."

We entered through the side door and were immediately greeted by the bar area a couple of yards in front of us, jutting out from the wall to our right. There were booths to our right and left, and on the other side of the bar was a collection of raised tables and chairs. A small dance floor was shoved into the corner, but I only saw it used when it was really busy or there was a DJ for events. Most people just used the jukebox next to the bar, beside the double doors leading to an enclosed patio.

"Well, well," a voice called over music that thankfully wasn't blaring so loud you had to scream to hope to be heard. "Look who it is!"

Grinning, I waved at the bartender. "Well, hey there, Dominic, I thought you quit?"

The older man behind the counter shook his head, long gray hair flopping around his shoulders. "Went on vacation."

"For a month?"

"Had it built up. Told the old bastard that I worked here for three years and took a whole two days off when I got sick, and he could give me all of my vacation time at once. Took my sister and my nephew to Hawaii for a couple of weeks, then went over to Greece to see some extended family."

"Well, damn, look at you, world traveling," I chuckled, gesturing to Adam. "This is my friend, Adam."

"Another friend, eh?" Dominic asked, and I repressed the urge to sigh.

"Not *that* kind of friend," I said, leaning over the bar. "He's straight, be nice. I've known him since we were kids."

"Ahh, well, nice to meet you either way," Dominic said, looking Adam over, then around the bar at some of the other patrons. "Though, not too smart bringing someone looking like that in here. You know how people feel about fresh meat."

"Fresh meat?" Adam asked, and I didn't have to turn around to know that his thin brow was pushing up his forehead.

"Two of my usual," I told Dominic before turning around to face Adam. "Welcome to the only gay bar for miles around. Everyone either knows everyone else or is used to seeing the same faces."

"I'm meat?"

I had to hold back the urge to laugh at his confused and almost slightly insulted expression. "You're a good-looking guy they've never seen before, do not be surprised if someone tries hitting on you...more than one person, actually. As for your meat, well—"

"Oh god," he groaned, bowing his head to shake it.

Honestly, the less I said about his meat, the better. I took the two drinks from Dominic and slid my card across the bar to start a tab. "Don't worry about it. I'm sure you'll get through the night without getting too molested."

"I know you're just saying this shit to get a rise out of me. It won't work," Adam said, taking the drink I offered him and sipping it. "Jesus, Bennett, I'm supposed to be the DD."

I laughed. "You'll be fine. Nurse that for a little while. I like to get a decent dose of booze in me and then stretch my drinks out over the rest of the night. Gets me a good buzz but doesn't usually fuck me up."

"And if it does fuck you up?"

"Well, there just so happens to be a motel up the road that usually has vacancies. I've stumbled into their front office a few times in the past."

"They know you as well as the people in here do?"

"Thank god, no. Otherwise, I'd be really worried about myself," I said with a snort, taking a drink and blinking. Okay, the drink wasn't usually *this* strong. Apparently,

Dominic was either feeling generous or was interested in getting Adam drunk before the night was over.

I was going to think the best and go with the former.

"C'mon, let's go get a seat and scope out what's happening," I told Adam, nodding toward the raised tables.

"Am I going to watch you have game?" Adam asked wryly as we found a seat in the corner, pulling ourselves up into the chairs.

"I'm not here to get laid," I told him, taking another drink. "I just like getting out once in a while and chatting with people. If I were trying to get laid, I would not have brought my gay-for-pay best friend with me."

"Gay for...excuse me?"

"Porn category. Gay men love them some straight men."

Adam eyed me, unimpressed. "You're going to have to try harder than that to get to me, Bennett."

"Well, the funny thing is, none of what I've told you is made to get under your skin. You really are fresh meat in their eyes, and gay guys really do like them some straight-to-gay porn," I said with a shrug. That my younger self had indulged in my fair share of it plenty of times, along with books and fanfictions to feed into my feelings, was something that would have to go left unsaid.

Adam shook his head in response and went back to taking small sips and looking around. He no longer looked as rough as the first day I'd seen him and woken him from his stupor. Color had returned to his face, and his gaze didn't tend to slip out of focus as he stared into the distance. I liked to think part of it was because I was around him again, but I was willing to bet it had more to do with the work he'd been doing lately. Ever since I'd sent him Isaiah's way, I'd heard from more people interested in having Adam swing by to help them with something.

"So," I said, cocking my head, "have you been enjoying your busy week?"

"I have," he said, side-eyeing me. "Which I'm sure you could have answered for yourself since you planned it that way."

"Me, planning? Never," I said because that's exactly what I had been doing. That it was so far proving to be a spectacular success was fantastic. "But you know, since you've already got, what was it, three weeks of appointments?"

"Four now," he said, smirking. "Also not your doing?"

"Okay, look, Isaiah wasn't even my fault, alright?"

"Uh-huh."

"It's not! I mentioned what you were doing, he said he was interested, I passed the message along."

"That does sound pretty innocent, but from the look on your face you're either holding something back or just remembered something important."

"Well," I drew out, "I might have told him I'd tell you, but only if he promised to pass along to other people what you were doing if you did a good job. So really, this is your fault for doing a good job."

"Right. Of course, silly me."

"Act grumpy all you want," I told him. "I know for a fact you're happy as hell to have work again."

"Yeah, well, I haven't had any work in months. So it's nice to have something to do besides stare at bills and new motions from Bri's lawyer," Adam said with a sour expression and then blinked. "Sorry."

"Don't be," I said quickly. "But, uh, why haven't you had any work?"

"The fun thing about going through a rough divorce is you start to lose a lot more than you think you're going to," he said with a chuckle that carried no humor whatsoever. Adam picked up his glass and looked it over, turning it in the faint overhead light. "I had a business that I'd been running for a while. We mostly built furniture and things like that."

"You were a furniture maker?"

"Eh, it was a side thing. Just something to, I don't know, have fun with?"

I smiled, thinking of the hobbies I'd picked up over the years. "Something to flex a little creative, fun muscle with."

"Basically," he said, taking another sip, this one heavier than the others, "it was just, well, what I'm doing now. Go out and fix someone's porch. Fix someone's doorway and do everything in a kitchen or bathroom that didn't involve wiring. Build a shed, whatever."

"Huh," I said, a little nonplussed at first. For the first few years, I knew he'd been working at different shops and union jobs and thinking about going into business for himself. It had been his reason for going to college here and there over a few years to get an idea of running a business. "Got around to fulfilling that dream, huh?"

"Yeah, I wasn't sure how well it would work out. I mean, there were plenty of services in the field, so it wasn't like I was doing anything special," Adam admitted with a shrug that I wasn't too fond of. "Even Bri wondered how the hell I managed to make it work, and I couldn't give her an answer."

"Easy to say for someone who already had an in with her law firm," I said, just loud enough for him to hear but not to interrupt. I'd only met her once, and there'd been something sharp and icy about Brianne that I hadn't been comfortable with. Still, she'd warmed up when Adam was around, so I'd simply chalked it up to the sort of awkwardness that came from meeting your new partner's old friend.

"I pointed that out to her once after she expressed her 'surprise' one too many times," Adam chuckled. "She was never fond of when I mouthed off to her."

"Mouth off? What were you to her, a sassy eight-year-old?" I asked with a scowl.

"I used to tell myself she was just used to working in an environment where she had to be strict, demanding, and a little rude," he said with a shrug. "In the early days, she wasn't like that with me for the most part. But as time went on—"

Saying something didn't feel right. Not only because I didn't know the woman well, but I didn't want to interrupt Adam now he was finally talking. Honestly, if I'd known that dragging him to a gay bar a couple of towns away would get him talking, I might have done it sooner.

"But things went downhill, and the divorce got nasty." He wrinkled his nose. "Well, it's still nasty. I could tell which way the winds were blowing, and I just...I don't know. I've tried so hard to make this as painless as possible. Not that I always did. Sometimes she'd dig in deep, and I'd find myself digging right back. It was part of why I decided to come to Fairlake. Maybe the distance would make it easier to stop hating each other so much."

"I hear divorce can get pretty nasty," I said, realizing I was well out of my depth. What did someone like me know what it meant to fall in love with, marry, and then fall apart from someone so heavily that it required legal proceedings to duke it out?

"It was nasty before. The lawyers just make it official... and a little more targeted," he said, taking a bigger drink. "Truth is, I was willing to let her have that stupidly big apartment she insisted we had to have, most of the crap in it was hers anyway. I'd keep my tools, clothes, books I'd had since I was a kid, and stuff like that. Everything else could be hers. But then she tried to go after our vehicles. She had to fight over every penny in our shared bank account even though I was willing to give her most of it. And then—"

I knew where this was headed. "She wanted your business."

"That she did," he said, and for the first time I heard not irritation but actual bitterness and anger in his voice. "She never wanted anything to do with the damn thing, the thing I built before I even knew she existed. Hell, she used to bitch about me coming home smelling like sweat and dirt, dragging in sawdust and everything else. She set foot in my shop two whole times, but when it came down to it, I could tell she was setting her sights on *my* business."

"So what'd you do?" I prompted.

"The first of only two things I did that I knew would really piss her right off," he said with a smile I'd never seen on Adam's face before. It was victorious, but it was ugly and mean, and I wondered if I had really been missing out all that much when it came to romance if this was what it could turn someone into. "I burned that fucker down."

I blinked as he drained his drink. "Uh, ethical dilemmas aside, did you just admit to arson to a police officer?"

He laughed, and this time I could hear his humor return as he shook his head. "Not literally. I couldn't have brought myself to do that, no matter how pissed off I was, and I was pretty pissed. No, I arranged the sale of everything in the store, dissolved the business, and sold the location to someone who'd been sniffing around for ages trying to get it from me for some pizzeria or something, I can't remember."

"Oh," I said with relief. I wasn't sure what I would have to do if I found out my best friend had committed a felony. All things considered, I would have been torn between the ethics of my job and my respect and loyalty to my friend. "Can't that backfire on someone in the middle of a divorce?"

"Not if you're honest about what you're doing. I informed Ted, my lawyer, what was happening, and he did everything to ensure she and her lawyer knew what was happening. She proved my suspicion right by immediately trying to stop me, but she had a hard time doing it. Other than being married to me, she didn't have a stake in the business, not the slightest bit of control," Adam chuckled. "I bet she regretted it at that moment. She couldn't stop me in time, and yeah, all that money went into the same lump sum that was being split between us but hey, she didn't get my baby, so that's what matters to me."

"Even now?" I asked, sliding my drink toward him as I saw him glance around. I figured he could do with a few more drinks tonight than me. I was pretty sure I could drive his beast of a truck when we needed to leave.

"Even now," he reaffirmed, taking my drink without a second thought.

"So, what was the second thing you knew would piss her off?" I asked, motioning to Dominic when I caught his gaze and held up the glass Adam had polished off.

"Well, pretty sure the judge knew what I was doing, so he wanted to know why I was so intent on liquidating my successful business. So, I told him that, simply put, I wasn't interested in staying in the Boston area anymore. Truth was, I was moving to the other side of the country, and I didn't see a point in trying to run a business from afar when I had been successful because I'd been running it by being there all the time."

"And that pissed her off?"

"Funny thing, all of this, or stuff like this. Bri and I...we grew apart and grew to hate each other. We couldn't be together, I know that now, and she does too. Thing is, she'd never leave me alone. First, it was her contacting me when we were supposed to be separated, and then when the lawyers got involved there were constant requests and demands and blah blah blah."

"She wanted to keep in contact. She couldn't let you go," I said, guessing where he was going with this.

It was something I'd witnessed before with other couples. No matter how clear it was that neither of them was good for the other, one or both kept finding ways to come back around, to hold fast to the other person. I used to find myself wondering why people would hold so tightly to something that was just going to bring them pain. Why would people want to stay close to someone who hurt them, drove them crazy, or didn't give them what they needed or wanted?

Then I'd remember my long-standing complicated feelings toward Adam and would quietly remind myself to mind my own business and shut the hell up.

"That's what I figured too," he said with a shake of his head. "And that's just...I just wanted it to be over, you know? I wanted to move on, leave it all behind us and have our lives continue."

"Yeah," I said softly, having felt something like that several times when it came to Adam. Admittedly, there had never been any reciprocity from him when it came to feelings, but sometimes I had wondered what it would be like not to have to feel so stuck on him, to feel myself swerving back to him every time. It reappeared when I realized Adam was drifting away from me, and I realized there was nothing I could do about it. At times there had been something like relief as if that was finally my chance to move on with my life, but most of the time I just felt that dull ache in my chest.

"We built this whole life together. We were supposed to be partners in crime, life, or whatever. And I don't even know where it started to go wrong," he said, staring up at the ceiling and barely moving when Dominic set two more drinks down before disappearing. "Maybe there isn't a single point where things like that happen. Fuck knows I've tried to discover it. I've run myself into the ground trying to figure it out. Maybe it just starts with the little things. The stuff you don't pay attention to. Like the white caps on waves that flicker in the distance that tell you it's a bit of a windy day. They're so far away it doesn't seem to matter. But you should pay attention. Those waves can be a lot bigger than you thought when they finally reach shore. If you aren't paying attention, they can sweep you off your feet. That's what happened to us, I think. We didn't pay attention, and we didn't take precautions. It feels like I've been dragged out to sea and barely know how to swim. Now those waves I thought weren't that big a deal have been throwing me all over the place, and all I can do is hope not to drown."

I sat, listening to what was easily the longest speech I'd ever heard from Adam, and my heart ached for him. It had spilled out of him so easily and smoothly that I wondered just how long he'd thought about that speech. How many times he'd practiced it in his head, debated with himself about the wording, and how many times he had felt it tear at him as he realized he was having an internal discussion about the dissolution of the life he'd tried to build.

"Is that what happened when you came back here?" I asked once the silence had gone on long enough to feel confident he was done talking. "Like, those first few days?"

"Something like that," he said, stirring his drink mindlessly before finishing it off and grabbing a third one. "I just stopped trying to stay above water. It was like, without her around to constantly badger me, push me or throw me around, I decided there was no point trying to tread water anymore. I turned my phone off, found my dad's liquor supply, and let myself sink for a little while."

"I'll be honest, I'm torn between saying it's perfectly alright to mourn and feeling like staying down there wasn't the best idea," I admitted, taking the last drink for myself. As much as I was okay with him getting plenty of alcohol, I also didn't want to see him overdoing it.

He seemed to have the same thoughts as he held onto his third drink, considering it. "And then this dumbass search and rescue guy showed up, tooting his horn to the tune of a terrible pop song, and dragged me up to the surface."

"And again, having conflicting feelings."

"Look, I let myself sink, and I probably would have stayed there for the longest time, a lot longer than I probably should have. It felt like I'd been mourning for so long without actually mourning. Things just kept happening, back-to-back, and I never had a chance to really…I guess, appreciate what was happening."

"And you are now?"

"I am. I finally have the chance to look around and see my life for what it's been for the past couple of years, even before all the lawyers and courts got involved. It's depressing as all hell, but it's manageable now."

"Just needed to sink down there for a little while?" I asked with a small smile.

To my surprise, he reached over and squeezed my elbow. "I think I needed to be reminded that there are people willing to drag my mopey ass up and remind me to take a deep breath."

The gesture touched me, and I smiled at him, laying my hand over his and squeezing back. Physical touch had never really been our way of showing affection, as neither of us had been touchy people. For me, it marked just how much he meant what he said and how appreciative he was.

"Well, I don't know about all that, but I'm glad I could be of service," I told him with a smile.

"And I know we still need to talk about—"

A cry went up, and we both turned toward the bar just in time for me to realize that one of the cries had been my name. I snorted hard when I saw Isaiah waving feverishly from the bar, his face red and wearing a broad smile.

"Jesus, how drunk is he right now?" Adam asked in amusement.

"Very," I confirmed before waving at Isaiah to come over since it was clearly what he wanted to do. "Not that it takes much. He's the definition of a lightweight."

"Hope he's not driving," Adam intoned, frowning.

"Nah, that whole group is with him, and I'm sure he's probably got someone driving him," I promised him and then frowned as I saw all of them coming over. "Oh crap, I was just going to say hi to him. I didn't realize he was going to bring the whole posse over, sorry. I know you were going to say something."

"It can wait," Adam snorted, leaning back once more. "Go ahead and shine, you social butterfly."

"Fine, but don't drift away too far to hide in the background," I teased.

"I'll be right here," he told me.

ADAM

Bennett and Isaiah's friends liked to touch...a lot. Not me, necessarily. All of them had looked me over appraisingly from the moment they were introduced, but only a couple kept checking me out after Bennett had destroyed any of their brief hopes about me. I hadn't heard what he said, but I imagined he told them I was straight. His comment about some gay men's love of straight men kept intruding every time I found one of them watching me for too long.

No, they really liked touching each other and Bennett.

It was the last part that bothered me as the night went on and the drinks continued to flow. Bennett had *never* been physically affectionate. Playful, energetic, and always willing to lend a helping hand, but touch had never been his way of showing he was close to someone, not unless they were upset and in desperate need of a hug.

These people, however, had their hands on him constantly. For some, it was just a small thing like a hand on his arm or shoulder. Others felt the need to actively hold his hand when they talked to him or place their hand on the small of his back. No matter where their hands roamed, Bennett never seemed to notice. Or at least, he didn't seem to care.

It left me with the uncomfortable feeling that something about Bennett's life had somehow changed him in a way I hadn't noticed. In the grand scheme of things, it really shouldn't have bothered me. After all, wasn't it a good thing that my friend had become more comfortable with being touched, even if he wasn't the one touching anyone?

I tried to tell myself it wasn't a big deal and I was just suffering from the aftereffects of spilling my guts to Bennett before the party started. The annoyed part of me was far more insistent, however, that it shouldn't sit right with me. Bennett had always been particular about touching or being touched, and this group of guys did it without the slightest hesitation.

Bennett leaned in, raising a brow and speaking so only I could hear him. "You alright?"

"Hm? Oh, yeah, I'm fine," I told him quickly, motioning to the collection of guys that had dragged us out onto the patio so a few of them could smoke. "Just watching the…shenanigans."

It wasn't the first time Bennett cornered me to ensure I was alright. The little check-ins reminded me I needed to get my shit together before he really noticed something was up. Bennett wasn't neglectful when it came to social situations, but he wasn't one to check in as often as he was. Something was telling him something was wrong with me, and while he wouldn't push it with other people around, his radar was still pinging.

"Well, hey there, stranger," a new voice piped up, and I tensed as I felt someone drape themselves over my shoulders. I craned my neck to find Isaiah's face a few inches from mine. "Still Mr. Sits-in-the-Corner-and-Glares-at-Everyone I see."

"I wasn't glaring at you when I was at your house," I reminded him, trying to lean away without being obvious. Isaiah had been the picture of polite and well-behaved when I'd been at his house, and I was left with the impression he had zero interest in me.

"Isaiah's house too?" one of the men said, whose name escaped me because remembering names had never been my expertise. He was the only one in the group who looked like he'd walked out of the mid-2000s, all the way up to his frosted tips that stood straight up. "You wanna come to my house while you're at it?"

"He was fixing my porch, Derrick," Isaiah told him, his voice scolding.

"Oh, so he's good with wood?"

"Quit being horny."

"And what fun is that?"

"The kind where I tell everyone why you needed to call me last spring," Bennett piped up from the nearby table.

All interest in other topics of conversation immediately diverted to whatever the mystery of Derrick's call for help had been. The comment earned Bennett a dirty look from Derrick, who only smiled benignly back at him. Had I been so inclined, I would have warned Derrick that irritating Bennett was the last thing anyone wanted to do. The man had a sharp mind, and while he wasn't usually the type to harass someone, he could be dangerous when pushed.

That Derrick's comments to me counted as pushing Bennett at least went a little way toward making me feel better.

"Don't mind them," Isaiah told me. "They're good guys most of the time, but they—"

"What?" I asked, turning to look at him again. I was

forced to pull my head back a little more so I wouldn't go cross-eyed while talking to him.

"Eh, a couple of them have egos. So they're just, uh, trying to bring you down a peg or two," Isaiah told me, speaking softly. The only noise was the conversation from everyone who'd congregated outside, with the music drowned out by the walls, so he could afford to speak quietly.

"Bring me down, what the fuck for?" I asked with a flash of annoyance. I had done nothing to these men except sit around, occasionally talking to whoever spoke to me. Was this some sort of distrust because I was the only straight guy in the group?

Isaiah sighed, sliding off my shoulders, which I was grateful for, and plopping down into the seat beside me. "Well, don't go telling anyone this, but some of them kind of have a thing for Bennett."

The thought irritated me further for some reason. "So? He's single. I'm straight. What's stopping them?"

"Bennett is," Isaiah said with a light snicker and then eyed the drink on the table near him. "Is this mine?"

"Pretty sure you drank yours already."

"Nu-uh! It was full when I saw it last."

"And then stopped being full when you kept drinking it."

"Dammit." He sighed heavily, taking the drink anyway. "Finders keepers, right?"

I raised a brow. "You're a goofy drunk, aren't you?"

"A little." He snickered. "And I thought you'd talk more when you drank. But you just been sip sip sippin' away without anything but a li'l wobble in your step."

"I didn't wobble," I said, jamming the straw into my mouth.

"Sure ya did," Isaiah said with a contented sigh as he took a drink of his stolen cocktail.

"And what do you mean, Bennett's stopping them?" I

asked, glancing at the nearby group of chatting men. If any of them were paying attention to our conversation, they were doing a damn fine job hiding it.

"I mean"—he paused to take a drink—"that Bennett just doesn't…do anything with them."

"Anything?"

"Well, not what they want anyway. Just cuz he's willing to sleep with them doesn't mean he wants anything else."

This conversation was doing nothing to improve my mood, but I found myself oddly fascinated all the same. As uncomfortable as it was to get details of Bennett's sex life, *extremely* uncomfortable in fact, I found myself hypnotized. I was an onlooker to a crash scene, wishing I didn't have to see something so upsetting and unable to turn my face away.

"He's…slept with all of them?" I asked quietly. "All of you, I mean?"

"Nah," Isaiah said with a shake of his head. "He's not really the 'sleep around with every hot friend he has' type. We went on a date once, but I think we just did that because we thought we should. We figured out pretty quickly that we should just be friends, and nothing else has happened. He's like that with most of 'em, actually. But there's been a few he's fooled around with. Nothing serious, but some of 'em want it to be serious."

"They want him all to themselves," I said with a grunt.

"Pretty much," Isaiah said with a chuckle, now entertaining himself by poking at the ice in his glass with the straw. "They want it, he doesn't."

"So?"

"So? So they want it, and they're not being given it. Makes them a little bitter but doesn't stop them from trying."

"What, they don't know how to take no for an answer?" I asked, not caring that I sounded almost as annoyed as I actually was.

"Ehhhhh," Isaiah said with a wiggle of his free hand. "There's 'no,' and then there's no. I mean, aren't there women who don't mean no when they say no? I've known a couple."

"Not in my world," I said with a snort. "No is no."

"Really? Huh, I've known a couple who actually get upset when a guy took no for no, at least when what they wanted was for the guy to know it meant yes."

"That's…too fucking complicated and stupid as hell. If she says no, she means no. If she didn't mean no, then she should've said something else."

Not that I hadn't run into that sort of weird wordplay with people before, but I'd stayed right away from it from the beginning. For all Bri's issues, she'd always been clear on what she did and didn't want. That wasn't without its own issues, but at the very least, I usually had a clear idea where she stood.

"Well, they're persistent," Isaiah said with a shrug. "But Bennett is Bennett. He just keeps letting them down gently."

"Sounds about right," I grumbled, irritated with Bennett's happy-go-lucky, people-pleasing attitude. It wasn't the first time in our friendship, but it was the most recent. Sometimes I wished the man could tell people to fuck off and leave him alone. "They should just accept it and move on."

"Well, that's where you come in," Isaiah said, fishing out an ice cube and popping it into his mouth.

The angry squirming in my stomach flipped, and I felt something flutter. "What do *I* have to do with anything?"

"I mean, he doesn't even get close to them. Like, especially the ones he's slept with. They know some things, but they don't *know* him. We're all friends to him. Hell, I just get the 'good friend' moniker," Isaiah said with a smile that said his words didn't bother him in the slightest. "Then here you are, all six foot…four inches?"

"Three," I grunted, unsure what that had to do with anything.

"Right, six foot four inches of you. All dark and handsome, with just the sort of grumpiness people like."

"I'm not grumpy," I said with a frown. "I just don't talk much around people I don't know unless it's a business thing."

"Ooh, so add mysterious and silent on top," Isaiah said with a laugh. It was high and clear, and despite his laughing at me I found it hard to be annoyed. His laugh fit the image of this lighthearted, slightly silly guy who was just having a good night.

"I'm not mysterious," I said with a roll of my eyes.

Isaiah looked pointedly at Bennett, who was leaning over to hear something someone was whispering in his ear. "Maybe not to him, and he's probably not a mystery to you. So yeah, you being straight and not his boyfriend? That kind of is the problem."

My eyes lingered on the whispered conversation, my brow furrowing. "Wouldn't that be a *good* thing?"

"Not really," Isaiah said in a strange tone. "It just means that you, a straight guy, get to know more about who Bennett is than the people he's slept with, than the guys who want to date him. These guys would happily get closer to Bennett, but lo and behold, the one guy off-limits to Bennett is the one he chooses to confide in."

I glanced at Isaiah, surprised when I saw a thoughtful expression on his face. "So, because I'm off the table for Bennett, and Bennett trusts me as his best friend, I'm an issue?"

"Nah, not an issue," Isaiah said, turning his thoughtful expression on me and looking me over. "They're *jealous*, Adam. You might not have noticed, but Bennett is kind of a good catch. He's cute, funny, has a solid job, his own house and car, knows how to make people feel special."

"I'm straight, not fucking blind," I grumbled because, *yes*, I had noticed, thank you. It was kind of hard not to notice. Anyone with a pair of eyes and a few functioning brain cells would have been able to come to the same conclusion. "Bennett will find someone when he's ready. Anyone else can fuck off and leave him alone until then."

Isaiah cocked his head. "That so?"

"What?" I asked, hearing the defensiveness in my voice.

"Nothing," Isaiah said quickly...a little too quickly. "Just a little impressed at how quickly you're jumping to defend his honor is all."

"I'm not defending shit," I grumbled. "But if someone tells you to fuck off, you should fuck off. That's just how things should work. If he doesn't wanna be with anyone, no one should force him."

"Oh, I'm not so sure he doesn't want to be with someone," Isaiah said, and almost immediately I watched his face freeze.

I arched my brow. "Said something you weren't supposed to?"

"No," he said with the same haste as before.

"Somehow," I said slowly, looking him over, "I don't believe you. Who's he interested in?"

"I didn't say I knew anyone specific," he said, averting his eyes. "I'm just saying, a man's gotta have *someone* they're into once in a while, right? I don't know why Bennett would be any different."

"You're a terrible liar," I said, narrowing my eyes. "And you definitely know more than you're trying to let on."

"Nope," he said lightly, leaning back in his seat and busying himself with his drink.

"Liar," I growled.

Not that there was any point in trying to grill him further, Isaiah was clearly trying to avoid the subject and would probably bolt if I pushed it. Well, it would probably end up causing a scene, which I'm sure half the guys would probably enjoy. The last thing I wanted to do was call attention to myself and have Bennett wonder what was wrong.

"I need a refill," Isaiah proclaimed after a couple of tension-filled minutes, pushing up from his chair.

Which left me to stew in our conversation as I finished my drink. I had no idea how many I'd polished off, but I could feel the liquor working through my body. What had previously been a pleasant warmth and lethargy was now replaced by a brittle, sharp-edged annoyance that kept prickling at the edge of my thoughts.

Was this really how I found out that Bennett was into someone else? I knew I hadn't exactly been the best of friends with him in recent years, but to actively keep something important from me?

He was my friend, and maybe I hadn't proven to be a best friend again just yet, but I would have still liked to know. The whole subject just turned the alcohol in my stomach sour, and I ended up putting aside my drink, refusing to touch the rest.

Maybe it was just a good reminder that I didn't know Bennett like I once had and that he still didn't trust me with something this big. The idea that he would have someone he was interested in and keep that fact from me sat in the center of my thoughts as the night wore on.

It was only another hour before some of the group began to split off. Some, like Isaiah, wandered out with a wobbly gait that showed just how much they'd had to drink. Others managed to walk out seeming sober, while I spotted a few, including those I hadn't met, walking out with other people.

"You ready to go?" Bennett asked, appearing at my side with a smile.

"Sure," I grunted, peering up and wondering what else he'd been keeping from me.

Which of these guys was possibly the one Bennett was interested in being with? There had been plenty of guys in the little mini-party, and most had been pretty good-looking. All of them had known Bennett and were friendly with him. Was the guy Bennett had his eye on even in this group? Was it someone I even knew?

"Okay," Bennett said, a little crease forming in his brow before nodding his head toward the door. "Let's get going then."

"Sure," I grunted, pushing myself upward.

Bennett shot me a curious glance but said nothing as he turned to the remainder of the group to say his final good-byes. Considering I hadn't spoken to most of them, I decided to head back in to the bar, dropping off the glasses I'd accrued for the bartender to clean.

"Have fun?" he asked, looking me over.

"Thanks for the drinks," I told him, reaching into my wallet and sliding twenty bucks onto the counter.

"Bennett's already covering the drinks," he told me.

"It's a tip."

"He tips pretty damn good."

"Then have some more money."

The man grinned, taking the bill and tossing it into a beer pitcher containing a handful of bills. "The day I turn down an extra tip is the day I need to be sent to the looney bin."

That dragged a small smile out of me. "Out of everyone I met today, you're easily my favorite."

"I'd take that as high praise, but I know some of the losers you could have met, so I'm not going to be too flattered," he chuckled.

"That's mean," Bennett announced, having apparently come in just in time to hear the conversation.

"Yeah, and you're one of them," the bartender said with a smirk, winking at me. "You get tired of hanging out with this idiot, come on in and spend time with me. I'll show you what fun really is."

"It sounds like he's being *horny*," Bennett explained, accepting the printed drink bill and picking up a pen. "But he actually wants to test your knowledge about movies. The man is a film-obsessed nut."

"It's called being *passionate* about something. You should try it."

"I'm passionate about getting out of here before I get stuck in another rant about how older movies were better before color and sound."

"There was nuance and subtlety that you don't—"

"Dominic," Bennett said with a smirk, pen hovering over the tip line on the receipt. "See where the pen is? Think long and hard about how long you want to pin me down with a rant about old movies."

"Kids these days have no taste," Dominic said with a sniff. "Take a bottle of water with you. Your boy looks like he's been enjoying my drinks a little too much."

"That's what I thought," Bennett said, jotting down a tip almost as much as the bill itself. Clearly, Dominic wasn't kidding about Bennett being a generous tipper.

Dominic grunted, slapping down an unopened bottle of water in front of me, shooting me a look that brooked no argument as he took the bill. I rolled my eyes, making a show of opening the bottle and taking a deep drink. Personally, any effects from the alcohol were long gone, but if it spared me any hassle I would drink the bottle of water.

I followed Bennett's lead and headed out to the parking

lot. Despite feeling like my buzz was gone, I tossed him my keys. He caught them easily with a snap of his hand, again shooting me a questioning look as I continued toward the truck.

Avoiding eye contact as we both got into the truck, I snapped my seat belt into place. Bennett hesitated before putting the key in the ignition and bringing my truck to life. There was another moment of hesitation, and I tensed, sensing he was gearing up to say something. Finally, after a few heartbeats, he leaned back in the seat and pulled the truck out of its parking spot, heading for the road.

I noticed he didn't turn on the radio to fill the silence as we drove, and I wondered if it was intentional. I couldn't help but remember the times near the end when Bri and I had constantly argued. If it happened in the car and we lapsed into a furious silence, she would always snap the radio off, refusing to let anything but the sound of the car and wind fill the gap in our anger. It had always felt personal, as though she wanted me to focus on our tense silence rather than be distracted by music.

With a huff, I reached out and turned on the radio, letting it pipe out through the speakers I'd installed the year before. Bennett never moved to change it as he pulled onto the narrow freeway that would take us straight to Fairlake.

Sadly, the music did little to assuage the bad mood I'd started building earlier. I could barely glance at Bennett without feeling the ugly mix of anger and frustration combined into a sickening mix with the guilt and shame I felt. I hated that he'd kept something so important from me, but I couldn't shake the feeling that it was ultimately my fault he had done so in the first place.

Would we ever find a way back to the friendship we'd had before, or would the past constantly hang over us like a specter? Honestly, was I doomed to continually be forced to suffer through the mistakes and missteps of my past?

Only then I realized—how could I not suffer for them? They were my mistakes, after all. Maybe I could be as frustrated as I wanted with Bennett, but could I well and truly blame him for keeping things to himself? Sure, he'd kept something important, but what had I been keeping from him for years?

Maybe it wasn't completely unfair. On the other hand, maybe I was being completely unfair.

Maybe the whole damn thing was fucked and would never be fixed.

"Alright," Bennett announced after twenty minutes, "enough of this."

"What?" I barked, more out of surprise than anger.

He reached out, turning the music down. "You're pissed off or upset about something."

"No I'm not," I said, refusing to react so I didn't give him even more ammunition.

"It doesn't take an expert in Adam to know something's eating at you," he said evenly.

"And I said I'm not mad," I retorted tightly.

"Right," he said in a tone so sarcastic I was left to wonder if I'd ever heard it before. "Of course. My mistake."

"Don't be a dick," I snapped.

"This coming from the man who spent the last hour at the bar glaring around like he wanted to set the whole place on fire," he said.

"I didn't—"

"You did. And you know what? I get that it probably wasn't your scene. Too many people, strangers, too much noise. I get that. That's on me. But I'm really curious about what you and Isaiah were talking about," he said, sounding calm once more.

"What the fuck does that matter?" I asked, feeling caught out.

"Because I've seen Isaiah drunk more than once."

"I'm sure," I muttered.

Bennett hesitated before continuing. "But that's the first time I've ever seen him act like a skittish cat after talking to someone. He practically took off and then avoided you for the rest of the night."

I was impressed and annoyed with how much he'd noticed. Usually, I was the first to warn someone that Bennett was the type to notice a lot more than he let on. "I'm supposed to know why he was acting weird?"

"He acted weird *after* he talked to you," Bennett answered in a voice I was now beginning to recognize was just a little *too* in control. "So now I'm wondering just what you said to him."

"Why does it have to be what I said?"

"Because he hasn't acted like that with anyone else before."

"So that makes it automatically my fault?"

"I'm trying to understand," Bennett said in that same maddening tone. "I'm not accusing you of anything, and I'm not trying to piss you off. At least not more than you already are. I'm just trying to understand what has you so upset and what got to Isaiah."

"Nothing," I ground out. "So now, are we done with the interrogation? Because if I wanted that, I would have stayed married to Bri."

"Like *hell* are you going to push that on me," Bennett said with a sudden injection of heat to his voice. "I am not your ex-wife, and you know better than to treat me like an inquisitor."

"Sure feels like one."

"Now you're the one being a dick."

"Fuck you, Bennett."

Inexplicably, Bennett snorted. "Wouldn't that be something?"

"What?" I snapped in confusion.

"No, I don't have to explain shit to you," he said, and I could see his jaw tightening. "You're going to sit there and play dumb, pretending you don't know what I'm talking about. Why the hell should I explain anything to you?"

"Right, of course." I snorted. "You want to play mind games without—"

"Fuck *you*," he growled. "The only one playing here is you. Playing like I don't know that you're upset, playing like I don't know that something happened, playing—"

"You don't fucking know me," I snapped back.

"And whose fault is that?" he barked, surprising me with the sudden crack of his voice. His next words were punctuated with the slap of his palm against the steering wheel. "Whose. Fucking. Fault. Is. That?"

"Bennett," I began, immediately recognizing I had crossed the line in the heat of the moment.

"No, *no*. Don't you 'Bennett' me in that sad, kicked-puppy voice you do so well," he snapped, finally glancing at me.

"I'm not—" I began, but stopped.

Kicked-puppy voice?

"You're an absolute bastard sometimes, I swear to fucking god, Adam," he snarled, gripping the wheel so hard his knuckles turned white.

"Look, I know I haven't exactly done things like I should have."

"You think? I wonder what could have given you that idea."

"But you're the one who acted like everything was fine!"

"The *fuck* I did," he snarled.

"Then what would you call it?" I demanded, sitting upright to face him.

"I'd call it finding my old friend, who I was still pissed off at, hurting and lost," he told me, his eyes locked on the road ahead. "And despite wanting to rip him a new asshole, I knew he didn't need that right then. So I said 'fuck it,' and decided my issues with him could wait until he was steady again, until he was ready to deal with things again."

"Noble," I ground out in the most sarcastic way I could manage.

"You can mock me all you want, you absolute dick, but it was more than you ever gave me in the past few years," Bennett snarled. "Even now. I'm *still* trying to be your friend, and you're throwing shit back in my face, so yeah, fuck off."

"So much my friend you couldn't tell me there was someone you're interested in?" I shot back.

To my surprise, I watched some of the color in his cheeks drain. "Excuse me?"

"You fucking heard me," I snapped, not even caring that we were pulling into Fairlake. "You wanted to know what Isaiah and I were talking about, right? Well, he fucked up, while he gossiped about the people you'd fucked, he mentioned there was someone you were interested in."

"He said that?" Bennett asked in a tight and brittle voice.

"Didn't fucking mean to." I snorted, glaring out of the passenger side window. "That's why he took off. He didn't want to answer my questions."

"Fuck," Bennett muttered as he took the next turn a little too hard.

"Right. So act like you're still trying to be my friend while still keeping me at arm's length. Keep acting like you're trying to build a relationship when you're going to keep something like that from me."

"Jesus Christ, Adam."

"What?"

"Why the hell do you even care in the first place?"

It was a valid question, and I felt stumped as we turned onto a semi-familiar street. I had been obsessing over why it mattered so much to me, and I still couldn't figure out the answer. I just knew that the whole thought made my stomach twist and my chest feel so tight I couldn't breathe.

"Because you kept something important from me," I finally said, knowing full well that wasn't good enough, but it was the only thing I could think of.

"My dating life is somehow important to you?" he asked in disbelief.

"Your life should be considered important to me. I thought you knew that."

"Oh, the fuck it does!"

I held the handle over the door as he snapped the truck into his driveway with a terrifying yet impressive level of vehicular control. "Fuck's sake, Bennett!"

"Cry about it," he snapped, slamming my truck into park and yanking out the keys. He tossed them toward me with a snap of his wrist before banging out of the truck. "C'mon, you drunk bastard, you can sleep in my guest room and fuck off in the morning."

Despite the obvious anger in his voice, I found myself hesitating. Was he still going to insist I slept here despite everything?

"Bennett," I called as I stepped out of the truck.

He stopped at the beginning of the walk toward his porch. "No, there's nothing else you need to say. Honestly? I think we've both said enough."

"You think so, huh?" I asked, feeling my anger spark again. "Just like that because you said so?"

"What the hell do you want me to say?" he asked, whirling around on me. "That you leaving hurt like hell? That being

114

apart sucked like nothing has ever sucked? That you deciding I wasn't worth your time anymore was the worst thing of all?"

"That is *not* what I did," I contested hotly, even though it felt like a weak argument.

"Really?" he snapped, stepping closer. "Because that's exactly what it looked like to me. We were still doing pretty good, and then you started getting your nice life in the city. You met yourself a girl who was everything you thought you wanted. You got your business, your money and apartment. And suddenly? Well, suddenly, little ol' me was left to stay here."

"It wasn't like *that*," I snarled at him.

"Oh, so you just *forgot*." His voice was a simpering irony that cut deep. "You just forgot your best friend. You forgot the person who stood with you no matter what? Is that what happens when you move away from home then? All the people who matter, those who cared, just get shunted to the back of your mind?"

"I didn't forget," I said, feeling like I was right back in time, arguing with Bri once more. She could rant and rail with the best of them, and I'd almost forgotten how forceful Bennett could be. I'd never been on the receiving end.

"So you didn't care then," he continued, his eyes going hard. "All that mattered was what *you* wanted, what *you* valued, what *you* thought about. Because it sure as shit didn't include the rest of us."

"It wasn't that simple!" I finally screamed back at him. "I had to build myself from the ground up. I was alone! And now I'm back, and you're acting like everything should be a-okay without any issues!"

To my complete shock, Bennett surged forward, his hands hooking into the front of my shirt, shoving me back. The harsh clang of metal against my back was nothing compared to the surprise of feeling Bennett handle me not only with ease but with an anger I had never seen in him before.

"Cry me a fucking river," he hissed in my face. "You left. You left *me*. And I don't mean leaving this town. I mean in every way you can leave someone. And you come back here, battered, broken, tail between your legs, and you think that somehow gives you the right to treat me like shit? Are you fucking kidding me?"

"Let go of me," I finally managed.

"You left *me*," he repeated, and my heart skipped a beat at the crack in his voice. "And then you come back here. And now you stand there, pretending you have a right, a goddamn *right* to know what's going on in my life?"

"Why are you avoiding it?" I snapped back, reaching out to grab his shoulders and shake him. We had never laid hands on one another in our entire friendship, but here it was. This is what we had become. "Are you just punishing me? Is that it?"

"Fuck you," he snarled, but I saw a small, trembling thing in his eyes. "You don't know shit, and you never fucking have!"

"Then fucking tell me! Because it sure as shit sounds like you've been holding shit back. You've been lying to me this whole time, Bennett?"

"Fuck you!"

"Fuck *you*."

I should have expected it when his arm cocked back, and his fist drove into my face. Pain raced up my face, and I had a brief moment to appreciate that he really could fuck me up if he wanted to. I had height and weight on him, but he was no weakling, and he'd been trained to deal with people in a physical confrontation. My head rocked back, cracking against the passenger side window of my truck.

He reached out, gripping my head with both hands, and I stared at him in a daze, feeling emotions I couldn't describe rolling through my gut. His eyes, which I'd always associated with joy and playfulness, pierced into mine. I knew what was coming. I knew he was going to continue, I knew he was going to—

Kiss me?

BENNETT

What the hell was I doing?

I was kissing Adam. I was fucking *kissing* him.

Every adolescent fantasy, every dream, was culminating in a moment immediately after I'd punched him, for god's sake. I could feel the heat of his face against mine, the tightness of his lips as he stood in complete shock against the side of his truck. This close, I could feel how firm he was, how he felt exactly like I'd always imagined.

It *should* have been everything I'd ever dreamed of, but reality was gradually reinserting itself. Christ, I was kissing *Adam*. It hadn't been prompted by anything but high emotions and a passion that had nothing to do with my feelings. I had attacked him, only to kiss him, and now he was standing in one place, letting me do it.

I needed to back off.

I needed to run away.

I needed to—

Was he *relaxing*?

Oh god, he was. I could feel the tenseness in his body bleeding away as our lips pressed together. I could feel the way his fingers on my shoulders flexed as if torn between pulling me closer and wanting to let go so he never had to touch me again. I could hear the sharp gust of his breath as he...pressed closer?

Fuck. Fuckfuckfuck.

With a heaving gasp, I pushed away from him as the horror of what I'd done came crashing down around me with the crystal clarity of a bitter ice storm. All the times I had ever wanted to do something like this, every time I had ever wanted to be closer but had held back, knowing it was a terrible, rotten, destructive idea.

All gone, dust in the wind.

"Bennett?" Adam whispered, sounding breathless and shocked.

"Fuck," I whispered, turning away from him.

I couldn't stand to see whatever emotions showed on his face. To see the results of the boundary crossing I had finally done. Years of self-control and self-admonishment down the drain.

"Let's go inside," I said roughly, sucking in a breath and marching toward my porch.

I felt drunk despite not having had a drink for a couple of hours as I staggered toward my front door. My head swam with the realization of what I'd done, and my shoulders felt dragged down by the weight of what I'd allowed to happen.

I was surprised to find him trailing behind me as I fumbled with my house keys. I wouldn't have blamed him for turning and immediately going back to his truck or simply walking to his parents' house, prepared to come back in the early hours to retrieve his truck and never see me again.

Good god, what had I done?

The jingle of my keys was loud and sharp in my ears as I finally managed to get the lock open. I shoved the door with more force than I meant to and stumbled inside. Mutely,

Adam followed me, stepping around me as I turned to close and lock the door.

"Guest room has fresh sheets and pillows," I told him, looking anywhere but at him. "Go get some sleep."

Just as quietly, he lingered beside my couch for a moment before walking off as if in a daze. I could see the line I had crossed in his slow, unsteady gait as he moved away from me. Standing there in shock, I listened to his soft footsteps and the squeal of the doorknob I kept meaning to replace. It was only when I heard the door shut that I finally let out a low, slow breath.

"Fuck," I muttered again, turning and almost slamming into my bedroom door before remembering to turn the knob and open it. I stumbled in, mindlessly pulling off my clothes before yanking on sleep pants.

I flopped into bed boneless, turning only to stare at the blank wall. Playing the conversation and argument repeatedly in my head, I wanted to cringe until nothing was left of me.

Until that last moment, I could see each point where I'd been pushed and pushed. Hearing him accuse me of so much, feeling the fear of what he might have found out from Isaiah and the culminating anger.

God, I had been so angry, so furious. To think that I had been trying so hard not to emphasize what he had done, or rather what he hadn't done, only to have it flung back in my face. And for what? Because he hadn't known that for years and years, it had been him, and only him, that I'd ever wanted?

How could I tell him that? How could I possibly tell him that the only man who'd ever been enough for me had been the straight man who was like a brother?

My emotions had got the better of me, and in the end, I lost my temper.

Shit, I'd *hit* him.

I had no idea how long I drifted there, soaking in my thoughts, before I heard a soft rap against the wood door. Jolting back to reality, I jerked my head toward my door, which I realized I'd kept open. I could just see a shadow through the crack, and I winced.

"Bennett?" Adam asked in a soft voice.

"Need something?" I asked in a painfully polite voice as I shifted onto my back.

"To talk."

"Oh."

Shit. Was I ready for whatever he was about to say? Probably not, but I'd thrown my choice in the matter out the window the moment I kissed him, so I couldn't complain.

"Sure," I said, pushing myself back and leaning against the headboard.

Adam pushed the door open to let himself in. He had stripped himself of his button-up, revealing an undershirt I hadn't realized was there. From the sound of his footsteps as he entered, he'd removed his boots and possibly his socks. His eyes darted around the room, and I realized this was the first time he had ever entered my bedroom.

"There's a chair," I said, pointing toward the desk in the opposite corner where I kept my computer.

"Right," he said, shuffling toward the desk and easing himself into the chair. I almost laughed when the chair suddenly dropped with a hard thunk, and he jerked in surprise.

"I'm...overdue for a new chair," I explained apologetically.

"It's alright...just surprised me."

"It does that. Still gets me once in a while when I forget."

He smiled crookedly, and all at once I remembered why we were in this awkward position and looked down at my lap. I wrapped my fingers in the soft comforter, squeezing it for comfort as I prayed I didn't say anything stupid.

"So," he began, drawing the word out.

"So," I replied simply.

"I uh—"

"You—"

"Look—"

"What?"

He gave a deep, heaving sigh. "I don't know how to say this nicely or gently."

I braced. "So don't."

"You kissed me."

"I did."

"After hitting me."

"I did."

Adam's eyes felt like they were burrowing into me. "How long?"

"Huh?"

"How long have you wanted to do that?"

"Hit you or kiss you?"

I saw his lips twitch. "Both?"

"I've wanted to hit you for a couple of years now, but the worst was when I saw you in that goddamn bed of yours. Wasting away because of…it doesn't matter," I said with a shake of my head.

"Are you, uh, sorry you hit me?"

"I am, but I'm not."

"Okay. That's fair. No, wait, that's actually really fucking fair."

I smirked. "Kind of is, isn't it?"

"Yeah."

I waited several heartbeats before finally biting the bullet and taking the plunge. "The kiss."

"Yeah?" he asked, tone soft.

"Years."

"Years?"

"Yeah."

"When?"

"When what?"

"The first time."

"We were fifteen."

Something shuddered and shook in Adam's eyes, and I resisted the urge to look away from him. "Fifteen? It's…it's been that long?"

His question finally made me look down at my lap. "Yeah."

"Oh."

How to explain that the kiss had been everything I had ever felt, culminating in a moment of passion? God, how much I'd craved to do something so close to what I had done. To feel his lips against mine, to feel his body pressed to mine, to know the heat of his body in a way that so few others had before.

"Hey, uh, Bennett?"

"Yeah?"

It felt like an eternity before he spoke again. "Am…am I the one Isaiah was talking about?"

My heart stuttered and threatened to stop, but I swallowed hard to answer. I had already gone too far as it was. What else could I do now but tell the truth?

"Yeah," I said, still watching the blanket twist between my fingers.

"Oh."

"Yeah."

I wished there was a clock in my room that would break the silence between us with its incessant, dependable ticking. Instead, I was left with a silence so heavy I felt it would crush me.

"Who else?" he asked.

I looked up, confused. "What?"

"Who else knows about how you felt?"

Not the question I expected. "Oh, uh, Chase probably knows. I never told him. But—"

"You were dating him?"

"No. We're friends. We just—"

"Slept together?"

"Sometimes. He's not...he's not ready to uh—"

"Be open? Be you?"

"Something like that."

It was more than I ever wanted to say about Chase, but in the end, I'd always known Chase's heart belonged somewhere else, just as mine had. It was only recently that Chase probably figured out where mine had belonged, whereas I had yet to know where his truly lay. However, I suspected that, much like myself, his heart lay with someone in his past.

"Isaiah?" he asked.

"We're friends," I told him firmly. "We had a date once, but...no, we're friends. That's all we'll ever be."

"Just like Chase?"

"Just like Chase."

Another tension-filled several seconds.

"Bennett?"

"Yeah?"

"Are you sorry you kissed me?"

"Yes."

"Why?"

I snapped my head up, glaring at him. "Because it's not something I should have done."

His face was slack, but he stared at me intently. "Why?"

"I don't know, Adam," I snapped, feeling my anger return. "Maybe because you're straight? Maybe because, despite it being everything I've wanted to do for so goddamn long, I knew it wasn't something I should do? Maybe because I did it after being so pissed off that I was willing to hit you."

"I deserved it," he said.

That made me smile a little. "You kinda did."

He cocked his head. "Would you do it again?"

Snapping back to reality, I stared at him in shock. "Hit you?"

"Kiss me."

I continued staring at him, no longer hiding my surprise. "What?"

To my growing surprise, he pushed out of the chair and moved closer to me, sitting on the edge of the bed. "Kind of a simple question."

"Not really," I retorted without thinking because…it really wasn't.

To kiss him again? God yes, and fuck no.

Bad. Good. Right. Wrong.

And here he was, staring at me intently, almost interested.

"Adam?" I asked softly, trying to reassert my grasp on reality.

"It wasn't…bad," he said softly, tearing his eyes away from me. "The kiss."

"What the fuck?" I asked in the most helpful way possible.

"Do it again?" he asked in the smallest voice I'd ever heard from him.

What could I do with that?

I kissed him, of course.

Reaching up, I slid my fingers over his cheek, feeling the prickle of his facial hair before coming to rest at his jaw. Curling my fingers, I hooked them into his jaw and pulled him closer. To my surprise, he pulled closer as I sat up, inevitably drawn toward him.

"You're straight," I offered.

Adam gave no retort as he drew closer to me, and I felt

my pathetic resistance weaken. I kissed him then, drawing our lips together and feeling him turn into it. The tension from the first kiss was gone as our lips met. I could feel his confusion, how lost he was in this new experience, and guided him by parting our lips.

Our mouths crushed against each other as he leaned against me, his teeth clicking against mine. Almost immediately, we righted ourselves, and he caught the side of my face to hold me steady.

"Mmph," he grunted, his fingers curling against the back of my head as I felt the kiss deepen naturally.

I felt him fall against me, and I let myself tilt backward, my back hitting the soft bed. Adam followed me effortlessly, his mouth latched to mine before our lips parted further, his tongue sliding over mine. His hesitant yet bold exploration sent a spark of anticipation through me, and I clutched him tighter.

All the walls I had built inside myself over the years began to fall away, and I pulled him closer. My hands slid down his back, feeling the muscles I had watched many times in the past, feeling the sudden spike of desire from him I had always wanted.

"Adam," I breathed.

Again he said nothing, moving so he hovered over me as he kissed me hard again. For the first time in my life, I could feel his hunger and desire, and it was for *me*. I felt his body press against mine, and my mind flew into overdrive.

He was hard.

He was *hard*.

"Fuck," I grunted, unable to stop myself reaching between our bodies to cup him.

He was big. Not monstrous or inhuman, but big enough that I doubted there was a partner in his past who hadn't known precisely when he entered them. The thought shot through me with electric anticipation, and I soaked up the groan he gave as I gripped his hardening shaft.

"Bennett," he whispered in my ear, and I thought I might come right there.

"I've got you," I promised, not even sure what I was promising.

He rutted against my hand as he shoved his face into my neck. For a moment I thought he would lay there and then gasped as I felt the press of his lips and then the bite of his teeth.

"Fucking hell," I groaned, quickly trying to remember my skills to undo the snap of his jeans and his zipper. Then I felt the brush of rough hair, and I realized. "Are you not wearing underwear?"

"*No.*"

I didn't have the breath to swear as I lost all hesitation, pushing my hands into his pants. There was no holding back the loud moan as I wrapped my fingers around his hard shaft. To my absolute delight, I found him not only painfully hard but with a distinct wetness at the tip.

"You want me," I breathed, unbelieving.

"This. I want this."

I had never heard him so delirious, so absolutely and completely aroused by something. And it was for me, because of me.

"Bennett, please," he groaned in my ear, and I almost lost my mind right then and there.

"I've got you," I promised again, pushing so he was forced to roll on his back.

Immediately I was assaulted by the image of Adam on his back, his shirt riding up to reveal his stomach with its light dusting of dark hair that I'd lusted over for ages. His cock jutted up from his pants, thick and hard, and I felt myself salivating. Best and most distracting was the look of hazy lust on his face as he gazed up at me with need.

Whatever remnant of common sense and sanity I had left crumbled to dust at his expression. Whether or not this was a good idea was quickly irrelevant as he gazed at me in the way I'd imagined hundreds of times before. It turned out reality was so much better than any hormone-driven fantasy. Adam could have asked me for anything at that moment, and I wouldn't have hesitated to give it to him.

Which was precisely what I was going to do.

Reaching to take the base of his cock in my hand, I drew him back as I scooted forward. My eyes flicked up, catching his gaze as I bent my head. My heart hammered in my chest as I placed my tongue against his leaking head, tasting him for the first time. A shiver ran through me, and I closed my mouth over him, letting the blunt head slide over my tongue.

Adam squirmed beneath me as I sank further, inching him into my throat as far as possible. I had never mastered the art of deep-throating, and there was no way in hell I would manage to take all of him. Finding whatever would bring him the most pleasure was more important than torturing myself. Sure, I would've loved to make this last as long as possible, but a sense of urgency was nagging at the back of my head. Maybe, just maybe, if I took too long, Adam would find his own common sense, remember this shouldn't be happening, and pull away before we finished.

Trying to ignore the ticking clock in my head, I took him deep once more, creating suction as I slowly backed away. I tried to take my time, learning what made his legs tense beneath me and what made his breath catch in his throat. After a couple of minutes, I managed to make just enough of a mess of his length that I could comfortably slide my hand up and down his shaft.

I felt him shudder at that, letting out a low groan that

threatened to undo me. Emboldened by his new reaction, I began working my hand and mouth together. When I bowed forward to take as much of him into my mouth as I could, my fist sank to the base of his dick. When I reared back, letting him leak over my tongue, I brought my grip up to rest under the sensitive head.

In no time, I was steadily building a rhythm with what I considered a classic but effective technique. From how Adam was steadily becoming more restless beneath me and the growing noises from him, I could tell he was enjoying himself. I'd wondered more than once if he'd be silent or noisy, resigning myself to never knowing. It turned out he was somewhere in between, neither shy about expressing his enjoyment nor making a theatrical show about it.

I could feel the way his cock throbbed against my tongue as I built up speed. Adam's groans became deeper, and I almost lost it again when I felt his hand slide into my hair and try to find something to grab onto.

"B-Bennett," Adam panted as I felt his fingers scramble against my scalp, his hips beginning to twitch.

I knew better than to stop what I was doing or alter the pace in the slightest. The sounds were a little sloppy, but I focused on the increasing groans as Adam placed another hand on the other side of my head, holding firmly. His body stiffened, and I could feel the shudder run through him as I felt his cock throb harder in my mouth.

I couldn't help the moan that finally escaped me as the first spurt hit the back of my throat hard, nearly choking me. Swallowing, I bent forward further, allowing as much of his dick into my throat as I could. Another groan escaped me, making him jerk at the vibration surrounding him as I held myself in place and allowed him to finish.

When I sensed he was done, I carefully eased my mouth back so I didn't brush too much against his sensitive dick. I still felt him jerk a couple of times at the sensation, but there wasn't much I could do about how much he managed to fill my mouth.

"That," he began, head tilted back on a pillow, eyes closed.

I honestly had no idea what I was supposed to say, so I leaned back, curling my legs under me, and watched him. The rise and fall of his chest gently eased as he stayed in one place. His cock was slowly softening, laying against his stomach as his breathing calmed. I could feel my own straining against my pants, but I ignored it. Far more important than any desire on my part was just how well Adam would deal with what just happened.

Alcohol or not, I was pretty sure the haze surrounding his thoughts had burned away now he'd found his release. That the same release had come from not only another guy but from me was sure to be a jarring realization now he was probably thinking a little more clearly.

I couldn't help but watch him, waiting for the inevitable meltdown. I honestly had no idea what it had to be like to do something that went entirely against who you thought you were or what you were about. My sexuality had always been set in stone in my mind, just as I was sure Adam's had been for him. I didn't know what I'd be like if I found myself on the receiving end of sex with a woman, and I couldn't predict how he'd deal with what we'd just done.

Finally, the tension grew too much for me as the minutes ticked by, and I cleared my throat softly. "Adam, we should probably talk about what just happened."

His silence continued, and I fought the urge to squirm. As nervous and terrified as I was, I didn't think I'd be doing us any favors if I was obvious about it. The last thing either of us needed was for me to start unraveling. Plus, Adam had always preferred to deal with things, even problems, as calmly and carefully as possible.

"I don't know what's going on in your head right now," I continued softly, hoping that maybe if I talked enough, it might spark something. "After everything that's been going on in your life lately, and then I go…deck you, now this. It's gotta feel like a lot of things thrown at you all at once. I'm not sure if I'll be able to help you much, considering I'm part of the problem, but if you let me, I might be able to."

His silence was starting to settle deep into my nerves, tightening and twisting them. My gut felt tied in knots, and I thought I might lose my mind if he didn't at least grunt or say *something*.

"Look," I began, leaning forward to get closer to him. "I think this is something you should at least talk about. It's not something you can just ignore and—" I looked closer at him. "You bastard, did you fall asleep?"

Now almost sure, I leaned forward and watched him in the dim light. Even with the movement of the bed as I shifted around, Adam didn't stir. His chest rose and fell in slow, even movements, and I could hear the soft whistle of breathing from his nose.

"Unbelievable," I grunted and then snorted in amusement. "Get your first kisses from a guy, your first blowjob, and you pass out in bed immediately afterward, dick still out. Christ, you are *such* a man."

Sighing, I carefully tucked him back into his pants and decided to leave him there. The night had been eventful enough as it was. I didn't see the point in waking him up. He would just be disoriented and of no use to either of us. It was probably better to let him sleep off the drinks and the whole night.

I, however, was not going to sleep anytime soon, and I knew it, so I left him sleeping peacefully in my bed. With a heavy sigh, I went to the kitchen and considered the six-pack of beer still in the fridge. After a moment's thought, I opened the fridge and dug out the bottle of whiskey I kept in there instead. I was old enough to know that alcohol wouldn't make my problems any better, but maybe I could count on it to help take the edge off or at least help me sleep at some point.

I made my way out to the back porch, grabbing a glass as I went. Walking across the deck Adam had repaired, I dropped onto the steps leading to my backyard. Cracking open the bottle, I poured myself a decent measure and took the shot.

"Oof," I grunted as it slid down my throat, turning into a wave of fire in my gut. "Smooth until it's not."

Gazing up, I watched clouds weave back and forth over the moon. The stars glittered overhead, and I felt the sudden urge to be out in the woods surrounding the town. Fairlake wasn't a large or bright town, but there was enough light to block out some of the night sky. Once you were a couple of miles out of town, the entire sky came to life with millions of stars and the strange milky streak that stretched around them.

The smile on my face faded as I tapped at the side of my glass, wondering just what I was going to do. In a matter of minutes, I'd managed to throw everything I'd worked so hard at out the window. Now Adam practically knew everything, and not only that, but I'd given him a blowjob.

"God," I groaned, rubbing my face vigorously. I poured and drank another healthy dose of whiskey. I would most likely regret it in the morning, but at least the liquor's bite felt like it was managing to cut through the worst of my thoughts.

I knew I would need to talk to someone before I had to face Adam in the morning, and I dragged my phone out to see if Chase was awake. If he wasn't, I would just have to stop by his place in the morning if he was available. All I knew was there was no way I could deal with all the thoughts and feelings in my head without a little help. Admittedly, when it came to Chase, I was probably going to have to deal with being called an idiot, and probably a horny idiot at that, but that was part of being friends with Chase.

"Fuck me," I muttered, hanging my head and staring between my legs. "What am I going to do?"

I had no idea, but all I could do was hope I hadn't managed to screw everything up and that I still had a friend when the sun rose tomorrow.

ADAM

The first thing I felt was the urge to groan as my consciousness groggily crawled toward the surface. A nasty taste coated my tongue, making me smack my mouth in disgust as I peered around the room. The gears in my head spun with clanking slowness as I tried to understand what I saw. The room looked somewhat familiar, and I had a faint memory of sitting in that chair.

Looking around, I blinked as I caught sight of my jeans on the floor where I'd tossed them the night before. With an almighty lurch of realization, I remembered exactly where I was and, more precisely, what I had done before falling asleep.

I bolted upright, only to groan and grab my forehead as my skull throbbed. It wasn't quite the bolt of searing agony I could have been hit with, but it was still enough to remind me that maybe I had been deeper in my drinks than I'd thought. Probably didn't help that I could distinctly remember Bennett hitting me and vaguely that I'd had it coming.

Moving slowly, I swung my legs around and pulled

myself to the edge of the bed. I wasn't sure where my boots were, or my socks for that matter. They weren't on the floor of what I now realized was Bennett's bedroom. I seemed to have kept everything else on, and I quickly buttoned and zipped my pants back up as my face burned at the memory.

I had no idea where I'd dropped my boots, but I clearly remembered staring down and watching Bennett—

Shit, Bennett.

Pushing myself to my feet, I stumbled into the living room in the hopes of finding Bennett. Instead, I found the TV on low, showing some cartoon I didn't recognize.

"Bennett?" I called, making my way toward the next room and opening the guest room door. I had clearly been in his bed, and though I couldn't be sure, I didn't think he'd spent the night with me. The thought was as uncomfortable as the guest room was empty, but I did find my socks and boots on the floor at the end of the barely rumpled bed.

After taking a moment to yank them on, shoving the laces into the boots rather than tying them, I resumed my search. The kitchen and bathroom were both empty, and his backyard wasn't big enough that I couldn't scan it through the back sliding door to see that it too was empty.

"Shit," I grumbled, turning to find my phone and stopping when I saw a small note stuck to the coffee machine. Next to it was a bottle of water and a small collection of pills.

I picked it up and read it aloud. "Adam, if you stick around after you get up, flip the coffee machine on for yourself. Also, take these pills with some lunch meat or something. Drink the water. I'll be back in a little bit. Bennett."

I was impressed that he'd managed to fit all that onto the small post-it note. Doing as I was told, I flipped the coffee machine on and made my way to the fridge to grab a few pieces of the lunch meat, chewing my way slowly through them as I sipped the water while the machine gurgled and brewed.

While I forced my unhappy stomach to tolerate even that small amount of food, I looked over the note. There wasn't much in it to tell me what was going on in Bennett's head, save for the opening line.

Did Bennett really think I'd take off the moment I woke up? Admittedly, I wasn't exactly sure what I would say when I saw him, but I couldn't picture slipping away like a thief in the night. More and more of the night was coming back to me, including how much of an absolute bastard I had been to him on the ride back. It was little wonder he'd finally lost his temper, a first in all the time I'd known him, and decided to knock me a good one.

Everything that happened once we were back in the house, however...well, that was almost completely crystal clear. I remembered sitting on the end of the bed in his guest room, staring at the floor and thinking about him kissing me. I had been so absolutely shocked by what he was doing I hadn't even thought to react at the time. It was only when I watched him walk away, his shoulders slumped in what felt like defeat, I realized just what had happened.

All this time, Bennett had been...had feelings for me? Last night the thought had been amazing, even awe-inspiring. Partly because I was impressed he'd managed to hide it from me but also that he'd held on to it for so long. I had no idea what that meant for me, but god, what it must be like to live that way. I couldn't help but wonder just how often he had let it torment him or how many times it had haunted him against his will.

Once the coffee finished, I poured myself a cup and decided to sit out on the deck. I paused long enough to see a bottle of whiskey sitting on the step alongside a glass. Picking it up, I realized nearly half of it was gone, and I wondered just what kind of night Bennett had after I'd fallen asleep.

Passed out was more accurate. Not only that, but I'd passed out after my friend, almost once again best friend, had given me a blowjob. I honestly had no idea what to do with that information, so I plopped myself into one of the deck chairs. The food had helped to calm my stomach a bit, and I hoped that between the water and the pills, the caffeine in the coffee would help ease the throbbing in my head.

A blowjob...from Bennett. Never in all my life would I have ever imagined doing anything like that, which was probably more than could be said for Bennett. I could only imagine how he must have felt after everything that happened last night, especially the part where I passed out like a drunken idiot.

Leaning back in the chair, I set the coffee on the arm and made myself comfortable. I didn't know where Bennett had disappeared, and I was afraid to message him and find out. For all I knew he was out clearing his head, though I hoped he wasn't driving around after I'd found his bottle of partially drunk whiskey.

What was more important was keeping myself calm and getting my head back on right. The last thing I wanted to do was be a jumbled mess when Bennett eventually showed up. I had been the one to start the whole mess last night, and I needed to be in full control of myself when I saw him again. So, I needed to take a deep breath and even myself out.

Deep breathing exercises were probably the only thing I remembered from the multiple failed attempts at couples therapy Bri had dragged me to. I couldn't say they worked a miracle and made me immune to getting upset, but I found them good enough to ensure I didn't stew for too long. Brooding over things that bothered me had been a lifelong habit of mine, and at least I had *some* way to take the edge off.

I didn't know how long I was there, trying to focus on my breathing rather than my obsessive thoughts, but it was long enough that I didn't pay attention to the sound of a latch. It was only when Bennett spoke that I realized he was there. "Did you really fall asleep again?"

My eyes flashed open, flicking to where he stood in the yard beside the deck. He was dressed in his running gear, and I could see he'd worked up a good sweat. His cheeks were red, probably from all the exertion, and I couldn't quite read his expression. I had never seen him look so guarded and closed off, even while he managed a small smile.

"I wasn't asleep," I said, leaning forward and clearing my throat roughly.

"Just closing your eyes for a few minutes?" he asked, his smile taking a wry twist.

"More like trying to get my thoughts together," I admitted, reaching out to take hold of my coffee and finding it cool. Apparently, I'd zoned out longer than I thought, and it probably was a miracle I hadn't fallen asleep. "Why are you coming in through the back?"

"Eh, it rained last night, and part of my path was muddy. Was coming back to rinse my shoes off," he said, walking around the deck to show me his shoes, which were indeed covered in mud. It had splattered up his socks and his bare legs.

I felt a flutter of nerves as he pulled his shoes and socks off, draping the latter over the railing before turning on the hose to wash the former. I noticed the way his eyes slid to me, only to dart away nervously as he bent to clean his shoes in a way that was just a little *too* studious and careful.

"Sleep late?" I asked, watching his arms as he twisted the shoes around to wash them.

"Not really," he said with a shrug. "Why?"

"Well, I saw the time when I grabbed the coffee," I

explained, wishing I'd gotten through one cup before it went cold. "Seemed kinda late for you for a run."

"Was it?" he asked. "You, uh, been paying attention to my schedule?"

"I pay attention to a lot of things about you," I said with a frown.

"Huh," he grunted, sounding thoughtful as he turned off the hose. "And I wasn't just running. I went to Chase's beforehand."

"Oh? Why's that?" I asked, trying to ignore the irritated flash that shot through me.

Bennett glanced at me before shrugging. "I needed to vomit some things out, then use the run to clear the rest of the gunk out."

"And you couldn't do that here?" I asked, even more annoyed now.

"Well, you were asleep," he said slowly, dropping his shoes on the deck. I couldn't help but look him over as he mounted the steps and moved toward the back door. The same awkward, fluttery feeling I remembered from the first time I'd seen him like this rose, and I wondered where the hell it had come from in the first place. "And I didn't want to word vomit all over you."

"You used to do it all the time."

"First off, and I don't mean to be a dick, but I haven't been able to do that with you in a long time."

Okay, that stung, but at least he was trying to be honest with me without being a dick about it. "Okay, fair."

"Right, and Chase is someone I've talked to about a lot of things in the past. I don't know what your problem with him is."

"There's no problem."

I could hear how quickly I said it, but thankfully Bennett only raised his brow. "Okay. Well, he's my friend. And secondly, when it comes to, well, last night. It's better I talk to someone else before I talk to you. Clearly, I can't be trusted to think right when that subject comes up with you around, so—"

Wishing I could pretend I knew what to do with that statement, I fell silent as I mulled it over. I watched Bennett take my mug into the house with him and sat back in the chair. It wasn't like I could argue with him. He had been dealing with his side of things longer than I'd even known they existed.

I could only imagine what it must have been like to not only feel like that but also watch that person drift away from you. Had it perhaps been easier in some ways to watch me get so wrapped up in my life that I forgot so many of the things I'd left in Fairlake? Or had it just been more salt added to a wound I couldn't comprehend?

"You're brooding," he announced, returning with my refilled mug and a mug of his own.

"Thinking," I corrected, taking the mug.

"With you, the line is so thin it might as well not exist."

"Well, I suppose that's a far nicer way of putting it than Bri did near the end."

"I'd rather we didn't talk about your ex-wife after your dick was in my mouth."

I choked on my first attempted careful sip of the coffee, pulling the cup away from my mouth to set it down before I spilled it everywhere. "Bennett!"

He sat down, looking at me over his cup. "Was that too blunt for you?"

"Christ," I said, wiping at my mouth. "I just wasn't expecting it."

"Yeah, I know that feeling," he muttered, taking a sip. "But Chase was right. If I pussyfoot around everything, it's just going to be awkward and stupid for both of us."

I winced. "Told him, did you?"

"Yeah, we talked."

"Told him…everything?"

"Well, I had to tell him the relevant details. But if it makes you feel better, I didn't share that you're well-hung or describe the face you make when you get off."

"I have this nagging feeling you're enjoying being this blunt," I grumbled, even as I absurdly felt myself want to preen at the compliments. Or at least, I hoped the second one was a compliment.

Huh. I hoped it was a compliment. That was…new.

"A little," he admitted. "Being a bit of a shit makes me feel more in control. Chase called me out on it."

"From what you've told me about him, he does seem the type."

"Yeah, but he was…different today."

I cocked my head at his strange tone. "What's up?"

"He's, uh…do you remember Devin Mitchell?"

I thought about it for a minute. "Oh. Really, *really* quiet kid? Like, I don't think I ever heard him say anything other than 'here' when the roll was called."

"Yep, that's him. But all things considered, I can't say I blame him."

My eyes widened as I remembered. "Oh fuck. Wasn't he the kid whose dad killed his mom?"

"It was never proven," Bennett said with an angry flicker in his eyes.

"Does that matter? I remember that bastard, Andrew wasn't it?"

"Matters to the courts. And I bet it mattered a lot to Devin growing up, especially because he was stuck in the house with that bastard. And yeah, Andrew."

"I, uh, never really paid much attention to those rumors," I admitted with a shrug. Devin had been a couple of years

141

younger than us, and I was long gone before he'd even left high school. "I remember everyone in town gave him a huge berth when he was around, and we were always told to stay away from him. I remember you and my mom telling me someone finally shot his dad."

"Shot him?" Bennett asked with a heavy snort. "Someone shot him practically on the police station steps. In the middle of the day."

I tried to remember the story but only shook my head. It had happened right after I arrived in Boston, and everything seemed to be happening at once for me. If I wasn't taking time to talk to Bennett about things, I was constantly juggling so many other aspects of my life. Everything else had simply faded into the background, regarded as unimportant.

"Wait," I said, realizing how Bennett had said it. "Someone? Like, they don't know who did it?"

"If someone other than the shooter does, no one's told," Bennett said with a strange look in his eye. "Chief Price looked into it and launched an investigation. He won't talk about it, but I've heard things."

"Like what?" I asked, finding myself drawn into the conversation despite having more pressing concerns. Despite how gentle and peaceful Fairlake was, it was a town like any other. Take any quiet, friendly town and scratch the surface, and you're bound to find a nest of secrets and sometimes some nasty surprises. Andrew Mitchell had originally been one of our more quietly held secrets, and now I was finding out there was even more.

"Like the fact that there were at least a dozen people who were around when it happened, and not one person claimed to have seen anything. Said they heard the shot and tried to get away from the sound, didn't see a thing," Bennett said, arching a brow.

"No one?"

"No one."

"You can't tell me anyone believed that, right?"

"Couldn't prove it. Like I said, the chief won't talk about it, but from what I heard, he didn't try too hard either. Andrew Mitchell made it his business to make other people's lives hell. There was that business when he was younger. A couple of girls accused him of assaulting them."

I leaned forward. "No shit?"

Bennett nodded grimly. "He was a teen, and so were they. But just like so much, things got buried, but if you know where to look and who to listen to, you learn things no one wanted you to learn. That's not even including all the fights, both drunk and sober, he got into. He had no problem terrorizing anyone. Plus, even outside his wife's 'fall down the basement stairs,' he took his fist to Devin more than once. But, like I said, no one talks about it."

"Just like they don't talk about whoever it was that had enough of his shit and gunned him down in the street," I said wryly.

"I can't really say if that's the real miscarriage of justice or the fact that he was allowed to keep getting away with shit. He was always freed on some technicality or because no one in town would talk out of fear of him," Bennett said sourly. "I guess there's a sort of divine justice that when it came time for someone to commit a crime on him, there was no one willing to speak out for him either."

"A grim sort of irony," I said with a snort. "Not that I'm all that upset about the loss of someone like him."

"Yeah, neither am I. It just...I don't like the way it had to get to that point."

I had to smile at that. Bennett had *always* had a sense of fairness and justice, and I hadn't been surprised when he'd announced his plans to join the force. Maybe he would have done "greater" things in some big city, but I knew Fairlake was where he belonged. He might not have been born here as I was, but I knew he had every intention of living his life here and being buried in the plot of land just outside town where Fairlake cemetery waited.

"Anyway," he said with a shake of his head, "Devin and Chase were really good friends back in the day. And no, I don't know the story because Chase doesn't exactly share much. But I guess after the incident with his dad, Devin couldn't stay in town anymore and moved on. Chase tried to keep in contact with him, but Devin, well—"

I saw the conflicted expression on his face. "What? Is it bad?"

"I saw Devin today," Bennett said, chewing his bottom lip. "He looks like hell, absolute warmed-over hell."

"Abuse?"

"Probably."

"Shit, drugs?"

"Pretty sure."

"Fuck. What's he doing here?"

Bennett sighed. "Devin called Chase. Out of the blue. Now Devin is staying with him, and Chase is trying to help him get sober and, you know, not keel over and die from withdrawal."

"Jesus," I hissed. "That's not—"

"His job? Yeah, I'm not telling him, fuck that. I might be goofy, but I'm not stupid," Bennett said, features thoughtful. "I've never...there was something different about him."

"Devin?"

"Chase."

"Oh, like what?"

"It's hard to explain to someone who doesn't know him. He was somehow both crankier than usual, yet softer."

I couldn't help the arch of my brow. "His...other parts?"

144

Bennett rolled his eyes so hard I wondered if he was going to pull something. "I told you we're not like that."

"Anymore," I added.

"Yes," he said slowly, eyeing me. "Anymore. Are you—"

I waited before grunting. "Am I what?"

"Anyway," he said, taking another sip of coffee, "there's a lot more to that story. I don't know what the rest of it is, not right now anyway, but there's a story that Chase hasn't told me. Christ, I've never seen him get so mad at me like when I told him he needed to get Devin into rehab, a hospital, something."

"He should," I said with a frown. "He's being—"

"Stubborn. He knows, just like you know when you're being stubborn," Bennett said, a small, somewhat sad smile on his face. "It seems I have a type."

It seemed our little gossip session was done and over, and we were circling back to the original topic. "A type, huh?"

"I guess we should start with the most important question," Bennett said, rubbing his forehead. "Just how much do you remember from last night?"

I scowled at him. "I wasn't *that* drunk."

"So you remember coming into my room, having a heart-to-heart, and then having gay sex?"

"Wait, hold on, we didn't—"

"Not *anal*. Hate to break it to you, Adam, but any sex as a guy with another guy is automatically gay. Doesn't matter if it's anal or not."

Properly chastised, I huffed and leaned back in my seat. "Yes, I remember that part. And the conversation."

I had hardly been able to believe what I'd heard. In all the years we'd known one another, I'd never even questioned if there had been a time when Bennett might have found me attractive, let alone be several steps ahead of simple attraction. He had never said anything about it, and not once had he ever made me feel like he was feeling anything other than friendship.

I suppose for someone else, that thought would have been unnerving or uncomfortable. Most people probably wouldn't be too thrilled with the idea that their best friend was attracted to them. Maybe at a different point in my life, I would have been one of those people.

But last night? I had been anything but uncomfortable.

"Brooding," Bennett warned, examining my face.

I flipped him the bird. "I'm allowed to think a bit when I'm dealing with the fact that I let a guy suck me off last night, alright?"

Bennett sighed heavily. "Look, I know it's a lot to take in, and for what it's worth, I'm sorry I kissed you."

"But not that you hit me first?" I asked with a smirk.

"We already agreed you had that coming," Bennett said with a frown. "Both for slowly starting to act like I didn't exist, like our friendship had never existed, and then being a—"

He trailed off, and I cocked my head. "Bastard?"

The confused fog in his eyes disappeared, and he nodded. "Yeah, that."

"That wasn't what you were going to say, was it?"

"I don't know what I was going to say," he said, but I noticed the way he averted his gaze. "Look, I shouldn't have done that, and well, things went a lot differently than I thought they would."

"Have you really—"

"Adam. You might as well just say it. This conversation is already going to be pretty awkward as it is. You might as well not make it more awkward by trying not to say certain things."

"Have you really…been in love with me all these years?"

"Heh, that would be the first question you ask," he said with a snort. "That's…a complicated answer."

"Try me."

"I love you. That's never been in question. But there's this weird middle ground between my romantic feelings for you and my love for you as my best friend. Am I *in* love with you? I honestly can't say. It's all muddled up in my head," he said with a vague, spinning gesture of his hand at his head. "I mean, I don't think it's possible to be in love with someone until you've…been with them. Sure, you can have all the components lying around, but just because you have a pile of lumber, tools, and a plan doesn't mean you suddenly have a full-sized deck built and ready to go."

I had to smile at the comparison. "Thank you for dumbing it down to something I would understand."

He plucked a stray twig from the deck table and flicked it at me. "I'm trying to make it make sense to me too, alright? I've never…look, I've never really analyzed it, okay? I've known I was attracted to you for ages. And that's not exactly hard to analyze."

"That simple, huh?" I asked, finding myself interested in his answer.

"Are you fishing for a compliment right now? Do you want me to tell you I've thought you're hot since pretty much the moment puberty started affecting us? That even when you were fifteen and were in that weird gangly, clumsy stage, I still wanted to kiss you stupid? Or that when I saw you lying in your old childhood bed a couple of weeks ago, hungover and looking like a disaster, I still found myself distracted by all the skin?"

Suddenly the interest I'd had only moments before felt intrusive and nosy. "Oh."

"Yeah, oh," he said with a shake of his head. "And you know, that part is easy to deal with. Okay, sure, it's a little weird to have the hots for your best friend, but being turned on by someone? Plenty of practice with that."

I scowled. "I guess that's good."

"You really know how to make it sound good," he said with a roll of his eyes. "It's just...everything else I've never thought too hard about."

"Why?"

"Why haven't I thought about it?"

"Yeah."

"What was the point? I had to deal with feeling it all the time, and thinking about it, breaking it down wasn't going to make it easier to deal with. Whether or not I figured out if I simply could be instead of was in love with you wouldn't make my life a whole lot easier."

I wasn't sure I agreed with the sentiment, but I kept my mouth shut. Bennett had always been better at rolling with the punches life gave him, either going with the flow or finding a new angle to get out of the current. I was the one who had to tread water and try to figure out where the current was taking me or analyze the way the waves were moving in order to discover whether I wanted to do something about it or not.

Instead, I just shrugged. "I'm not going to hold you kissing me against you. It was a heat of the moment thing and, well, it's not like I—"

I had confronted him, at first, to understand how that could have happened in the first place. His answer had been surprisingly frank, though considering that was just how Bennett was, I shouldn't have been all that surprised. Yet under the surprise was a growing amount of curiosity and wonder.

"I can't even say it was a temptation thing," Bennett said quietly, now looking down at his cup. "One minute we were arguing, and the next thing I knew, I was kissing you."

MY BEST FRIEND'S SECRET

"Well, if it makes you feel any better, it took me a little longer to figure out what was happening," I said with a shrug.

"That doesn't make me feel better, no," he said with a snort. "I honestly thought you came into my room to give me an earful. I wasn't expecting you to start asking questions."

"Well, I knew that's what I was going to do."

"You really weren't pissed?"

"Did I seem that mad to you?"

"No, you were…I don't know how to describe what you were like. Well, not at that point. I can find a few words to describe what you were like after that."

"After I asked if you'd do it again," I said quietly, feeling my heart rate pick up.

This was the part of the conversation I'd known was coming, and I still wasn't sure how to feel about it. From the look on Bennett's face, the attempt to conceal his feelings, and the poorly concealed hurt and fear, I wasn't alone in that.

"Yeah, after that," he said. "I'm not sure what to say about that."

"I wish I could say I knew what to say instead," I admitted softly.

"I just…like I said, it's a lot for you to take in. You've already been going through enough as it is, and I won't blame you if you need to step back and think about things," Bennett said in a steady, even voice.

"What?" I asked, looking up in surprise.

Bennett arched a brow, but the wryness was ruined by the sad tilt to his knowing smile. "C'mon, that's kind of who you are, Adam. Something happens that takes you by surprise or bothers you. You retreat, get quiet, and have to sit there, pick it apart, and figure out how you feel about things. I used to think that's what you were doing when you started going quiet on me. Wasn't until it went on long enough that I realized it was just the new state of affairs."

I didn't know which of those two statements to deal with first. On the one hand, we really did need to talk about my gradual disappearance from his life. On the other, we had something else we were dealing with at the moment, and I had to tell myself to deal with one thing at a time.

"I'm not trying to back away, and I'm not going to walk out of here and not talk to you for days," I told him with a frown.

"And do what instead? Brood around here while you try to figure out what it all means?" Bennett scoffed.

"Bennett," I began slowly, setting my cup aside and leaning forward, "last night, while unexpected, and definitely has me wondering what the hell was up with all of it, doesn't freak me out."

And with that, I finally managed to stump Bennett, catching him completely off-guard. I could see the way he stiffened, eyes widening in surprise as he stared at me.

"You…you…I gave you a *blowjob*," he said, no longer with the same casual indifference he'd said it earlier. I now suspected that under all that casual coolness there had been a far more terrified and worried voice repeating it in his head.

"Yes, you did," I admitted, feeling a twist in my stomach. It was only now that I realized it wasn't a twist of discomfort but the sudden tensing of my muscles at a pleasant, erotic thought. "For the record, you're good at it."

Bennett's mouth dropped open. *"Excuse me?"*

I almost laughed, but I had to remind myself we were treading into some weird waters. "Look, I'm not sitting here saying that…well, I don't know what I'm not saying. I'm not having some huge epiphany or something, but last night didn't bother me. Well, except for the part about you having strong feelings for me all these years."

"Look." Bennett ducked his head, and I immediately had to backtrack.

"Not because it makes me uncomfortable," I said hastily. "You've *never* made me feel uncomfortable, Bennett. Not in our entire friendship, and you sure as hell didn't last night. I just…it bothers me that you were going through that, and I had no idea, even before I was an asshole who stopped being your friend for a while there."

A small measure of the tension left Bennett's shoulders. "You're allowed to be uncomfortable with what happened."

I couldn't help it and rolled my eyes. "Yeah, sure, fine. But in case you forgot, you might have kissed me, but I was uh…I was the one who started the rest of it."

"You were also pretty drunk."

"Not *that* drunk. If I was, I probably wouldn't remember most of what happened."

Including how irritated I'd been after my conversation with Isaiah. Now that I knew that, *apparently*, the person Bennett had been interested in was me, the conversation took on a whole new perspective.

"Jesus," I groaned. "Isaiah knows."

"I haven't talked to Isaiah today."

"No, but when he accidentally dropped a hint that there was someone you were interested in, he was talking about me."

"Oh." Bennett's cheeks colored. "Right, yeah. We talked about it a few years back. Got drunk, hung out, got to talking about guys we'd been with. That led to me spilling my guts a little."

I rubbed my forehead. "Isaiah, Chase, is there anyone else?"

"Well, I told my mom once," he said with a wince. "*That* was mortifying. She made this whole thing about it, asking if I was okay, making sure I understood you were straight, wondering if maybe I was better off distancing myself from you. I honestly thought she was never going to stop."

"Yeah," I agreed with a wince. "I can see that."

"Oh, and I'm like, pretty sure your mom knows too."

"You told my mom?" I asked incredulously.

"What? Hell no! I'm just pretty sure she figured it out, is all. Don't ask me how, but—"

"Do I wanna know what makes you say that?"

"Just call it a hunch."

I sensed there was more to it but decided it could wait. More important in my mind was that he understood. "And Bennett? I'm not uncomfortable about what happened."

"Yeah, you said that," he said in a tone that clearly said he wasn't sold on the matter.

"Look," I said, repeating his chosen phrase for this conversation and scooting my chair closer to him. "I was anything *but* uncomfortable last night, alright? I'm not sure where all that came from or what it all means, but...I wasn't uncomfortable."

Bennett eyed me, and I could see him fighting an internal battle to believe me. "Yeah?"

I hated seeing him struggle so much, and I reached out, first taking his fingers with mine and giving them a tug. There was a moment of hesitation on his part before he eased his hand forward, and I closed my hand around his. This was just as strange and awkward for me, though for different reasons, I needed him to understand that I was okay.

More than okay, actually.

"After the initial shock of what happened and then being kind of blown away by our conversation, everything after that was good," I told him.

"Good?" he repeated, and I wondered if perhaps his brain was starting to short-circuit.

"I can even admit it was great, fantastic even," I said with a small smile. "It's, uh, it's been a while since I was with someone, well, with someone who made me feel special and taken care of."

"Even when I thought you were the world's biggest dickhead, you've always been special to me," he said, and I could see some of the lines easing on his face.

"And I'm sorry I did what I did the past few years," I told him with a heavy sigh. "But I'm not sorry about what *we* did last night."

Bennett looked over my face for several seconds before swallowing hard. "What…what does that mean?"

"At its most basic, it means I'm not bothered, uncomfortable, or upset with you. It also means that I, uh"—I cleared my throat, feeling a pool of warmth forming in my gut—"definitely enjoyed what happened."

"Well," he said with a shy smile. "It seemed like you were enjoying yourself."

That was putting it lightly. I had never seriously considered what it would feel like to get blown by another guy. All in all—other than the fact that I could clearly see it was a guy, and when we kissed I could feel the aesthetic differences for sure—sensation-wise, it was almost like any other blowjob I'd received. Admittedly, this one had been a high-ranking one, and I had to hand it to Bennett, he knew what he was doing.

The fact that it was another man was strange, but I'd barely thought about it at the time. All I could think about was how good it felt and how good Bennett made me feel. He had been so ready and willing, eager to make me feel good, and I'd felt taken care of in a way I could only dimly remember from the good years with Bri.

"I really did," I said softly as the thoughts trickled through my brain. "You made me feel good, and I don't just mean… physically. I was a little freaked out at first because I didn't know what the hell I was doing, but you just took care of things."

"And it really didn't bother you that a guy, more specifically, *me*, was giving you a blowjob?"

"That's the funny thing. I think if it had been any other guy, it probably would have bothered me. I'd probably have done exactly what you thought I was going to do in the first place, retreat to a quiet place and have a mental breakdown over it. Or at least have an existential crisis. But the fact that it *was* you? I believe that's the reason I'm okay."

As soon as the words left my mouth, I knew they were true. I truly believed no one else could have done something like that with me and left me feeling as comfortable and safe. In all honesty, I didn't think I had *ever* been made to feel safe by another person before, at least not a former girlfriend or my ex-wife.

"So, what do we do?" Bennett asked, and I could tell he was still lost and struggling to deal with whatever thoughts he had in his head.

"I don't know," I admitted honestly. "I'm not bothered, but that doesn't mean this makes a lot of sense to me. I just know what I know. Everything else is a mystery."

Bennett sighed. "This kind of puts a weird thing between us, doesn't it?"

I hesitated. "Does it have to?"

He looked up, frowning in confusion. "What do you mean?"

"Does it have to put anything between us? I mean, it happened, it was good, and we're good as far as I'm concerned," I told him.

He looked me over, and I wondered what was going through his head as he took his time to reply. "Adam, um…I hope this doesn't make this weirder for you, but, uh…do you want it to happen again?"

I would have been a damned liar if I tried to claim that the thought hadn't been sitting in the back of my head through a good chunk of our conversation. Every time I thought about the night before, my stomach flipped and tightened in a strangely pleasant way.

"I mean," I said slowly, trying to figure out just what emotions were working through me, "it *was* a good experience, and I don't regret it."

"That's not the same thing as wanting it to happen again."

"No, I guess it isn't, is it?"

"Well, I might have an idea of what to do."

"If you've got a workable idea, I'm all ears."

"Alright…you trust me?"

I cocked my head, frowning slightly. "Yes."

Nodding, Bennett scooted forward until he was kneeling before me. Confused, I leaned back to see what he was doing, only to be stopped by his hand on my arm. As he grew closer, my heart began to race as I realized what he was doing. His eyes felt like they were burrowing into mine as he leaned into my personal space. I felt myself swallow hard when I watched his tongue dart out to lick his bottom lip nervously.

My eyes fluttered closed when he grew close enough that I felt his breath brush against my lips. Half a heartbeat later, his lips were against mine, light and feathery, simply letting them sit there. Even then, I could feel the light brush of his stubble as his head moved slightly and hear the slight exhale as he let himself sit there.

Far faster than I had the night before, I realized I didn't want just to sit there and pressed forward, kissing him in return. His stubble scraped against mine, and I couldn't help the small laugh at the sensation. Then, without thinking, I reached out, sliding my hand along his neck to cup the back and pull him closer.

I ended up knocking him off-balance and bringing his

body between my legs. I was a little surprised at how well he managed to nestle there and appreciated that I didn't have to bend as far forward as I was used to in order to kiss him. He caught himself on my thighs, and I felt a zing of anticipation rush through me as his fingers dug into the muscles of my legs.

"That," I began roughly as he pulled away, "was your idea?"

"I'd ask if you enjoyed yourself, but—" Bennett stopped, and I jerked in surprise when he wiggled his thumb and brushed against the hard-on I didn't even know I had.

"Huh, would you look at that?" I said, both surprised and not. It tracked that if I had enjoyed what we'd done the night before, I would probably enjoy it more the next day. It was still a little strange since I'd never shown even the slightest hint of being into a guy, particularly Bennett, but it wasn't unnerving.

"I have," Bennett said, and I felt my stomach curl pleasantly at the warm, heated tone in his voice. "Ten out of ten would definitely recommend."

I snorted, pushing him with a laugh. "Please don't leave a review on my dick."

Bennett caught himself, sitting on his legs. I knew he was getting comfortable, but for a moment, I wondered what it would be like if his position were just a little less innocent. "So, you enjoyed last night, and you just enjoyed that?"

"Seems like I did," I said, rubbing my jaw thoughtfully and adjusting my position so I wasn't uncomfortable. "Not sure what it means."

"Maybe it doesn't mean anything."

"Pretty sure it has to mean something."

"Okay. Do you have to figure out what it means immediately?"

I cocked my head. "You know as well as I do, there's no way I could leave something like this unanswered."

"True," he drew out. "But does it have to be figured out immediately? Like, right now, life or death, your whole world will be tipped upside down if you don't."

I rolled my eyes. "No. Like I said, it doesn't upset me...just kinda confuses me."

"Well, maybe the answer will come in time?"

"That's a very confident response on your part."

"Oh, shut it. I'm not exactly walking in territory that I understand all that well. My point is, well, uh—"

His confidence faltered, and I frowned. "What?"

"What if we just kind of played it by ear?" he asked, looking wary, but at least he wasn't looking like a kicked puppy as he had earlier.

"Meaning?" I asked though I had a very good idea of what he was aiming for.

"Meaning if you enjoyed those things, we can do them when we feel like it," he said with a shrug, though I suspected he was feeling far less nonchalant than he was letting on. "Maybe it'll clarify things, or maybe you'll get your answer."

"That's...that doesn't sound like much fun for you," I said with a frown, thinking of everything he'd told me.

Bennett raised a brow. "You kidding? If you take out the moments before and after that were filled with panic, last night was fun."

I scowled. "That's not what I meant."

To my surprise, he gave a thick chuckle and slid forward, once more entering my space. This time he let his chest press against my groin as he peered up at me. "Look, Adam, I'm a big boy, alright? I don't need you to treat me with kid gloves, and I don't need you to be extra gentle with me because you feel like shit because of the whole 'ignored me' thing."

"That's not it at all," I argued, even as I struggled to hold onto my irritation while he just knelt there looking…different.

"Good, then when I say you don't need to worry about me in that regard, you don't have to worry. I know what I'm saying. I know what I'm offering. I don't have to break it down to know what's up, alright? I'm asking that you trust me in that regard and just worry about whether or not that's something you want," he said.

I wasn't sure which made it more difficult to make an informed decision, my worry about him or his proximity. When it came right down to it, I did trust him. He was the one who had a right not to have any trust. And really, he *had* made me feel good the night before, and not just because of his skill. Here he was, offering me something and putting himself at risk to make me feel comfortable and perhaps get a little more enjoyment out of life.

"And if this…changes things?" I asked cautiously.

"Then we can deal with that when it happens."

"When, not if, huh?"

"Had I said 'if,' you probably would've found a reason to argue. Stick to the topic at hand, Adam."

I took a deep breath. "There's an eject button for both of us. If it's too much for either of us, we say so, and we get out."

Bennett's brow rose. "You're…serious?"

"Well, unless you have a better—"

"No, you're actually going for it. Like, my offer."

"Yesss?"

"Seriously?"

"Why are you the surprised one here?"

Bennett snorted, pushing away with a laugh. "I've never been comfortable telling you this, but sometimes your denseness isn't frustrating, it's adorable."

"Thanks?" I asked, mildly offended.

"You're welcome," he said, adjusting himself as he stood. "And I'm not arguing with your logic, just a little surprised."

I grabbed his hand before he could go back into the house. "I'm serious."

"I know," Bennett said softly. "But it's probably not a good idea to make too big a deal about this little…agreement. We both know it's there, and we're going to roll with things in the best way we know how. So in the meantime, I'm going to go wash off my jogging sweat, you're going to finish your coffee, and maybe we can go get some real food in you from the diner later. I can gossip over fried food about how I'm pretty sure Chase is half in love with Devin."

I sat up straighter. "Wait, is that the rest of the story you think you're not getting?"

"Ah ah, no more spoilers until we're eating lunch," he chided, stepping into the house.

"Bastard!" I called after him.

ADAM

I wasn't sure what to expect, but it took another week before anything else happened between us. We saw each other just about every day, but for the most part we were kept pretty busy. Word of my skills started spreading through Fairlake, and I was seriously considering opening a small, proper business. It would involve some running around with the government, but having done it once, I was sure I could do it again.

Bennett was as busy as ever, including getting into trouble at work. Somewhere in the middle of the week, he'd announced he would be staying late to clean. When I'd asked why he was doing that instead of the janitor, he informed me it probably wasn't right that poor Colin had to clean up rubber glue and paper.

I honestly thought it was better not to ask for more details.

Yet even with how busy we were, we still allowed ourselves to have the weekend and planned to spend it at his house. Which meant drinking more beer than was necessary, watching junk shows and movies, and being slobs while ignoring the rest of the world. It had been Bennett's idea, but I'd been all for it, thinking it was almost exactly like we used to do when we were younger and had spare time to spend together.

"Well howdy, stranger," Bennett called when I finally pulled into his driveway and hopped out of my truck. He was bent down around the bushes, pulling out weeds. "Thought you were going to be here an hour ago."

"I texted and said I'd be late," I said, plucking the twelve-pack of beer I'd bought on the way over from the passenger seat. "Maybe pay attention to your phone."

"I got...distracted," he admitted, looking over his pile. "I see you brought the beer."

"And you were supposed to get the food," I said, arching a brow.

Bennett grinned, standing up to wipe his dirty hands on his pants. "Pizza's in the oven, should be just about done."

"Ooh, frozen pizza," I said, raising a brow as I looked him over. As usual when he was at home, he'd found something loose and comfortable to throw on. Back when we were kids, I used to tease him that he was the world's worst gay man about his appearance. "Feeling fancy, I see."

Bennett flipped me the bird as he climbed the steps. "It's from Margie's, so you know that shit is good, don't be a bitch."

It was then I noticed that as loose as his shorts were, they weren't loose enough to conceal his ass as he mounted the steps. It was also then that I realized I was noticing his ass in the first place. "Oooh, I forgot all about Margie's, shouldn't be surprised they're still around. When did they start selling frozen stuff?"

"Few years back," he said, opening the door and holding it until I followed him. "Guy at the bakery, Grant, was the one who told them it would be good for business. They went for it, and it worked out."

"Oh, sounds like that guy knows what's up," I said, jamming the beer into the fridge and grabbing two bottles.

"He showed up a couple of years after you left," Bennett explained, pulling out the pizza and looking it over. "Opened up the bakery, and well, word got around town. Then one of the kids convinced him to do some social media. Some of his shit got popular across the world. Still gets custom orders from all over the country."

"Huh, we have a celebrity in Fairlake. Who would've thought," I said, cracking the beers open and holding one out to him.

"Don't say that around him," Bennett chuckled as he set the bottle aside to cut up the pizza. "He gets this weird look on his face. Nice guy, a little weird, but he's almost kinda scary when he looks like that."

"Noted." I chuckled, taking a drink and watching him as he moved around the kitchen to grab plates.

I felt the anxiety and stress bleeding out of me as I heard him start humming to himself. For the first time in weeks, I felt like my life was starting to come together. I had my work starting up again, along with the idea that if I was going to settle back in Fairlake for good, I could have a form of my old business back.

My parents were no longer watching me out of the corner of their eyes, and if my little handyman business kept going, I could comfortably give them back their house in a couple of months. I couldn't blame them for worrying; my whole life had come crashing down, and it had probably looked like I was going to stay in the flames.

But now? Now there was a sense of normalcy, and a large part of it came from the somehow adult dork humming "Tiptoe Through the Tulips" while he cut up a pizza.

"Alright!" he proclaimed, handing me a plate before gathering his food and drink to head toward the living room. "Trashy action movie or trashy horror?"

"Horror, then action. And since you have the worst taste imaginable in movies, you pick," I told him, dropping onto the couch.

"Fine, but you're enduring *Sharknado 2*," he told me, sorting through his film library with a remote. "You can laugh at Tara Reid's awkward screaming when her arm gets bitten off."

"Pretty sure those movies are intentionally bad."

"You didn't require me to pick one that was unintentionally bad."

"Fine, but the action movie has to be unintentionally bad."

"And that, my dear friend, is easy enough. I'm thinking *Ultraviolet*."

I had no idea what that meant, but I wasn't nearly as explorative as him when it came to movies and shows. Only when I was sure it was something I'd like and hadn't been dragged by reviews would I finally watch something. Which meant I had an admittedly smaller collection than Bennett, but it was curated and of higher quality.

At least, I liked to think so.

I had to give Bennett credit, *Sharknado 2* turned out to be as dreadful and cheesy as promised. Even though it was meant to be as bad as it was, it didn't change its cringeworthy nature. That didn't stop me from laughing while we ate the rest of the pizza and downed a few more beers each.

"Yeah, that was...not the best scream in the world," I said once the film finally ended.

"The real debate is whether or not it was intentionally bad or just bad acting."

"I can't really say I can recall any memorable acting from Tara Reid, to be honest."

"Yeah," he agreed, flipping through the digital library again. "I think it was the sex appeal that got her through most of it."

"Never saw it," I admitted, tipping my bottle up to finish it off. "She always looks…lost and confused. Like, I didn't want to fuck her. I wanted to ask her if she was lost and lead her to safety."

"Very…sexy," Bennett said with a laugh.

"Exactly my point," I said, returning to hand him a new beer. "Start her up."

"Ah yes, prepare for over-the-top action, terrible, stilted acting, and actually a pretty decent art budget," he said with a happy sigh, turning on the movie.

It didn't take me long to see what he meant. Admittedly, it was shaping up to be a pretty bad movie, and the action sequences, while over-the-top and flashy, weren't enough to save the rest of it

"Good lord," I muttered after twenty minutes. "You were not kidding."

"Told ya." He chuckled, dropping his empty bottle onto the table and flopping down onto the couch next to me.

"Easy," I grumbled as I bounced.

"Shush," he chided, curling up beside me and flopping his head onto my lap.

It was the first time he'd done anything innocently phys-ical with me since I came back. While physical affection had never been our thing, we'd occasionally had our moments, generally when we were most comfortable and laid back.

Usually, it was just sitting or laying like this, his head near my knee, and sometimes my hand resting on his side or arm. This time, however, he was halfway up my thigh, and I only hesitated a moment before resting my hand in his short hair. There wasn't much to hold on to or pull playfully, but I could run my fingertips through it to massage his scalp. If he thought it was unusual, he showed no signs as he rested his hand on my thigh and made himself comfortable while the movie continued to play.

After another fight scene, I found my attention drawn away from the terrible dialogue and acting and back to Bennett. He had barely moved, which was unusual for a man who struggled to sit in a chair for more than five minutes. In fact, his eyes were half shut as he watched the movie while my fingers moved back and forth through his hair with firm but gentle strokes.

Huh, apparently he liked having his head stroked, never knew that.

A zing of interest shot through me, and I set my half-drunk bottle to the side, using that hand to resume stroking his head. With the other hand free, I rubbed down his neck and shoulders. Bennett rolled his shoulders and immediately settled back down as I pressed my fingers into his muscles.

Touching him was different than anyone else I'd touched this intimately before. There was the short hair, of course, and the ever-present stubble that I swore was more stubborn about leaving than my own. There was more firmness to the muscle he built up and kept toned, but his skin was still warm and soft.

Without thinking, I slipped my hand down his shirt, smiling at the unsurprising lack of anything soft on his chest, finding only a firm plane of skin, muscle, and a smattering of hair. I didn't find the chest hair unappealing as I ran my fingers through it, finding it a little coarse.

Flipping my hand out of the collar of his shirt, I ran it down his torso to pull up his shirt. I was barely thinking about what I was doing as I ran my hand up the flat, firm stretch of his stomach. Much like me, he had a patch of hair that was softer than the few hairs on his chest. I could feel the muscles jump slightly under my touch, and had to appreciate how warm he was as he nestled against me.

"Having fun?" Bennett asked, breaking me out of my trance.

"Oh," I said, freezing with my hand on his stomach. "Sorry."

"Not complaining about getting a groping out of nowhere, but what's all this about?"

"Uh, started thinking about how different it felt to touch a guy. Then got caught up in finding out what else was different. Kinda fell down a mental rabbit hole there."

Bennett rolled over onto his back, facing me. "And the results of your examination?"

I stared down at him, my eyes flicking to his lips, and felt my pulse speed up. "I think...I wanna try something."

Bennett's pupils swelled noticeably, and I realized I'd aroused him. "Such as?"

"Hold on a second," I said, trying to twist my body around so I'd be lying across the couch. That was easier said than done because grace had never been my strong suit, which I displayed in full when my knee smacked Bennett in the back of the head when I tried to get one leg around him.

"Ow! God, I like it a little rough but not that rough," Bennett said with a laugh as he tried to sit up.

"Shut up," I grumbled, grabbing him to pull him back into me so his back was against my chest.

Though I might have to file that information away for later.

"Bossy," he said lightly, but I felt him still when I wrapped my arm around his waist and cupped his groin. "Adam?"

"I might as well find out what else feels different, right?" I asked in a low voice, hoping he couldn't hear my nerves. Sure, I'd done this with myself plenty of times in the past, more times than I'd ever had sex, that was for sure. That didn't make me an expert doing it with someone else, though.

"Sure," he said, voice wavering as I untied the knot of his shorts and pushed my hands under the waistband. I could feel him straining against the fabric of his underwear, and I smiled when his breath caught at the lightest brush of my fingertips.

Deciding there was no point in drawing things out, I gently pushed my fingers into his underwear. Then I leaned forward, kissing the side of his neck as I reached in and wrapped my hand around his cock. Bennett immediately pressed back into me, pushing his hips forward and making it easier for me to pull his dick free.

And it was...a dick. More specifically, it was Bennett's dick. It was smaller than mine, but by no means little, but it was different to hold a dick other than mine in my grip. He was rock hard, however, and I could see he was already leaking pretty heavily despite the fact that I hadn't done much of anything yet.

Carefully I stroked him, unsure if he was the type to jerk off without lube like I occasionally did, and not wanting to hurt him. After a few strokes, however, I felt him buck into my hand subtly and realized I was doing *something* right.

"Just pretend it's yours," Bennett breathed, pushing his shoulders back against me.

"I can be a little rough on mine...and don't always use lube."

"Like I'm patient enough to dig out lube all the time or clean it up afterward."

Also information that I might be able to use again.

I wrapped my hand around him firmly this time, allowing my hand to pull the skin back and forth, my grip sliding up over the underside of his head. It was a rhythm I was used to, and despite going slow at first to make sure it *really* was what Bennett was into, I found myself getting into a groove easily.

Bennett barely moved against me, save that he let his head gradually drop back onto my shoulder, and his hips shuddered. For the first minute or so, I thought he was just the quiet type, until I heard him give a grunt that almost wanted to be a groan.

"Oh no, I wanted to see different things," I told him, bending my head down to nip at his ear. "Let me hear what's different too. You don't have to hold back."

"Adam," he all but whined, and I continued to nip at him, at any part of his neck and jaw I could find.

Whether from my "permission" or the new sensation, Bennett started making noises. They were soft at first, whimpers that threatened to drive me crazy as I continued stroking him, feeling his shaft throb in my grip. Little by little, the soft noises became low groans that were altogether new to me in their timbre, but I found them just as encouraging as the higher-pitched noises I'd heard from women.

I heard his breath shudder, and I kept up what I was doing, knowing what was about to happen. Bennett's body grew harder against me, and he pushed himself back with more force than before, his hips stuttering up into my grip. His cock pulsed, he cried out softly, and I watched and felt warmth spreading down over my hand and his shaft as he came.

"Fuck," he breathed, sagging back against me.

My heart hammered as I realized what I'd just done, and I gently released him. My hand was still covered, and I held it out as if I'd done this for myself and wondered where I might find a paper towel or a cloth.

"One second," Bennett said with a laugh. "Not to leave you with jizz on your hands. But it's been a minute, and I needed that."

"You haven't got off since...oh god." I stopped, realizing. "I never returned the favor, did I? I passed out and left you with blue balls."

"That was the least of my troubles that night," Bennett said with a chuckle, reaching down to tuck himself away. "Let me find you something."

I eyed my hand for a moment and then cocked my head. Before I could second-guess the idea that flitted into my head, I drew my hand closer and, after a moment's hesitation, licked one of my fingers.

"Huh, a little salty but kinda sweet too," I said, turning my hand around.

Bennett stared at me, his face a mask of shock. "Did you just—"

"What?" I asked, blinking. "It was there. And it's not like I haven't done anything else with you. I just jerked you—"

I was interrupted as he practically leaped on me with a vigor so renewed that I was seriously wondering what his rebound period was like. Then our lips parted and I felt his tongue slide over mine, and I realized his rebound period could be whatever he wanted it to be. Then his hands grabbed my jeans, which I'd barely noticed were painfully tight, and I knew that if this was all it took to unleash whatever the hell this was, I'd happily do it again.

"C'mere," he grunted, pulling my dick out of my pants before grabbing my cum-covered hand. "Jerk off while I make out with you like a horny teenager."

Not in a position to argue, I did as I was told, marveling at the sensation of using another guy's cum for lube to jerk off and making out with my best friend. There was certainly no denying the sheer pleasure of the moment as our lips met once more. I wasn't quite sure if the kiss was a kiss or a battle, but I loved it all the same. Even the scratch of his stubble was new and exciting while I pumped away at myself.

When he broke away, I stared at him in confusion until I watched him sink down, and my eyes widened. "B-Bennett?"

"Shush," he said, and I groaned as his mouth closed around the head of my dick.

Jesus, was he really going to do this right after I—

He sank lower, and I practically lost my mind. So many new things were happening in succession I could barely fit them in my head. All that mattered to me at that moment was watching him work me just as enthusiastically and skillfully as before, except he wasn't waiting until there was enough spit to lube me up. The thought that he was probably tasting me right along with himself flicked some switch inside my brain that I hadn't known existed.

Without thinking, I took hold of his head and began moving my hips in conjunction with his movements. I could feel the familiar heat racing through my body, and I didn't care in the slightest that this wasn't going to take long. All that mattered was the sight of Bennett, the sound of him moaning on my next thrust, and the sensation of his mouth and hand working to get me off.

Which is precisely what happened a minute later. I jerked upward, pushing my cock deeper into his mouth as I came with a shuddering groan, my body overflowing with pleasure before I sank back onto the couch. My chest heaved, and I swore my head was spinning as I stared at the ceiling.

"Jesus Christ on a stick, what the *fuck* was that?" I finally managed to ask, piecing together everything that happened.

"You jerking me off, eating some of my cum, then me using your cum as lube to suck you while jerking you off," Bennett summarized.

"Never knew you were kinky," I muttered.

"Adam." He slid forward, kissing me on the lips. "You probably think anal is kinky, and that's just standard fare for me. You don't know what kinky is."

"Bastard," I muttered, then frowned as he got up. "What're you doing?"

"Getting some wet wipes and a towel. I have cum in my hair," he snorted. "Your hand isn't clean either."

"Oh," I said, looking at it and grimacing. "We made a mess."

"We can clean it up."

"Good idea. Hey, Bennett?"

"What's up?"

"Uh, more cuddling when we're clean?"

I could hear the smile in his voice from the other room. "Sure."

* * *

A COUPLE OF WEEKS LATER, I was finally comfortable enough to consider an apartment or a house. I had enough money to put down for a small house, but if I wanted to go the business route again, I'd need the nest egg I'd accrued for that and need to go with an apartment instead. I was back and forth, and while no one had said anything to push me, I could tell my loved ones were watching.

"What?" my mother asked as she walked past me sprawled out on their living room couch. "No work today?"

"Mr. Clein canceled," I said, flipping through the few listings in Fairlake. The apartments weren't the greatest, but some of the houses for rent were possible if I was careful and maybe waited another month or two to build up more money. "Kind of a shame, doing a man's whole roof is worth good money."

"Oh, he's just a cheapskate. He'll call around a couple of places, find out that you're doing more than right by him, and come crawling back," she told me with a scoff, dropping an overflowing basket of clean clothes onto the love seat.

"Don't you dare let him haggle you down either because he'll try."

"I know I'm working under cost," I snorted, pushing myself up and setting my phone on the coffee table. I scooped the laundry basket up and brought it over to the couch, where there was more room. "Just tell me to move next time."

"Oh, you were comfortable. You've been working hard," she said with a shake of her head.

"If it was Dad, you would have kicked him off," I chuckled, grabbing a shirt and folding it like she'd taught me many years ago.

"That's because it's your father, and it's good for him," she said, and I rolled my eyes when she cocked her head.

"Keep goin'. I'll show you what's good for you," my father called back from the kitchen.

"And what's that? A bunch of grumblin' and moanin' while you putter about the house?" she called back.

"I don't putter!"

"You get anything done today?"

"I'm workin' on it!"

"Working on another pot of coffee, he means," she grumbled. "Honestly, doctor tells him to mind his heart, what does he do? Drinks more coffee and throws half a pound of salt on everything. Honestly, I know you got your daddy's looks, thank God, and too much of his personality, God save us all, but I hope you're smarter about your health."

"That's why I have people like you and Bennett around, Mom," I told her with a smile. "People who keep me from getting *too* hardheaded."

She snorted. "Only one who's had any luck with that is Bennett, bless him. It's so nice to see you boys spending time together again. Goodness, with how much time you've been spending together, I've had to look in the mirror and check to see if a few of my wrinkles are gone. I half expect my teenage son to come in the door when you've been out with him."

"It hasn't been that bad," I said with a laugh, though she wasn't far from the truth.

"Bad. Who said anything about bad?"

"That frequent. It's not the same."

In more ways than one. In the past couple of weeks, I'd discovered just how much fun having a physical relationship with someone like Bennett could be. The man was as enthusiastic and assertive with sex as anything else. I was a little slower-paced about things, but I didn't think I could be blamed when I was new to the whole thing. And despite what Bennett tried to say, my first few times giving a blowjob were nothing spectacular.

He'd come, of course, but I couldn't say that was because I was any good at it.

Not that sex was all we did, and in many ways, my mom was right. It was like being a teenager again. He was as goofy and playful as ever, and sometimes I couldn't mind my own business without him deciding it was a perfect time to attack me. Other times we were perfectly content to play games together, eat junk food, and occasionally work out.

Working out together was an *interesting* experience, and I wasn't sure if we really got much done.

"Oh, it's just nice, is all," she said with a flap of a shirt as she slapped the wrinkles out of it. "Seeing you two be like boys again. I know how much he missed you when you were gone. He tried to hide it, but you know how Bennett is, not very good at hiding much of anything. I always told that boy not to play poker."

It made me think of what Bennett had said a few weeks prior about what he suspected my mother had figured out. "Hey, uh, Mom?"

My quieter tone got her attention. "Yes?"

"You never told me what you thought about Bennett being gay."

"Oh. Well, I thought it was pretty obvious."

"Well, you never treated him any different...for the most part."

She sniffed indignantly. "I'd like to think it was the whole part."

I chuckled. "You did fuss over him a little more than usual after he told you guys."

"God, I remember that. Standing in that kitchen there, looking nervous as a hare in a trap, while you stood behind him, *glaring*. As if daring us to say anything against it." My mother chuckled, a warm smile on her face. "You two were always so sweet."

"You never...worried about anything from him?" I asked, still unable to bring myself to say it. As good as Bennett's instincts usually were, I didn't want to spill his secret to her, just in case she didn't know.

"Worried about what?"

"I don't know...anything?"

"What, like doing something with you? Sweetheart, that boy might've been—" She stopped, snatched up two socks, and glared at them as if evaluating whether they matched.

"Mom."

"Yes?"

"Those are two very clearly black socks of the same length. With no markings on them."

"Of course."

"Mom?"

"Yes?"

"What did you stop yourself from saying?"

"Nothing," she said, waving the socks at me before folding them over onto themselves and setting them neatly aside. "I

174

never worried about him doing anything with or to you that…well, you wouldn't have been comfortable with."

"Uh, Mom?" I asked, suddenly startled by the implication.

She rolled her eyes, swatting me with a hand towel with a sharp snap of her wrist. "Oh, stop it! I know full well that you're into ladies. I didn't mean anything else by it."

"Geez, Mom," I said, rubbing the spot where she'd hit me. "Almost made me wonder."

"Oh *no*, if I thought for even a minute that you were getting thoughts in your head, there is no way I would have let you boys sit around unsupervised."

"What?"

"Oh, what, you think just because you couldn't get pregnant I was going to leave two lovebirds to sit alone in a room without being watched? No, sir, not until you're well into your adult years. And even then."

"Mom!"

I jumped when the front door swung open with the enthusiasm that only one person could muster. Decked out in his uniform, Bennett strolled into the house and beamed at us. "I heard the indignant call of an outraged son. Mrs. Jensen, what did you do? Give me all the details."

For a moment, I was left speechless at the sight of him and felt my heart trip over itself as I took it in. It wasn't the first time I'd seen him in uniform, but somehow seeing him stand in the early evening light, a big grin on his face as he beamed at my mother. He looked perfectly content, like he'd walked into his own home where he was both wanted and expected.

Which, I had to admit, was precisely how things were, and the thought made me smile.

"You're looking pleased with yourself," Bennett said, and I had to chuckle at the wariness in his voice. "What exactly were you talking about?"

"Nonsense," my mother said with a roll of her eyes.

"Apparently, if she'd ever got even the slightest whiff that I was into other guys, she would have treated us spending time together like she treated me spending time with my old girlfriends," I told him, watching his reaction carefully.

"Oh," he said, blinking rapidly. I thought it was pretty obvious he wasn't expecting that as an answer. For a moment, I wondered if he'd been taken completely off guard until I saw a familiar glint in his eyes. "Well, I guess we probably shouldn't tell them about the wild and sordid love affair we're having."

"Excuse me?" I sputtered, fumbling with the shirt I'd been trying to fold.

"Oh, don't try to hide it!" he proclaimed in a high falsetto, positively dripping with wounded pride and indignation. I stared at him, flummoxed, as he dashed across the room to throw an arm around my shoulder, taking my hand in his. "I'm tired of hiding the love we share for one another. Mrs. Jensen?"

"Yes, sweetheart?" she asked with barely a glance our way as she rummaged through the basket for the twin to the sock she held in her hand.

"I'm sorry you have to find out this way, but Adam and I are going to run off into the mountains together! Where we can live in happiness and peace from a world that doesn't understand our love!" Bennett continued in the same dramatic voice.

"What in the world is going on in there?" I heard my father's exasperated voice call from the kitchen.

"Adam and Bennett are madly in love and running off into the mountains together," my mother called back, beginning to set all the now-folded laundry into the empty basket.

"The mountains? Bennett wouldn't know what to do if he

had to survive in the mountains, and our idiot isn't any better," my father called back.

"Yes, well, they're madly in love."

"They're idiots."

My mother winked as she hefted up the basket. "He's a sweetheart, isn't he? That's why I married him, you know."

"I thought you married him because he's able to fix just about anything that didn't require a computer chip," Bennett said, letting go of my hand but keeping his arm around my shoulders.

"*One* of the reasons," she said with a wink, heading toward the stairs. "Bennett, will you be joining us for dinner? I've got a roast in the oven."

"You do know how to make a convincing argument," Bennett said, watching as she climbed the stairs and went out of sight. To my surprise, he turned and kissed me on the cheek before heading for the stairs after her. "Hold up! I'll help you put that away."

I listened to her lighthearted complaining because she didn't need any help, and he needed to sit down after being at work all day. Without thinking, I raised my hand to the spot where Bennett had kissed me, as bewildered as I'd been from the moment his lips had touched me. The gesture had been so casual, as if he hadn't given a moment's thought to what he was doing before he darted off to help my mother with household chores.

He really did fit in around here, even after all these years and even after he was left to wonder if we were friends at all. I knew the conversation we'd just had was in jest and that my parents didn't believe for a minute that either of us was anything more than friends. Even then, they'd accepted the joke without so much as a batted eye or a moment's hesitation.

In some bizarre way, it showed how little they were

bothered by the idea. I was their son, and they accepted Bennett as one of their own. Our lives had been so entwined within one another for so long, and now I saw history repeat itself. There was a great deal of comfort in that thought, and I couldn't help the small smile on my face.

"Hey, Adam!" my father barked gruffly from the doorway, and I spun to face him.

"Come back to Earth," he said with a frown, "and help me with the brakes on your mother's car. If I let Bennett anywhere near it, he'll set it on fire...again."

"That was one time, and I was fourteen!" I heard Bennett call indignantly down the stairs.

My father walked away, shaking his head. "Can't get you to hear me even after calling your name, but that one can hear one comment from a different floor."

I grinned, following after my father to help him and letting the sounds of home settle into me.

* * *

JUST OVER TWO WEEKS LATER, I found myself at Bennett's house again. If it were anyone else, I might have started to suspect he was taking advantage of my skills to help with his house. Not only had we replaced the shingles of his roof with a new layer, but we'd also managed a few changes in his bathroom to put in a new shower and had started expanding his bedroom closet.

But I knew Bennett. Not only did he usually struggle to sit still, even when there were dozens of things he liked to do, he just liked being active. Even when we were younger, he often tried to throw himself into a project that required him to move. When we were younger, that usually meant trying to help my father and me with whatever repairs or projects were around the house…except for anything involving cars.

Which meant he was bringing up new projects around his house because he just wanted to do something alongside me. He wasn't the most skilled worker, but he wasn't afraid to use his muscles or get dirty, so there was always something I could give him to do. It usually left us covered in something, sore, and ready to camp out in front of the TV for the rest of the night.

"So," Bennett began as we sprawled on the couch, staring at the TV, "I was thinking."

"Top ten things said right before a disaster," I said without taking my eyes off the screen.

"Blow me," he grunted, nudging me roughly with his foot.

"We're both covered in sawdust, drywall dust, and who the hell else knows what," I reminded him. "Maybe later."

Bennett snorted before spreading his legs over mine and reclining back. "Thanks for reminding me that we're on my couch like that."

"We did take our clothes off beforehand."

"Now there's a reminder."

I smirked as he continued to lay where he was, apparently perfectly content to let us be naked on his couch together without anything more. Not that I was going to complain, it was comfortable to lay around after spending all day working our butts off. That we were completely naked while we let the outside air flow through the open windows was just a bonus.

I would never have thought that simply lying around, half cuddling with Bennett, was something I'd love, but there I was, loving it all the same. I believed I'd reached the peak of comfort with Bennett, but little did I know there were whole new peaks to be reached. I was already about as comfortable as I could get being naked with him, including having sex.

Well, *almost* having sex. We hadn't quite conquered that final peak, but I knew that was more due to me than him. I had no doubt Bennett would be more than happy to take that final step, considering his enthusiasm for everything else we'd done. And it wasn't that I was necessarily against the idea. I just hadn't found the courage.

There was just something so big about the idea that I couldn't shake, even as the thought never entirely left my head.

"You're brooding," Bennett warned without looking at me.

"I'm waiting for you to tell me what this idea of yours is," I said, avoiding admitting to my thoughts, even as I felt them continue to brew in the back of my head. Sometimes it really did feel like a storm building whenever I thought about it for too long, and I never quite knew when it was finally going to hit the shore.

"Oh! Right, well, I think you should do it."

"Ah, yes, I should. Do it. The thing. The thing I absolutely know what you're talking about. Of course."

"You missed your calling as a comedian."

"My mom tells me I'm funny."

"No, she does not," he said with a snort. "And I think you should go and get your business license."

"Boy, I would have never guessed," I said with a wry arch of my brow. "It's not like you haven't been asking about it 'casually' for the past few weeks."

"I'm serious," Bennett complained, rolling his head to look at me with a frown. "You've been building a business as it is. All you're missing is a proper building to do business out of. I mean, don't get me wrong, the city will ignore it because not to would get a few angry calls from people."

"My mother being the first one," I chuckled, but I could see his point. They were ignoring it because I was a born and raised Fairlaker. Even then, they were still politicians and sticklers for the rules. Eventually, someone would have to say something, and I'd be in trouble.

"Look, just take advantage of the grace period you're being given," Bennett said, poking my ribs with one of his toes. "You know they won't make you wait, and you said you have the money for some places."

"I do have a couple I was thinking about," I admitted, batting his foot away before he found the ticklish spot between my ribs I knew he was looking for. "And there's a couple of nice places where I could probably afford the rent for a few months after the deposits."

"I've seen the houses you were looking at. Just let me know which one, and I'll take care of it."

"Bennett—"

"You've been in Boston for too long, my friend. While you're in Fairlake, finding someone with connections to all sorts is not hard. I'm sure I can get you a damn good deal on a place, so long as you're willing not to be a punk and let me do it."

"I'm not a punk," I grumbled, finally grabbing his calf. I felt a flutter in my chest as I felt the muscles in his leg shift under my grip. It wouldn't be the first time I wondered what it would be like to feel the same in his arms as I gently held him down and— "I'm just not sure, is all."

"I mean, what else are you going to do? Are you not planning on staying in Fairlake?" he asked, and I had to admit, if the thought bothered him, he was doing a good job covering it up.

"No, I mean, yes," I said, shaking my head. "I attempted to get out of Fairlake, and what did I get? A business I had to gut, no real friends that were mine, and a miserably failed marriage."

He looked me over. "Do you, uh…do you miss her?"

"I miss the people we were. I miss the good times we had," I admitted with a shrug. "But I also miss the days when you and I were twelve years old and used to run around here like little idiots. Both of those times are behind me now, and there's no getting them back."

"We can still run around here like idiots," he said with a shy smile.

I snorted. "*You* can do all the running for us, thanks. Those days are past us, but that doesn't mean we don't have the chance to make some new days."

"New days for us to look back on and miss?"

"Well, yeah, if my parents' report on the matter is any indication, we won't be able to do all the things we're doing now when we're their age. So, better to build up a lot of good memories while we can."

"While still making new days?"

"Exactly."

Bennett chuckled and flopped around as gracelessly as a drunk starfish before flopping on top of me. "I could get used to the sound of that."

My heart thumped a little harder, and I wondered why it felt like we'd just had two different conversations. "So no, I don't have a reason to leave Fairlake and several to stay."

"Good," he said, bopping me on the end of the nose with a dusty, white fingertip. "Then get the damn business license, get the building, start anew here. Quit trying to analyze everything and figure out if it's the best idea. Because unless you have other ideas, this is the one that gets you doing what you're good at, what you love, and is obviously in high demand around here."

"Is this the part where I'm supposed to say something along the lines of 'I'm just being practical?'"

"To which I would reply that being practical doesn't mean thinking everything to death while you stick around making no decision at all. You're going to keep feeling like you're stuck in a rut unless you start walking forward."

"I don't remember saying anything about being in a rut," I said, feeling him shift against me to get more comfortable.

"You don't have to," he said, leaning close enough I could feel his breath on my lips. "You've always needed a purpose, something to work toward. Without that, you've always been grumpy and even more brooding than usual. The only reason you haven't been lately is because you've been kept busy."

"And distracted," I said, reaching around to grab his ass and squeeze it.

"I'm pretty good at that."

"That you are."

It felt completely natural to lie there with him, our now hardening cocks pressing into one another's bodies as he leaned in and pressed his lips against mine. Strangely, it felt like an extension, a natural progression of everything we'd had before. I still wasn't entirely sure what it meant, but I knew that every day that passed, with each moment I accepted as normal, something else was building in the background.

The more immediately important thing growing at the moment, however, was the hunger building inside me as I kept my hand on his ass. I could feel the strength of his muscles as I pulled him closer, parting our lips. A shiver ran through me when he moaned heavily, rutting against me so our shafts slid roughly against one another.

"I want you," I admitted, feeling the heat growing in my gut as I realized just what I meant.

"I can arrange that," Bennett said with a little laugh. It was one of his quirks, laughing a little whenever things were growing heated between us. If I had been asked, I would have said it made complete sense because Bennett was just...Bennett.

"No," I said, knowing I was finally committing to the idea, and I felt my heart race even harder. To punctuate my point, I gripped his ass and gave it another squeeze. "I *want* you."

Bennett hesitated, pulling back as his eyes went wide. "Like—"

"Yes," I said, unable to help my smile at his surprise. It wasn't often I was able to catch Bennett off guard, but if I had to do it by telling him I was willing to fuck him, then I'd take it.

He narrowed his eyes. "You're sure?"

"Totally," I told him.

Bennett sucked in a sharp breath before pushing himself back. "Fine, but you're getting in the shower with me. No way in hell we're doing all that after spending all day getting covered in sweat and…everything else."

It wouldn't be the first shower I'd taken with him, and I happily pushed myself up from the couch to follow him toward the bathroom. I watched his ass a little more than usual as we walked, imagining what it would be like to see myself slide into him. I wasn't even sure if I wanted to see that while hearing him moan or if I would sacrifice the sight so that I could look him in the eye while we did it.

Bennett did make some very nice faces when he was worked up.

"Why do I feel like I'm being watched?" Bennett asked as he opened the door to start the new shower I'd helped him install. I hadn't stuck around when we were younger long enough to learn that, apparently, Bennett was quite good at saving money. Small-town cops didn't make a lot of money, and while he wasn't afraid to treat himself now and again, he still knew how to sock money away for when he needed something.

"Shush, you," I said, leaning in closer, waiting until I saw him draw his hand back from the water without reaching for the temperature dial. With a huff, I pushed him forward just enough that he had no choice but to step over the lip of the shower and into the stall.

"Bossy," he grumbled as I closed the door behind us.

"Didn't you say you liked it when I got bossy?" I said, running a hand down his slick side.

"I'm pretty sure I said it drives me crazy."

"Same thing."

"Yeah, pretty sure the context was different."

"Shame," I said, letting my teeth sink into the place where his neck and shoulder met. I knew immediately I'd done the right thing as I felt him shudder, pushing back against me.

"This is not a good way to get clean first," he said in a tight voice.

"Then let's make sure you're all nice and wet so we can soap you up."

"Jesus Christ, *what* is that tone you're using?"

Running my hands up and down, I covered as much of his body as I could with the water…just in case. Bennett leaned back into me as I grabbed one of the bottles off the nearby rack and poured bodywash into my palm. There was a loofah he insisted on using, but I ignored it as I rubbed the wash into his flat stomach.

Despite the deep, tightly wound, almost anxious desire stirring in my gut, I took my time to wash as much of his body as I could get to. From his chest all the way down to his dick, the latter earning me a low noise of pleasure as I cleaned it *thoroughly*. I washed his arms, sides, and back and then reached down to soap up his ass.

"You're in a mood today," Bennett said in a tone that told me he had no complaints.

"I'm enjoying myself," I told him, nibbling at his neck.

"Then enjoy," he said, turning around in my arms before sliding down.

My breath hitched as I stared down, watching him take me in his mouth. We'd yet to be able to shower together without something happening, but the half dozen times I'd seen this exact scene, it never got old. I had always been a big fan of watching what happened in as much detail as possible, and while Bennett was the first guy I'd ever found myself wanting to watch, I had to admit it was well worth it.

I could tell from the slow, languid movements that he was trying to take his time. Which was fine by me as I watched the head of my cock slowly disappear until half the shaft was gone. I could feel the squeeze of his throat around the head before he reared back, moving slowly. He kept his hand out of the equation, which was unusual, keeping it at the base.

"Tease," I said in a low voice, realizing he was trying not to get me off, wanting to save it for later.

His hum of agreement almost killed me as the vibrations brought a new level of pleasure. I was in no immediate danger of getting off, but I would have to make a note to see just how long it would take me to come when he was being a little tease.

"Maybe," he said, finally pulling off me. "But let's try and actually get clean before we lose ourselves. After all, I still have to soap you up."

I grinned. "I guess you do, don't you?"

The need inside me was growing even more demanding, but I was more than happy to put it off for the moment as Bennett's hands slid over my body. It seemed he was taking a page out of my book as he poured bodywash into his hands to clean me. He was more meticulous than I was, almost sensual in the way he made sure to get every nook and cranny.

I could only hope I managed to hold out until we got somewhere a little more comfortable for the full show.

BENNETT

It didn't matter how many times I was allowed to touch Adam, it always filled me with a thrill and total wonder. The man wasn't built like a brick shithouse, but he was still built. It seemed like he was made out of mostly muscle, and I never grew tired of searching, seeing just how big and thick they really were.

I could feel the way Adam's eyes bore into me as I covered every part of his body with soap. For a moment, I thought he might tense or even draw away from me when I reached around, returning the favor to wash his ass. To my surprise, he continued to watch, his hands resting on me with barely a twitch from his fingers.

Huh, well, maybe if tonight turned out not to be a disaster, I might see if he'd be willing to see the other side of things as well.

God, was I really going to sleep with Adam? I had been doing everything but that with him for weeks now, and just like our shared shower and groping sessions, it never got old. I'd never brought up either of us fucking the other simply because I knew Adam had to move at his own speed without feeling like I wanted something more.

"Now we rinse off," he said in that stupidly low voice that could have been a growl. I didn't hear it all that often from him, even when he was almost balls deep in my throat, but damned if it didn't drive me crazy every time I did.

"Yeah, yeah, Mr. Bossy," I said with a roll of my eyes, letting him wrap his arms around me and pull me under the spray. One thing I'd always loved about Adam, and loved even more now in moments like this, was that he was never put off or fooled by how I acted. I could accuse him of bossiness all I wanted, and he would still keep on doing it, not just because that was the way he was even when naked, but because he knew damn well I loved it.

Pulling me under, he kissed me, and instantly any resistance, even the playful kind I was fond of, disappeared. It didn't matter that we'd kissed several times over several weeks. Kissing Adam always blew me away far more than anything else we did. All the blowjobs and handjobs in the world couldn't compare to the sheer wonder of wish fulfillment that was being able to kiss Adam.

"Much as I'd like to," Adam said, drawing away and turning off the shower, "you're probably going to have to lead the way on this one."

"Not exactly knowledgeable in the ways of anal, huh?" I asked with a soft laugh as he grabbed the towels from the shelf next to the shower.

"Can't say it was something I did all that often and not all that successfully," he admitted in a far less aggressive voice as we dried ourselves off.

"I sense a story or three in there."

"Yeah, they can wait till later."

I chuckled, stepping out of the shower and taking him by the hand. "Well, don't worry. You're in good hands."

"I'll pretend the way you said that doesn't irritate me," he grumbled.

"And I'll pretend it doesn't turn me on a little to hear that," I shot back, even as I quietly wondered why.

It wasn't the first time I wondered what was going on inside his head or if he knew in the first place. I remembered how irritated and irate he'd been weeks ago after our night at the bar. At the time, I'd thought he was an ass, but after we'd fooled around, I wondered if it was something more. It was a dangerous thought, but part of me sometimes wondered if he got…jealous.

Which opened the door to something I had told myself a long time ago was a dangerous route to travel. If I thought he was even remotely capable of things like jealousy, then I would allow myself to believe he was capable of romantic feelings for me. Even now, with everything we'd done and were about to do, I didn't want to open myself up to the possibility, even as that door opened inch by inch with every passing day.

"C'mere," I said. "I'll show you it doesn't have to be scary."

"I'm serious," he said with a deep frown. "I don't want to hurt you, Bennett."

"Hey," I said, drawing him close and butting his forehead gently with mine. "I mean it. I'll show you this doesn't have to be scary. By the time I'm done, you'll be right back to all that growling and bossiness."

"Ass," he said, and I pushed him onto the bed. "Let's see just how you manage this feat."

"Easy," I said, opening the closet and pulling out a small box. "I'll use a little showmanship."

"Showmanship?" he asked, though I smiled when I sensed curiosity more than anything else.

"First things first," I said, pointing toward the bedside

table. "There's a bottle of lube in there I need, well there's two. And some condoms, if uh—"

Adam glanced at me as he looked through the drawer. "Do...we need them?"

It had been months since I'd last had sexual contact with anyone but Adam and my past couple of tests had come through clean. "I don't, no."

"Alright then. Silicone and water-based? Geez, Bennett."

"Water-based is for the show. Silicone is for you and me."

"O...kay."

He set one bottle aside and handed me the other, and I motioned for him to move back toward the head of the bed. I climbed onto the bed and opened the box, taking a moment before drawing out one of the toys. I had one larger and one smaller, but I thought the medium one would be perfect. Just enough to open me up and leave room for him to open me up further when I was done teasing.

Adam's brow looked like it was trying to crawl into his hair. "Toys?"

"Just this one for now," I said with a wink, opening the bottle.

In all honesty, I was hoping he didn't notice how nervous I was. It would have been easier if he just wanted to get to the main event. Now that I'd had the "brilliant" idea to show off, I could feel my nerves getting the better of me. With anyone else, I would have had no problem despite never having done something like this before. For all that we'd already done together, I had no way of being sure this sort of show would work for Adam rather than turn him off completely.

Which meant choosing whether to face him or turn my back, both of which carried their own risks. Deciding it was probably better to deal with his reaction, I lay on my back opposite Adam. Using plenty of lube, I took a moment to slide a finger into myself to make things easier before slicking up the dildo.

Making sure to keep my attention on what I was doing rather than whatever Adam was doing, I pulled my legs back to give my arms a better angle. Taking a deep breath, I positioned the toy, pulling it toward me. I was thankful I'd used the toys whenever I had a horny night alone in the past few weeks, all while imagining it was Adam inside me instead of a dildo. It meant far less of a fight to get the thing inside as my well-trained body worked with me.

It was still slow going at first, and I let out a soft grunt as the head breached my hole. Easing it in, I allowed myself to enjoy the feeling of being stretched open enough to accept the slight burn. Once I had a few inches inside, I slowly moved it back and forth, opening myself up further and pushing it in more as I went.

It was only when I realized I was getting closer and closer to the flared base that I remembered I was supposed to be putting on a show. My nerves tightened as I forced myself to look up. My hand jerked in surprise, shoving the dildo in further and causing a startled groan from me.

Adam was...enraptured. His dark eyes were wide as he watched me intently, his cock harder than it had been when I'd had it in my mouth. We were only a few feet apart, and I could see how badly he was leaking from the tip, practically covering the head as his cock throbbed with every beat of his heart.

His eyes darted up to meet mine, and he swallowed hard. Emboldened, I slid the rest of the dildo into me until the fake balls at the bottom pressed against my ass. I would almost swear Adam moaned at the sight, and I took that for the sign it was.

With the confidence I'd been lacking before, I eased the dildo out to the halfway point before pushing it back in to the hilt. Adam's eyes continued darting between the toy and my face as I began to pick up a rhythm, feeling myself opening up quickly.

The pleasure began to vibrate through my body, and I couldn't help myself. "I've done this quite a few times in the past several weeks."

"What?" he asked, sounding dazed.

"Used these toys. Always thinking of you while I did it," I told him, letting out a soft groan when it slid inside completely again.

"And before?"

"Before what?"

"Before we started doing all this. Did you ever do something like this?"

"Didn't have the toys," I admitted, now moving slowly so I could keep up with the conversation. "But when it was me and my hand…and sometimes when it was other guys."

"Fuck," he grunted, snatching up the silicone lube he'd left on the table and opening it. "You were right. You knew how to make this not scary in the fucking slightest."

My heart raced as I realized we were finally going to take the last physical step. "Good, because if I have to choose between this toy and the real thing, I will choose your cock every time."

Adam continued to mutter under his breath as he used what was admittedly more lube than necessary along the length of his shaft before moving toward me. I pulled my hand away from the toy, leaving it inside as he got on all fours over the top of me. Bending down, he kissed me fiercely, pinning my head to the mattress as he reached between my legs.

I couldn't help the pathetic groan that escaped me as he took the toy and pulled it out. Knowing that every inch of it was controlled by Adam made it all the more erotic. I thought the sensuality had peaked until I felt him push it back inside, filling me once more.

"Jesus," I groaned, hips stuttering in response. He reached out, taking my dick in his hand, and I almost came on the spot. "Wait, shit, Adam, you do that and I'm going to lose it right here. I come *so* fast when I'm being fucked, and I swear if you—"

Which is precisely when the evil bastard replaced his hand with his mouth instead. He was no master of the technique, but not only had he honed his skills in the past weeks, but I was already at breaking point. All that existed for me at that moment was the feel of his mouth sliding down my cock, and the knowledge that the large dildo inside me was being moved by his hand.

"Oh *fuck*," I groaned, not able to resist and not willing to try to stop him either. I bucked, pushing down onto the toy to send another wave of pleasure through me and then up into his mouth as I came harder than I could ever remember doing before. Just as he'd done many times before, Adam didn't pull away, instead holding steady as he swallowed.

Before I could get my thoughts together, I groaned as I felt the toy slowly pulled out of me and tossed aside. Dazed, I stared up as he hooked his arms under my knees, pushing my legs back. He didn't try to get them to my shoulders, but he didn't need to since he had the access he wanted.

And god save me, he looked as cocky as a man could be, and I loved it.

"I know you can recover pretty fast when you're this turned on," he told me, shifting to make himself comfortable.

I groaned as I felt the head of his cock push against me. "Damn right I do. Fuck me, Adam."

If he had something witty or clever to add to the conversation, he apparently decided to keep it to himself. Using one hand, he gripped the base of his dick and pushed forward.

There was barely any resistance as his thick head slid into me. Even having just come, I groaned as I felt him stretch me open further than the toy, and all without the slightest ache or burn.

"Holy shit," Adam breathed as he inched inside steadily. "Bennett, fuck."

I wanted to make some witty comment about that being the whole point, but then his cock pushed against the nerves inside me, and I lost the ability to speak. Each inch brought him closer until he was using his arms to hold himself up. It didn't take long before I felt his hips press against my ass, and I groaned, realizing it was finally happening, that Adam was inside me.

"Going to need a minute," he said with a slightly embarrassed chuckle. "Between the show and how fucking good you feel right now, I'm going to need a second...or several."

"Good thing I come fast when something's inside me," I said, reaching up to cup his face. "And if it's you, I don't care how recently I got off, I'm going to go off fast."

He kissed me then, his hips twitching as he dared to move. I didn't blame him for wanting to take it slow, but feeling him take his time as he eased back was torturous. It was just enough sensation to make me feel good but not enough to satisfy me. I knew the man was pretty big, but I felt pleasantly filled as he shifted back and forth, easing me open just a little more to make things comfortable for us both.

"Bennett," he breathed softly, saying my name so gently and reverently as he began to pick up the pace.

Adam wrapped his arms under my shoulders, pulling me close as his hips began to rock in earnest. For my part, all I could do was cling tight to him, low groans of pleasure and encouragement leaking out of me.

My mind swam with the understanding of what was

happening. The first person I had ever felt attracted to, the only man I had ever loved, who I'd spent years dreaming and fantasizing about, was finally with me completely. I could feel him inside me, his cock driving wave after wave of heated pleasure as we rocked together.

It was so much more than I ever dreamed it would be. The pleasure came from both body and mind, and I couldn't help but kiss him relentlessly, keeping him as close as possible as the seconds flew by. I reveled in the sounds of his pleasure, from the contained grunts to the soft moans in my ear.

The pattern broke when he pulled away, reaching between us to wrap his fingers around my shaft. The bolt of pleasure from that almost ended me right there as he reared back, beginning to pick up the pace with his hips. I could hear his breathing coming in short, sharp bursts, and I knew what was going to happen.

"In me," I whimpered, feeling my body tighten. "Come as deep as possible inside me."

Adam's hips stuttered, and he thrust up with a bark of pleasure. I cried out as I felt him throb before he buried every last inch inside me. Finally, my own body gave up its resistance, and I came hard as I felt him pouring deep inside me. In that moment of pure, shared bliss, I was his, and it felt as though he were marking me from the inside.

"Ho-ly *shit*," he gasped, bowing over me to stare down into my face.

Three words hung at the edge of my tongue, desperate to be released. I'd said them to him so many times in the past, but this wasn't those times. It wasn't the same thing. To say I loved him before was as friends, but now that line had been crossed into some strange no-man's-land, neither just friends nor something more. I couldn't bring myself to say them and risk what little I had right now, so I kissed him instead.

In that kiss, I hoped I managed to pour every last bit of feeling I had, holding him tight as I felt him soften. Almost immediately, I missed the feeling of him inside me when I felt him naturally slip out, and I groaned with lingering pleasure and longing.

"You okay?" Adam finally asked me, leaning back to look me over.

I couldn't help my laugh. "I'm beyond just simply 'okay.' I'm mind blown, more content than anyone has ever been."

"Good to know," he said with a small, crooked smile. "Still kinda worried about hurting you."

That time I laughed harder, pushing myself up to kiss him again. "Babe, you're going to have to fuck me a lot harder than that to hurt me."

The arch of his brow told me he was intrigued. "Is that so?"

"Oh yeah," I said, wrapping my arms around his neck and pulling him back down. "And considering how bossy and pushy you were earlier, I'm betting you could be much harder."

"I could," he said, giving no more information. That was pretty normal for him, though I wasn't sure if that was just his natural reticence at sharing private information or if he was mindful of my feelings.

"Tell you what, if you ever feel like pulling that act on me later, then feel free. You can pin me, toss me around if you want, hold me down, fuck me even more stupid than I am now, be my guest," I told him, gazing into his eyes and feeling a peace I hadn't known could exist. "Because I trust you completely and know you'd never hurt me."

"Maybe later," he said, but I could tell I had his interest.

He eased himself off and flopped down beside me. "Right now, I just kind of want to chill."

"Are *you* alright?" I asked him softly, placing my head on his chest without hesitation.

"Should I not be?"

"You did just fuck a guy for the first time."

"And before that, I fucked him with his dildo and sucked his dick, including swallowing."

I couldn't help but smile when I saw his soft dick get a little less soft. "Looks like someone likes that description."

His laugh rumbled up from his chest and into my ear. "I'm coming around to the idea that I might be a little bi."

"A little?"

"Enough to be willing to suck a dick and fuck a guy, enjoying both experiences."

"There's always taking a dick," I said, unable to help making the offer.

There was a moment of hesitation before he grunted. "I guess if there were anyone I would trust to get me through that without it being a scarring experience, it would be you."

I turned to peer up at his odd tone. "Uh, you have experience with your butt being fucked or something?"

He wrinkled his nose. "Not...not really."

"Uh-huh."

"It's nothing."

"Okay," I said, laying my head back on his chest. "I won't push if you're not comfortable—"

He shook his head again. "It's nothing like that. But it was...something Bri brought up a couple of times. I was never really all that comfortable with her doing it, so I put it off. Used to piss her off when I wouldn't give a straight answer. But I didn't want to hurt her feelings by telling her I didn't trust her."

"Oh," I said, wincing. "Sorry. Didn't mean to drag up a bad memory. Or her in general."

"Eh." He shrugged. "I don't know. I've been doing a lot of thinking about her, the relationship, the divorce."

I fought to keep my face neutral. "Oh?"

Absently, he reached to run a finger along my arm. "Yeah. I guess now I'm in a better place and I feel like my head's back on straight, I've started going through the memories. Kinda had to, I don't know, figure things out."

That didn't surprise me since that was just Adam. "And, uh, what did you figure out?"

He sighed. "We both fucked up. I didn't talk to her as often as I should have, and she didn't know how to express what she wanted. It left two frustrated people, hurting and blaming each other constantly. We didn't try to deal with it until we were already past the point of no return."

"That sounds rough," I offered a little lamely. I wasn't exactly the resident expert on dealing with long-term relationships, and I found the conversation unsettling.

"I know I made her out to be the Wicked Bitch of the West," he said, wincing. "And in a lot of ways, she was at times. But it wasn't any better for her. I could be a bastard without her doing anything to deserve it. Near the end, it was like we took all our love and respect for one another and twisted it to use as weapons against each other. By the end, we were ripping and tearing into one another, trying to make it hurt as much as possible. We were just…two heartbroken people. And I'm sorry for the things I said and did."

I took a deep breath. "Do you wanna tell her that?"

"One day, maybe. When we're not hurting so much. She's a good woman and deserves to know that I know I screwed up. Maybe it'll help us," he said with a shrug. "I don't know. Don't mind me. I'm just rambling now."

"Ramble as much as you like," I told him, watching as he closed his eyes and sighed contentedly.

I knew I shouldn't take the conversation personally. He was, after all, still processing everything that had happened in his life over the last few years. It was inevitable he would come back to his marriage and try to make sense of what went wrong and how it got that far. I was sure an expert would say it was perfectly normal and expected.

I couldn't help wondering if it was also the first step toward reconciliation between them. If things really were the way Adam described them, then there was a good chance something like that could happen. I tried to tell myself I was being ridiculous and not to ruin an incredibly special moment. Adam was here with me and not trying to have the conversation with Bri.

He was here so I was going to focus on how my own dreams were coming true right now.

* * *

I WAS STILL FLYING HIGH a week later as I once again stopped by the Jensens' place. Were it any other family, I would have said it was used as a guise to pick Adam up, but it was no secret that I adored Erik and Diane. To me, they were a second set of parents to complement my own. My dad was more lighthearted and less grumpy than Adam's, but just like his son, Erik Jensen was a big ole softy with a worse bark. Diane was as warm and welcoming as it got, but a long history of dealing with her had told me she had sharp eyes and a quick wit when she needed it.

Before I reached their house, I glanced at Chase's. I hadn't seen him for a few weeks and felt guilty at the thought. Admittedly, he had asked that I give him space while he dealt with his problems, but I still felt like I should have checked in with him sooner.

With a sigh, I slowed my car and pulled into his driveway. I probably should have messaged him to warn him I was coming, but I'd never had to before. The jerk would've probably given me shit if I had. So instead, I turned my car off and jogged up to the front door, knocking sharply.

I heard a familiar shout from inside the house but couldn't make out the words. I waited for the familiar sound of his heavy footsteps coming toward the door but only heard silence. That was until the handle jiggled slightly, and I heard the lock click before the door opened.

It took me a moment to recognize the smaller, dark-haired man who answered the door. Only then I realized I wasn't seeing the same horrible dark circles under the eyes, the sickly pale skin, and a body that no longer looked like it needed as many hearty meals as possible.

"Oh," I began in surprise, grinning even as I was met with a wary stare. "Hey there, Devin. Been doing alright?"

"Hi, Bennett," he replied, still looking wary but relaxing a little. "I guess 'alright' will cover it. Here for Chase?"

"Figured I should check in and see how you guys are doing," I said with a shrug. "Been a while since I've seen either of you, which is kind of my bad."

There was a ghost of a smile on his face as he backed up. "Chase! It's Bennett!"

"Bennett?" came his annoyed response from deeper in the house.

"Oh c'mon, it hasn't been *that* long," I called back. "Only, okay, a couple of months. Whoops."

"He's only made a couple of comments about that," Devin said softly.

"Which means he's probably pretty annoyed," I said with a grimace.

Devin actually smiled at that. "Yeah. If he wasn't bothered, he'd just bitch about it all the time."

"I can't begin to express how comforting it is that there's someone else in the world who has an insight into the grumpy bastard's mind," I told him with a wink.

Chase came around the corner clad only in a pair of loose basketball shorts. There was still grease staining his fingers and forearms from his shift at the garage and a smudge on the tip of his nose. It looked like his weeks of trying to help Devin hadn't worn him down too much. He looked more or less the same. Perhaps before anything had started with Adam, I would have thought that same thing with a tickle of arousal in my gut. Just because we'd mutually decided to be simply friends didn't mean the man didn't look attractive to me.

But now? Not even the slightest whisper.

"Hello, Grumpy," I called with a wave. "Figured I'd come by and say hi."

"What, so soon?" he asked with a frown.

"What, you don't have a phone?" I shot back, arching a brow. "Look, I feel bad that I haven't stopped by and checked in on you. I know you've been doing your own thing around here. But that doesn't mean you couldn't have texted me yourself if you were so worried about me."

"Who the hell said anything about being worried?" Chase demanded with a scowl.

To my surprise and delight, Devin rolled his eyes and began walking away. "He was worried. And he had his feelings hurt."

"I did not," Chase said, scowling at him.

"Yeah, you did," Devin said with a smile. "I'm going to get back to making dinner, alright?"

"Yeah, sure," Chase said, leaving me to stare at the sudden shift in tone from his usual grumpiness to something soft and almost submissive. "Make it as spicy as you want. You know I'll be fine."

Devin smiled, eyeing me. "You plan on staying? There's more than enough."

I shook my head. "No, but thank you. I'm going to go bug the Jensens for a bit, probably end up kidnapping their son for the weekend again."

"Sounds fun," Devin said before retreating to the kitchen at the back of the house. It was only then that I looked around and realized the living room was less cluttered and messy than usual. Chase wasn't a slob, but he wasn't exactly neat and tidy either, and it wasn't unusual to find clothing, cans or bottles, and plates sitting on the surfaces.

This was getting more and more interesting by the second.

"I take it that means you didn't come to your senses," Chase said, stepping out onto the front porch with me.

I frowned at him. "Just because it's not what *you* think I should do doesn't mean it's a bad decision."

"A bad choice is a bad choice," he said, trying to shove his hands into his pockets sullenly only to be reminded that his shorts didn't have pockets. "Doesn't matter if I think it is or isn't."

"It does when it's your opinion."

"And getting involved with a straight guy is just, what, not always a bad idea?"

I rolled my eyes. "Yes, yes, I get it. You're going to get all protective and grrr because you don't want to see me hurt. I got it, alright? Do you wanna flex a little, maybe make some threats about him while you're at it?"

His scowl deepened. "I'm not going to threaten him. When he ends up hurting you because he's *straight*, that's on you because you knew. I'll get you drunk and let you get your feelings out over it again. I'm only hurting him if he hurts you physically or does something really fucked up."

"Devin's right. You really are a softy," I said, patting his elbow.

"He didn't say that."

"Not in so many words, but I understood his meaning."

"Like hell you did."

I glanced over his shoulder. "How's uh, how's he doing?"

"It's been a ride. Those first few weeks were absolute shit, and I had to force him to go to the hospital once."

"Jesus, why didn't you call me?"

"I had it handled."

"Chase."

"What were you going to do, Bennett? There was nothing anyone could do but give him stuff to make it easier, and then I had to bring him back here. I've talked about rehab, and he might be coming around, but I think he just wants something normal. He hasn't...had a normal life. So, he cooks because I can afford real food for him to play with, and he's pretty good at it. He cleans up, gets on my ass about not picking up after myself, and is talking about maybe getting a job at the general store."

"Want me to put a word in?" I asked, arching a brow.

Chase shrugged. "Not like I can stop you."

Which meant yes. "So, he's good then?"

Chase twisted to look over his shoulder, and I spotted a couple of marks going down his shoulder blades. "As good as he can be right now."

"Oh," I said, finally putting things together and grinning, "I'd say he's more than just fine."

Chase's head snapped around to glare at me. "What's that supposed to mean?"

"It means I know what nail marks on a back look like," I said with a soft laugh, watching his expression go blank. "And I don't think I've ever seen you be outright nice to someone before. It's usually always with grumbling and bitching involved and a whole lot of your normal 'tough love' thrown in."

Chase glared at me. "Don't start."

"Is it serious?" I asked, keeping my voice soft and an eye out for Devin.

"Bennett," he complained, rubbing his face.

"What? I'm allowed to ask questions, aren't I?"

"No!"

"Too bad, I am. Is it serious or just fucking around?"

"I'm not going to just...fuck around with him," Chase said, the first flicker of genuine annoyance in his voice. "I'm not going to fuck with his head like that."

"Pfft, I didn't think you would, you're a bit of a dick at times, but you're not evil and manipulative," I told him with a snort. "But that doesn't mean I can't wonder if things are getting serious."

"I don't know what's going on, alright?" he said with a huff. "There's a...history, and it's complicated."

"Can't really say I don't know what you mean," I said, glancing toward the Jensens' house.

"Fuck, it's gotten worse, hasn't it?" he asked, sounding grim.

"I'll spare you the details, but I'll say that 'worse' isn't the word I'd use," I said with a shrug.

"He's fucked you, hasn't he?"

"Why do you assume I'm the—"

"He has."

"A few times."

Chase sighed again. "Christ, Bennett."

"Don't start," I warned him. "He's not a bad guy, even if he did do a dick thing by practically forgetting Fairlake for the past few years."

"I'm not saying he's a dick, but yeah, dick move. But it looks like he's getting back into the swing of things, and I heard he made an offer on one of the buildings downtown, so it looks like he's gonna stay this time."

"He did?" I asked in surprise.

"You didn't know?" he asked with an annoyed twitch of his lips.

"No," I said slowly, my hand falling to my pocket. "But he did tell me there was something good he wanted to tell me tonight. Three guesses as to what it was."

"Oh," Chase said, and I saw the regret on his face. "I didn't tell you."

"Oh, yes, you did."

"Ugh. Look, I'm not saying he's a bad guy. But good people hurt good people all the time. It doesn't have to be mean or on purpose. It just happens. And he's got all the markers of hurting someone without meaning to."

"Because he's straight."

"Good to see you're catching on."

I turned at the sound of a nearby door closing and watched as Adam walked out of his parents' house and headed toward the mailbox. He was wearing a pair of dirty jeans, which told me he'd been in the middle of something at his parents' since he usually changed when he got home from work. I couldn't help but follow him as he reached the mailbox, pulling a few envelopes out and glancing up. I could barely see the confusion on his face when he saw my car and then finally me standing on Chase's porch.

"Christ almighty, it's *that* bad?" Chase asked as I raised my hand in greeting, earning a slower one from Adam as he watched us.

"What do you mean?" I asked, glancing away only when I saw Adam go back indoors.

"You practically just melted into a puddle at the sight of him," Chase accused.

"I did not," I retorted, feeling self-conscious and playing back the moment Adam's eyes and mine had met across the street.

"Like hell you didn't," he grumbled.

"And what about you?" I accused, jabbing him in his bare chest. "Going all squishy and gentle when Devin talks to you?"

"Not the same."

"Feelings are feelings."

"Not when it's a straight guy."

I crossed my arms, leaning close so my voice wouldn't carry. "And some would say that getting tangled up with a recovering drug addict is the perfect way to get your heart broken too, but you didn't hear me pointing that out."

"Don't bring him into this," Chase growled in warning.

"Then ease up on trying to point out my potential mistakes so goddamn much," I snapped back at him. "I know you're trying to help, but there's a point where you have to ease off."

"It would help if you'd listen."

"What, to you?"

"Who the fuck else?"

"Right, just listen to you, Chase. You know what's best, right? Because I'm too much of an idiot to know what I'm potentially setting myself up for. Only you're wise enough to know."

"Fuck, don't put words in my mouth," he said, his jaw growing tight.

"Then stop acting like you're the only one who knows how to do things. I backed off and let you help Devin by yourself, even though I thought it was a bad idea. And I haven't said shit about what you're doing *now*," I said, glaring at him. "So maybe have a little of the same respect for me."

"Look, you're not going to listen to me, so what's the fucking point?" Chase snapped. "Why are you even standing here arguing with me about this stupid shit?"

"I'm not arguing. I'm telling you you're being an absolute bastard. So now I'm going to walk away and leave you alone. Maybe that'll give you time to realize you're being a dick," I said, turning on my heel and marching back to my car.

It felt ridiculous to pull my car out of his driveway with a little too much speed, make my way down to the Jensens' driveway, and pull in only two houses down, but that's what I did anyway. I knew Chase had already angrily closed his door and I stopped when I saw the garage open and Adam standing in the open doorway, wiping his hands off with a cloth while watching me.

"Good conversation?" he asked lightly, but I could see the way he was watching my every move and expression.

"No, Chase is being a dick."

"About?"

I scowled, shaking my head and glaring at Chase's house. I didn't want to relay my fears to Adam, not yet. Everything was still growing between us, and he'd yet to bring the subject up, apparently taking my initial advice to take things as they came. I didn't want to burden him with worry about whether or not I thought he was going to hurt me.

"Him and Devin are sleeping together," I told him, trying to shake off my bad mood. "There's a fun bit of gossip for you."

Adam's brow shot up. "Isn't Devin a recovering addict?"

"I don't even know if you can recover from that or you just deal with it," I admitted. I imagined there had to be some point where things became easier, though I remembered hearing that it never went away.

"Is that a good idea?"

"No, not really."

"That what he's being a dick about?"

"He's Chase. Sometimes he doesn't even know why he's being a dick," I said, unwinding my arms from my chest. I finally turned to him, looking him over and then at the open hood of his mom's car behind him. "Something wrong?"

"Just an oil change, no big deal," he said with a shrug, and I watched his shirt tighten from the gesture, leaving me to wonder if it was weird to be jealous of a piece of fabric.

"Your parents?" I asked, glancing around.

"Inside," he said, tilting his head slightly.

Deciding I knew the best way to make myself feel better, I moved toward him, smiling as he didn't move when I entered his personal space. I reached out, grabbing him by his shirt and pulling him closer. My knuckles bumped against his slightly soft stomach, and I kissed him. Adam didn't hesitate in the slightest, letting the kiss deepen with a deep rumble in his chest.

"Careful now," he said, and I felt his lips curl against mine.

With a smirk, I reached between us to cup his groin and give a light squeeze, feeling him harden slightly in my hand. "There, now I'm feeling better already."

"You're a perv," he accused, kissing the corner of my mouth. "And I have good news that might make you feel even better."

"Perverted and proud," I said with a shrug and then grimaced. "And, uh, I'm pretty sure I already heard your good news."

He frowned. "Sometimes I forget how easily things pass around this town, damn it."

"Sorry. I heard you made an offer on a building down-town," I said apologetically. "I guess you're going for that business license I nagged you about."

"I am," he said slowly, then smiled. "Is that all you know?"

"Wait, is there more?" I asked.

"There is," he said, hesitating when I heard a phone buzz. He reached into his pocket and pulled it out, only to mute it and put it back. "I got a call this morning. Turns out I'm going to end up even more broke soon because, as of next week, I'm able to move into that little rental on Druid Street."

"Are you serious?" I asked, eyes going wide.

"Yep, I'm even getting some of my rent shaved off if I promise to do any repairs or upkeep. I just have to send the invoices to them when it happens and get it approved," he said with a shrug. "Standard boilerplate, honestly."

"That's fantastic!" I said, kissing him again. "You told your parents?"

"I did—all of it. Mom's thrilled, and Dad tried to act like he wasn't but was quick to tell me he wanted to walk through the house with me to make sure there wasn't anything fishy," Adam chuckled. "I pretended like I wouldn't know more than him and agreed."

"You're so smart," I said, giving his arm a squeeze. "I guess that means we'll have to argue over whose house we'll be staying at."

"I'm sure we can figure it out," he said, reaching down and taking me by the hand. "Now, c'mon, you can help me fend off Mom over dinner while she tries to tell me all her ideas for my place."

* * *

IT ACTUALLY TOOK ALMOST two weeks for him to get moved in to the new place. It seemed that Erik's suspicions hadn't been too far off the mark when father and son had done a walk-through. They'd discovered a patch of mold in the bathroom and, upon inspection, found the whole bathroom had been full of it. Honestly, I was amazed it only took them a week to rip the bathroom apart and go through the process of putting it back together.

Then there was the time it took to move his things into the new house. Meanwhile, Adam had to go over the new building for the business as well because, of course, the owner accepted his offer in the midst of everything else. So he was also trying to deal with setting the place up and begin ordering all the things he'd need.

Finally, though, we managed to wheel in the last of his things and begin unpacking. The two-week process was a far cry from what we'd gone through touching up my house, but I wasn't going to complain. Everything we did with his place felt like a big step in the direction of making sure he had a real place in Fairlake and in my life.

We were borderline exhausted the first night we stayed there, but we didn't fall immediately into bed. Despite how tired we were, relief and excitement took over and Adam was eager to show me just how happy he was about the entire thing. Which meant he was also eager to show me he was no longer scared of the idea of fucking me, and we broke his new mattress in as vigorously as ever.

It turned out he could bring that aggressive, dominating attitude into the bedroom, and I wasn't the least bit disappointed. But in typical Adam fashion, he'd turned around and immediately started cuddling me. Not one to turn down a good cuddle, I was more than happy to take it and let myself get comfortable.

Only when I opened my eyes and saw sunlight streaming into the curtainless room did I realize I must have been more tired than I'd initially thought. Even Adam had stayed in one place, sprawled on his back, while I curled up at his side, head on his chest. Thankfully, we'd both learned from prior experience, and I'd tucked part of a sheet between our two bodies for the most part. Which meant I didn't have to peel my face off his chest as I pulled my head up to look around blearily.

Adam grunted softly when I moved his arm off my shoulders so I could grab my phone. There was a dresser, a box with a desk that still needed to be put together, and boxes full of his clothes. Making a mental note that we should probably consider washing his clothes before putting them away, I grabbed my phone and flopped onto my back.

It was later than we usually woke up, but I wasn't surprised, considering how tired we'd been. There was a message from Isaiah, which I couldn't make heads or tails of. Apparently, he'd screwed up royally at work the night before, and Julian had been hurt badly. It took me a minute to think of who he meant before I remembered a scowling face with red hair.

"Oh, that was his name," I said aloud as I typed a response.

Adam grunted to life suddenly, stirring beside me. "What's that?"

"Oh, sorry, didn't mean to wake you," I said. "Isaiah texted me. I guess he worked last night and got that new guy, Julian, hurt or something."

"What'd he do?" Adam asked, rolling over and immediately seeking me out to wrap an arm around my waist. One of the things I would've never guessed about Adam was that he was pretty hands-on. Apparently, it took him sleeping with that person in the first place, but I wasn't going to argue.

The man could get up and go with the best of them, but if he didn't have to get out of bed right away, he was more than happy to take his sweet time. That seemed especially true if I was physically close at hand like I usually was in the mornings we spent together.

My phone buzzed, and I read the message. "No idea, just

said that he screwed up really bad, and he's got to make things right. I guess he's having Julian stay with him while the guy recovers?"

"Wasn't that the guy you said was the living embodiment of if looks could kill?" he asked in the scratchy, sleepy voice I adored.

"That's exactly who he is," I said with a chuckle, typing back to Isaiah.

"Isaiah must have screwed up pretty badly if he's willing to put himself through all that," Adam mumbled, and I squirmed a little as his breath hit my neck, sending tingles down my spine.

"Not really. Isaiah could have accidentally made the guy stub his toe, and he would have bought him a gift basket to make up for it." I snorted.

Adam grunted, giving me a shake. "Put your phone away. It's Saturday."

"I noticed," I said with a chuckle, finding no place to set my phone, so I turned to drop it gently onto the carpet with a soft thump. "There, better?"

"Definitely," he said, somehow managing to pull me even closer and draping an arm and leg over me. "We're supposed to be lazy."

"Considering we haven't got out of bed yet, I think this counts as pretty lazy," I chuckled, setting my hand over his arm and turning my face toward him. "You realize it's after ten in the morning, right?"

"We earned it," he muttered, cracking open his eyes to stare at me as if daring me to argue with him.

"I guess we did." I snorted and then looked up at a buzzing sound. "Is that your phone?"

"Yeah," he said with a shrug. "Was buzzing earlier too, but I'm ignoring it. Whoever it is, they can wait."

"You sure?"

"If it was *that* important, they'd call you because everyone knows I'm always around you or my parents. Now lay down with me."

"Fine, fine, twist my arm," I said with a chuckle.

I stared into his sleep-rumpled face and found no argument I could summon. His hair was sticking up, and he looked like he barely knew where he was, but I found myself hypnotized by his dark eyes in the morning light. I couldn't help but brush my cheek against his, hearing the rasp of our morning stubble against one another. In moments like this, it was easy to forget that the rest of the world existed outside his bedroom.

"Hi," I said, unable to find anything else to say that would encapsulate the swelling warmth in my chest at that moment.

"Hi," he repeated in the same rough voice, closing his eyes and snuggling closer.

Never would I have ever thought I could have something as wonderful and comfortable as this. In moments like this, I could forget there was nothing set in stone between us and that we had defined nothing. Here, it was just the two of us, and it was so much bigger and better than anything I'd ever summoned up in my imagination in the years before.

"I didn't know it could feel like this," I muttered aloud before I could stop myself.

"What? Being lazy? It's pretty great."

"No, uh…just you know. Spending time like this with someone. Being this comfortable."

Adam cracked an eye open to stare at me for a moment. "You've never…been with anyone long term?"

"I mean, I've dated, had a couple of long term…daters. But nothing like whatever the hell we have going on," I admitted with a shrug. "It just never worked out for me, I guess. Nothing clicked."

"But something's clicking now?" he asked softly.

"I mean"—I let out a little laugh—"I've *always* clicked with you. I guess it makes sense that something like this would click too. And if the pleasant feeling I have going on in my ass right now is any indication, we definitely click in that regard."

"Noticed that, did you?" he asked wryly.

"Kind of hard not to when you're balls deep inside me." I snorted.

"God, have I ever mentioned how much I love it when you get a dirty mouth?" he asked in a low voice. At the same time, I felt his dick stir against my leg, clearly happy to make Adam look like he was telling the truth. It was little things like that I found absurdly comforting, like there was a good chance this was a little more than a new toy for him to explore and be excited by.

"You might have mentioned it a time or two," I said with a chuckle. The temptation was too much, and I pushed myself closer, kissing him gently. It was a test to see if perhaps I might be able to entice him into a little more.

Sure enough, I felt him stir even more against my thigh, growing so rapidly I couldn't help but feel my ego boost just a bit. Without any more prompting, Adam deepened the kiss, reaching to run his hands through my hair. There, they found a grip and pulled gently, pinning my head to the pillow as he slid over to hold the rest of me down with his body weight.

Not that I was going to try to get away, but I loved whenever he did this. His bigger size was incredibly attractive to me and something I rarely found in any other partner. Some had been a little taller than me, though that was rare, and others were stockier. But Chase and Adam were the only two partners I'd ever had who were both, and I absolutely loved feeling their bodies holding me down by sheer size alone.

I could tell he was still waking up by how slowly he

moved, parting my lips to run his tongue across mine. He ground his cock against my hip slowly, a low groan escaping him as his girth pressed against my stomach. I couldn't help but wonder what my younger self would have said if he could see us at this moment, and then I realized he probably would have run off somewhere private to take care of himself.

"I was a little rough last night," Adam informed me.

"I was there," I chuckled, reaching down to wrap my fingers around his dick and give it a few lazy strokes. There wasn't much about his body that I didn't love, but the sheer impressiveness of his dick in my hand, my mouth, or deep inside me definitely ranked in the top five. "And I told you afterward I was more than fine."

"Yeah, I believe you. You came hard enough you hit yourself in the face."

"First time I've ever given myself a facial, that's for sure."

A low growl bubbled up from his throat at the memory, which didn't surprise me. I was pretty sure he'd practically exploded inside me at the sight. "My original point was that I wanted to know if you're ready for another round or not."

"I am," I said, reaching around to grab his ass and squeeze it. "Or if you're feeling brave, I can show you what it's like."

I saw the hesitation in his eyes and said nothing, letting him mull it over in his head. Much like anything else, this was a big step for him, requiring him to go through his own thought process before making any decision. The best I could do was, much like now, occasionally prompt him to see if he'd come to a conclusion.

"What, uh, does that entail?" he asked slowly, and I could practically hear the gears in his head whirring furiously.

"It means," I said, nudging him onto his back so I could perch on top of him. "That you let the guy who knows what he's doing take care of things. All you have to do is tell me when something is or isn't right."

"You know I trust you," he said, though I could see his nervousness. That was alright, he could be as nervous as he wanted, so long as he was sure he was willing to try. Much like the first time he'd fucked me, I was pretty sure I knew how to ease his nerves.

I winked, taking him by the base of his cock and pulling the head toward my mouth. His nervousness didn't disappear, but I could see his interest spark as I wrapped my lips around his dick. As I lowered myself, feeling him leak onto my tongue, I could see the way the tension in his body eased.

It wasn't exactly hidden knowledge that a blowjob could be one of a man's favorite things in the world, but sometimes I wondered if Adam might be a particularly extreme example. I knew I was pretty good at giving head, but I'd never had someone who was almost always down for a blowjob quite like him. It didn't seem to matter what kind of mood he was in, being offered a blowjob always put him in the right mood, and after I was done, he was usually in a much better mood than before.

Not that I was going to complain. Watching him watch me was incredibly hot.

I worked my way back and forth, purposefully taking it slow. I knew taking my time always drove him crazy and in the best way possible. It was one of the few times I ever got to see him act impatient, and I knew it was a great way to make him forget his nerves. All it would take was a handful of minutes of this, along with getting my hand involved, and I'd have him ready for the next step.

It was only when the doorbell went off with a high-pitched chime that I realized how nervous *I* was about the entire thing. I nearly jumped out of my skin as I pulled away, looking up from his lap to frown toward the front of the house.

"What the fuck?" I asked. "Who the hell?"

"Either a nosy new neighbor, someone selling something, or wanting to invite me to their church," Adam growled. "Ignore them."

"Bossy, bossy," I chuckled, but who was I to argue? Even as I heard the bell chime again, I bent down to take him into my mouth, savoring the feel of his cock against my tongue. And even though I couldn't deep-throat to save my life, I still found some pleasure in the first couple of inches entering my throat to stretch it. It was so tempting to take this whole thing to the end but—

"Oh, for fuck's sake!" I snapped in annoyance as the bell rang again. "That is *not* just some random person."

Adam groaned, flopping his head against the pillow. "Probably my mom, dropping off food or something. I told her I was fine and to let me get settled in, but you know how she is."

"I do," I said with a sigh, swinging myself off the bed. "I'll go take care of it. If you answer the door in anything but jeans, you'll give your mom an eyeful with that thing."

Adam smirked, grabbing his dick which was still somehow hard, and giving it a wag toward me. "Let's be quick about getting rid of her. You've got something waiting for you."

"And you call me a perv." I snorted, yanking on the pair of sleep pants I'd brought to his house and a shirt. Unlike Adam, I didn't stay hard, so I knew I was safe to plod to the other side of the house and find out what was going on.

I had just stepped out of his room when the doorbell rang again. I didn't consider myself a particularly grumpy or short-tempered person, but to say I was in a grumpy mood as I moved toward the front door was an understatement.

Whoever decided they needed to spam the doorbell at ten in the morning on a Saturday was not someone I was going to be happy to see. Even if it *was* Diane, I honestly thought she'd know better.

I unlocked the door, yanking it open to look at the woman on the doorstep. "Yes?"

She jumped in surprise. "Oh! Bennett, hello. They said you'd probably be around."

I took a good look at her in momentary confusion and annoyance. It was only then I realized the last time I'd seen her, she'd been wearing heels instead of tennis shoes and had come up to my chin instead of somewhere around my chest. She had also been wearing what I had dubbed a "power suit," and her blonde hair had been neatly groomed rather than tied back into a ponytail. "B-Bri?"

"Hi, Bennett," she said with a smile. "I know I look different than the last time you saw me, but...this will do it."

It was only then that my overworking brain finally looked down and saw what she meant, and I wondered how I'd missed it. The biggest difference was not her clothes or hair but the absurdly noticeable bump.

Adam's soon-to-be ex-wife was pregnant.

ADAM

Even from across the house, I could hear Bennett's sharp tone when he answered the door, forcing me to suppress a smile. Bennett wasn't the type to get bitchy, but apparently when he was interrupted in the middle of foreplay, he could be as cranky as the worst of them.

At the very least, I knew I was presentable enough to see if he needed help and dug around for a pair of shorts and a shirt. If it *was* my mom, Bennett would inevitably feel bad for pulling a sharp tone on her and would be reluctant to send her away after being rude. Which meant it would be up to me to get my mother out of the house as soon as possible so we could go back to what we were doing.

That was if her presence didn't ruin my chances of getting any for the next few hours.

Before heading toward the front door, I swung into the kitchen to flip the coffeemaker on. We were bound to have to sit around and talk, and while Bennett had already managed to wake me up impressively, I suspected we'd both need caffeine to get through the next hour or two.

"Uh, Adam?" Bennett called from the front of the house.

I frowned at his tone. "Yeah?"

"I think, uh, you better come here. Bri's here."

He might as well have walked across the house to slap me in the face from how jarring that was to hear. Saying nothing, I made my way out of the kitchen and toward the front of the house. Bennett was standing in the doorway, slightly off to the side, and sure enough, there was Bri.

There were no words to describe the upsetting mix of emotions that ran through me. The familiar anger and resentment I felt toward her in the months leading up to my departure from our relationship and then Boston. The heartache that part of me still loved her, still missed what we'd once shared, and all the bitterness that came with it. Guilt and shame that I had been just as much a part of the failure as she had, and finally, sheer annoyance that she had chased me across the country.

Bennett's eyes were wide, and I could see panic and fear, which were incredibly out of character for him. His eyes were locked on mine, and I knew he'd probably just read every emotion that crossed my face. I would have to talk to him later, not only about this ugly surprise but a couple of other things as well.

Then Bennett shifted to the side, and I felt my entire world tilt on its axis. There was no mistaking the large swell of her stomach as she stood there on the front porch, looking wary and nervous.

"B-Bri?" I finally managed.

"I see you two really have been spending a great deal of time together," she said dryly. "You even greeted me the same. Now, can I come in? In case you haven't noticed, we have something to talk about. Or you can leave a pregnant woman standing on your porch. That's always comfortable."

Feeling faint, I nodded and gestured for her to come in. Bennett practically darted out of her way as if afraid to touch her. Bri shot him an amused look but continued into the house, looking around curiously as she went.

"They said you had just moved in, and it certainly looks like it," she noted as she entered the living room.

"They?" I asked faintly, still trying to wrap my brain around this.

"Your parents. Where do you think I stopped first?"

"They sent you here?"

"Well, I clearly have a convincing reason to need to talk to you."

Bennett's eyes were wide, following behind her as she moved to the couch and dropped down onto the nest of blankets and pillows Bennett and I had used the night before to relax before bed. If I didn't know any better, I would almost think his nervousness was on her behalf.

"Would you like coffee? I can smell it brewing," Bennett offered, and I could hear the high pitch of what was definitely a panicked voice. "Wait, shit, can you have caffeine? Is that bad for babies? It is, isn't it? Fuck, sorry."

Bri looked at him in amusement, and I felt a flare of annoyance at her. She'd dropped in unexpectedly with this… news. What right did she have to laugh at him for being shocked?

"I can have a small coffee," she said with a smile. "Not too much, though. Fluids already go straight through me faster than before."

"Right, right, sure, of course," he said, babbling as he darted out of the living room and into the kitchen.

She arched a brow. "Is he going to be okay?"

"I'll find out," I said with a frown at her, still unsure what to feel about everything.

"Don't mind me," she said, groaning as she eased back, putting her feet up on my new coffee table. "The less moving I have to do, the better. But don't take forever calming him down. We need to talk."

I bit back my retort, knowing that pointing out that she was *still* giving orders would only lead to another argument. I'd managed to live the past six months without an argument with Bri and didn't want to start another one. There was a reason I'd blocked her number so I wouldn't receive calls or texts from her anymore. There was a reason the divorce papers, the last I needed to sign, were already signed and waiting to be sent over to my lawyer on Monday.

I found Bennett hunched over the sink as he shakily poured a cup of coffee. His eyes were wild and wide when he looked up at me. "Is that really yours?"

My heart lurched nervously at the thought. "I don't know."

"I mean, it would have to be, right? Why else would she be here if it wasn't yours?"

"Who the hell knows?" I grumbled quietly, knowing my voice could easily carry to her sharp ears if I wasn't careful. "I wouldn't put it past her to bring something like this around to screw with me. I'm literally a scan and email away from being divorced. Maybe this is some last tactic on her part."

"To do what?"

"Screw with me?"

"What if she's trying to get back with you?"

That took me back, and I frowned as I considered it, wondering if that could really be what she was trying to do. Then again, I didn't even know if I was responsible for her being pregnant. I knew I'd found a couple of other partners during our separation and the divorce proceedings before I returned to Fairlake. Who was to say she hadn't done the same, and now it was suddenly my problem?

"How pregnant would you say she is?" I asked as Bennett stared at me intently.

His shoulders slumped at the question. "Nearly ready to burst. That's like, eight, almost nine months by the looks of it."

I frowned, thinking back to the months leading up to my leaving Boston, and then closed my eyes. "Fuck."

"Adam?"

"The timeline matches up."

"Does it? I thought you guys were separated for months before you came back."

"We…" I grimaced. "We were, only through the lawyers. But there was one night, a few months before I left, when we met up to talk. We decided to have a few drinks, help calm the nerves, and maybe not be complete assholes to each other. Well, it didn't work. We ended up arguing shortly after I arrived at our old place."

"And from how you're acting, I'm going to guess that arguing wasn't all you did," he said softly.

"No," I said through gritted teeth, turning to march back into the living room. Bri was still sprawled on the couch, her head back and relaxing. Finally, she opened her eyes and turned to me, her brow going up.

"Oh, you look nice and fired up," she said wryly.

"You were supposed to be on birth control," I finally said. "There's no way—"

"You know it's not totally effective, right? And we ditched the condoms two years before. We had one stopgap, and it failed…clearly."

"Is it clear?" I asked, cocking my head.

A crease formed on her brow, the first warning sign of a bad mood. "Are you trying to accuse me of cheating on you?"

"It's not cheating when we're separated," I told her with a scowl.

She snorted harshly. "I guess that tells me what you were doing while we were separated then, doesn't it?"

"What we did in our private time is neither of our business," I shot back. "I know giving people space is a foreign concept to you—"

"Foreign concept? Adam, you took 'private time' to an entirely different level. You should have tried to find a way to make an art form out of it. You would have made a killing," she snapped at me. "If I gave you any more space, then we would have been all but separated in name long before we actually were."

"Because having my own space and time while I was trying to run a goddamn business is some sort of crime. And I'm sure it wouldn't have *anything* to do with the fact that whenever we did 'spend time together,' it always involved you making sure to recite my sins for me."

"Your *sins*, Christ, you're so dramatic."

"Harping on everything I did because it didn't live up to your standards."

"My standards aren't that high. I just wanted you to do more, to be more involved."

"If I wasn't at work, I was with you. I couldn't be more involved unless I threw away what I wanted to do for you."

"That is *not* what I—"

"Hey!" Bennett barked, making Bri and I jump in surprise. He entered the living room with a scowl on his face. "Adam, stop arguing with her. She's freaking pregnant and hormonal."

"Thank you," Bri said with a smile.

I scowled. "Are you fucking serious right now?"

Bennett ignored me, using the same tone as he turned to Bri. "And you. You know full well how things were before Adam left. So don't act surprised that he's not happy to see you on his doorstep without warning."

"He would have had warning," she began with a scowl that said she was just as unhappy to be chastised as I had been. "But he decided to block me everywhere. I didn't even have his parents' number to contact him."

"Our lawyers still have contact, and mine has my new number," I said.

"I-I wanted to be the one to tell you," she said, looking unsure of herself. "This wasn't something that should go through the lawyers. It didn't seem right."

At least I couldn't argue with that, and I finally dropped into the armchair beside the couch. "Yeah, alright."

"There," Bennett said, handing us the coffee. "Now, both of you quit arguing like kids, especially because you apparently have an actual kid to talk about."

We both watched him leave, heading back to the kitchen. I suspected he was trying to give the appearance of giving us room to talk, but I knew he'd be listening closely. Maybe not downright eavesdropping, but he would be keeping an ear out to ensure we didn't devolve into bickering again.

"He became a cop, right?" she asked a few seconds after he was gone.

"That he did."

"Huh. I always thought that was a weird choice for someone as happy-go-lucky and nice as he is."

"I kind of thought the same."

"From that though...I'm starting to see how he could make it work."

"Same."

She chuckled, taking a sip of her coffee. "It's yours, Adam."

"You're sure?" I asked softly.

"Do you really think I'd come here like this and not be completely sure?"

Before our relationship had started dissolving around us,

I would have immediately denied that it was even remotely possible. Now I'd seen just how ugly the two of us could get, however, I found myself hesitant to respond. To say I thought she might be capable of that would be the truth, but would invite another fight. To say I didn't think so would be a lie, and she had always been good at knowing when I lied.

Bri grimaced at my delay. "I mean it. If you want the test after the birth, we can do that, whatever. But it's yours because, unlike you, I've not been with anyone else."

I felt a flash of shame at the accusation. Not just because I'd been with other women after Bri and I had separated, but because Bennett and I...well, I didn't know what we were yet. It was a subject neither of us had touched, even though I knew it was something we needed to talk about. Things had reached a level I hadn't expected, and it was high past time he and I settled things.

"Was that comment really necessary?" I asked her with a frown.

"The truth?"

"The judgment in it."

"You always think I'm judging you."

"Maybe I wasn't always right, but you can't say that if the shoe was on the other foot, you wouldn't accuse me of the same right now."

I saw her jaw tighten, but she glanced toward the kitchen and sighed. After a moment, she finally spoke through gritted teeth. "Yeah, I guess you have me there. Look, I know it shouldn't bother me that you've been with other people in Boston and probably here."

"It shouldn't," I agreed, keeping my tone neutral.

"But it does," she said with a snort. "And I can't help that. Are you with someone now?"

"I'm not...in a relationship," I said, guilt squirming in my gut. I technically wasn't, but I knew if I gave anything other than a firm answer, she would start asking questions. Bri wasn't supposed to be a part of my life anymore. Just because it looked like she would be for the next couple of decades didn't mean she needed to know the details of what my life had been like lately.

She searched my face. "I guess that's something, at least."

I stared at her stomach, confusion returning once more. "It's...it's really mine?"

"*He* is really yours, yes," she said, and to my surprise, she was smiling at the repeated question.

I looked up, eyes wide. "He?"

"You know me. I can't leave things a mystery if I can help it. I had it checked as soon as I could. Due date is mid-September."

"That's only a few weeks away," I said in wonder. "Why did you wait this long?"

"Well," she said, and I saw a shadow of fear cross her face for the first time in possibly forever. "The first few months, I was, well, I was—"

I leaned back, swallowing as I realized what she meant. "Wondering if you were going to keep him."

"Yes," she said softly. "It's so funny. I've been on board with that being an option my whole life, but when I was faced with making the decision, I couldn't do it. Maybe I could have if I'd really thought about it but, well, I still think it should be an option. But I realized it wasn't the option for me."

I said nothing, unsure what I could even say. The decision had never been mine to make, but there was a quiet sense of horror that it could very well have happened without my knowledge. We had discussed the possibility of having kids several times in our marriage, but it never felt like the right time. There was always something that felt like it was getting in the way.

"And the four months after that?" I asked with a raised brow, going for the easier, safer topic.

She screwed up her face and shrugged. "I struggled to decide if I wanted you to know or not. Can you blame me?"

"For *that,* yes, yes I can," I told her with a frown. "From the moment you decided to keep him, you should have tried to find me."

"Because you were so intent on sticking around."

"That is *not* fair," I snarled at her, no longer caring if I was going to get scolded or not. "I left because, as we both know, there was nothing left for me in Boston. It would have been entirely different if you'd told me about *this*. You can accuse me of a lot of things, Bri, and maybe some of those things are fair, but don't you dare accuse me of being willing to leave my child behind without a father."

For a moment, I thought she would do as she'd always done when I lost my temper and barked at her. Yet, instead of snapping right back at me, I watched her temper flare and then fizzle out in almost the same breath.

"I know," she said softly. "And I realized I was being a petty bitch. And before you say anything—"

"I wasn't going to," I said, for once managing to sound honest while I lied.

"I know I was a petty bitch with you more than once. But this wasn't about you and me. This is about our son. I might have been willing to rake you over the coals all day and night, but I'm not going to leave my son without a father who would want to be there for him. And while I convinced myself you were a prick, I knew you'd be a wonderful dad, so here I am."

For the first time in who knew how many months, I

smiled warmly at Bri. "Well, thank you for that much, at least."

"Yeah, well, don't let it go to your head," she said with a shy smile I didn't think I'd seen in almost two years. The same one she would give me when she was being genuinely sweet, as if somehow it embarrassed her to show me large displays of affection.

"Fuck," I said as the full weight of our conversation finally settled on my shoulders. "I'm going to be a dad."

"You are," she said with a snort. "Glad you finally managed to catch on."

I opened my mouth and then stopped when Bennett entered the room. He jammed a thumb over his shoulder. "I've got a quiche in the oven for you guys. Just go ahead and take it out when the timer goes off. I'd recommend letting it sit for about five or ten minutes before cutting into it, though."

"Someone got into baking in the past few years," I told Bri and straightened as I watched him gather up his clothes from the living room floor. "What're you doing?"

"I'm going to head out," he said lightly, but I could hear something strange and unnatural in his voice. "Might as well go for my normal run and probably do some grocery shopping."

"In this heat?" Bri asked with a shake of her head.

"Well, I normally go earlier, but I can deal," he said, and I stood up to follow him to the bathroom.

He saw me and didn't bother to close the door as he pulled off his sleep pants to yank on his underwear. Usually, getting a flash of his bare ass would have been distracting, but I had more important things to worry about now.

"What're you doing?" I asked him quietly.

"I just said," he said as he adjusted himself and headed toward the front door to slide his shoes on.

"That's not what I meant, and you know it," I grumbled.

With a sigh, he stepped out onto the front porch, and I followed, closing the door behind me. Bennett pulled his keys out, twirling them around his finger as he walked toward his car.

"Bennett, I'm serious," I said, walking after him, stopping just shy of the asphalt driveway to spare my bare feet from the August sun. "Hey!"

Bennett turned, giving me a strained smile. "Look, you've got a lot on your plate right now."

"That doesn't mean you have to leave," I said with a frown.

"Yeah, it kinda does," he said. "This is between the two of you, and you have to settle things. That doesn't involve me."

"It does involve you because you're—" I stopped, unsure what to say.

"I'm…what?" he asked, brow creeping up.

I fumbled with the answer and found that none of them sounded right. Just when had I started being unable to determine what we were and what we weren't? Had there been a line crossed that had simply passed without fanfare or notice on my part?

"I know things are complicated," I said and saw the slump in Bennett's shoulders. "And things just got *really* complicated."

"Look," he said, shaking his head and spinning his keys even faster around his finger, "your ex-wife just showed up out of the blue and dropped the bomb on you that you're going to be a dad in a few weeks. This shit is…well, it's more than I know what to do with, so I can't imagine how you feel. Just go in there and talk to her, okay? No fighting, no bitching, no sniping, just talk."

I reached out for him, only to stop when I saw him step away before I could touch him. "Bennett?"

He gave me a smile that broke my heart. "You've gotta take care of this, Adam. You can't just…this is your life, you know?"

"And you're part of that," I told him.

"Not this part," he said, eyes darting toward the house. "This is all you guys. And I know you, Adam. You'll need to take time to think things through, to wrap your head around it."

"I mean, I know a kid is a big deal and all, trust me, I'm still letting the full reality of that settle in," I protested.

"Really? And what are you going to do? Keep her here in Fairlake? Or is she going back to Boston? Then what are you going to do? Go with her? Stay here?" Bennett asked, and I felt any arguments I had wither away. Apparently, it showed on my face because Bennett grunted. "See? You haven't even digested what's happened yet. Let alone figured out what you're going to do."

"And you're just going to leave me with all this?" I asked in sudden disbelief. "Seriously?"

"I'm leaving right now," he said, but I saw the way his shoulders hunched, "because the two of you need to talk without me lurking in the shadows."

"Is that the only reason?" I asked with a frown.

He shrugged. "Not really."

"What's the other reason?"

"Because standing there, pretending like I'm just a part of the background while you talk to your wife about the baby you two are having is a little more than I can stand," he said, walking around his car.

He was running. Bennett was running away from me, something he'd never done before. I stepped forward, having to hop a little as my feet touched the hot asphalt. I tried to circle around to the driver's side as he opened the door and slid in. The car engine puttered to life by the time

I made it, and he grimaced before rolling down the window.

"Look, if you need me, you know where to find me," he said evenly. "I'll never turn you away, Adam, you know that. But right now, it looks like we both have to deal with our own stuff. It's no one's fault. Things like this were bound to happen eventually, that's just life, right?"

"Bennett," I began, suddenly alarmed at the way he was talking.

"Seriously, I'm alright, now go make sure you're going to be alright," he said, shifting the car into gear.

I could only stand there and stare as he backed his car out of my driveway, turning with a slightly jerky motion. It was only when I saw his face before he pulled away that I thought I understood what might have just happened. It was the expression of a man whose entire world had just crumbled around his feet, and he was desperate to get as far away from the source of the pain as soon as possible.

I knew it all too well, having seen it on my face more than once while facing the reality of my dissolving marriage, friendships, and professional life.

"Bennett?" I whispered softly.

I couldn't tolerate standing on the hot asphalt any longer and made my way back into the house. Bri was still on the couch, though it looked like she'd shifted to one side rather than the center.

"Everything okay?" she asked, looking me over and frowning.

"I don't know," I said, waving her next question off. "I don't know what just happened, Bri. But I can deal with it later. I'd rather deal with the two of us first."

"Sure, okay. I checked the timer in the kitchen. You've only got a couple of minutes."

"I'll get that out of the oven and let it cool. Then we can talk."

I could feel her eyes on me as I entered the kitchen and kept my expression completely neutral while I was within her sight. The last thing I needed was for Bri to see I was lying to her face because I thought I had a very good idea of what had just happened outside, but I couldn't stand to say it aloud, especially not to her.

It felt like Bennett had just said goodbye.

BENNETT

"Bennett!"

Stirring, I picked my head up from the couch to peer around and found Chase glaring at me from the doorway leading into the dining room.

"What?" I asked groggily, only then realizing I'd dozed off at some point.

Chase rolled his eyes and stomped over to my front door. I followed him, confused why he was disturbing me and when he got into my house. For the past week I'd tried to keep to myself, but Chase wouldn't leave me alone no matter what I did.

I blinked when I saw Devin appear from the dining room as well, smiling apologetically. "Hey. Sorry, Chase used his key to let us in while you were napping."

"Oh, I forgot he had a key," I said, flopping my head back down as I heard the front door open.

"Hey," I heard Isaiah say. "I take it he's still in here?"

"Yep," Chase grunted. "He's been in mourning on the couch the whole time."

"I am *not* in mourning," I complained loudly and considered whether or not I should throw something at him. That would require me to either move or give up my pillow, neither of which I was willing to do. "Jesus, can't a guy enjoy some peace and quiet at home?"

"Every day for a week?" Devin asked quietly.

I glared at him. "Traitor."

"Hasn't gone for his daily run. No one's seen him and Adam together," Isaiah began listing off, walking into the house. Apparently, Chase had decided he was in charge of who did and didn't come into my house. I needed to have a conversation about who paid the bills around here. "And let's not forget the oh-so-scandalous gossip about who Adam has been seen walking around town with."

"Yes, thank you, Isaiah, for that excellent reminder," I grumbled, taking the pillow out from under my head and slapping it over my face. Maybe if I ignored everyone, eventually they would go away and leave me in peace. "And why the hell does this whole damn town have to sit around and gossip about shit that doesn't concern them? Who the hell cares if Adam accidentally knocked up his ex-wife? Wife. Whatever."

"Yeah, you don't care in the slightest," Chase said with so much sarcasm I was surprised we weren't drowning in it.

"I should have never given you a key to my house!" I shot back, voice muffled by the pillow.

"Devin knows how to pick locks," Chase said, and I heard his heavy footsteps leaving the room.

"I really wish you wouldn't tell people that," Devin complained.

"C'mon babe, it's only Bennett I told."

"Ah ha!" I exclaimed, shooting upright and pointing an accusing finger. It just happened to land directly on Devin, who looked startled. "Babe, huh? I guess it was a lot more serious than *someone* let on."

Devin tilted his head. "Oh?"

"I've never, and I mean *never,* heard him use any sort of sweet, nice, or kind nickname for anyone in my life," I said, earning a scowl from Chase as he peered around the doorway.

"I told you to leave it alone," Chase told me.

I raised a brow. "Really? The guy who let himself in to nose his way into my business, bringing his boyfriend with him, and then letting Isaiah's nosy ass into my house? You really wanna talk about not leaving things alone?"

"Hey!" Isaiah protested but was ignored.

Chase continued to look annoyed as he crossed his arms over his chest. "I like to take him with me when I go places."

"So I'm right, he's your boyfriend," I pushed.

"Wait," Isaiah said, looking at the two of them. "You guys are dating?'

"It's nobody's business," Chase growled.

"Oh, so it's not my business, but my business is yours?" I asked, irritated all over again.

"*I'm* not the one hiding in my house over my business," Chase retorted. "Now leave my shit alone."

Devin turned, eyes wide. "Are we boyfriends?"

In what had to be the most surprising turn of events, I watched Chase's dark expression disappear in mere seconds. Not that I would have blamed the average person. Devin's big eyes and soft expression would charm anyone, but this wasn't anyone. This was Chase Everett, the man of a thousand grumpy expressions and one neutral one. This was the man who grumbled at stray cats even as he hid the fact that he shoved bowls of food out onto his back porch, knowingly attracting more. The man who would never admit he liked anyone or anything.

"I mean," Chase said, looking uncomfortable, "we were practically dating in high school."

Isaiah and I glanced at one another. This was news to us.

"That's not the same thing as dating now," Devin said softly, and I could hear the slight hurt in his voice.

Chase rubbed a palm against the back of the other hand, something I'd seen him do whenever he was agitated. "I... well, we hadn't really...I was going to...can we talk about this away from them?"

"Oh sure, we'll talk my business in front of everyone else, but yours gets to stay quiet," I said with a scowl.

Chase's face darkened. "Bennett, I swear to—"

"He's right," Devin said with a shrug. "We are being hypocritical."

"Seriously?" Chase protested.

"Ha!" I crowed.

Devin turned and frowned at me. "But we're still going to talk about this in your backyard if you don't mind."

Great, now I felt bad because I'd upset Devin. I had no idea what kind of witchcraft the man used, but apparently, it worked on more than just Chase.

"Sure," I said with a shrug, looking away. "And if you wanna take him back to his house and keep him there forever instead of in my house, I wouldn't argue."

"Nice try," Devin said and walked out with what I would swear was a chastised Chase.

"So," Isaiah said after we heard the sliding door close, "is it me, or did Devin just take advantage of the fact that Chase was off guard to get him away from you?"

"Probably," I huffed, swinging my legs around so I was sitting properly. "He's a lot sneakier than that innocent face would let you believe."

"And has Chase wrapped around his finger," Isaiah said, sounding as awed by the idea as I had been moments before.

"Miracles do happen, I guess," I said with a shrug, looking

around for my drink. "Oi, where's my drink? I know I set it down on the table."

Isaiah peered around, disappearing for a second and returning with my glass. "They said you were sleeping when they showed up, but this looks brand new."

I took the glass, sniffing it to find the pleasant smell of whiskey and cola wafting out, and noted that it was indeed filled to the top and had new ice cubes. "Huh, I think Devin made me another."

"Do I have to point out that you're drinking after work?" Isaiah asked, dropping down in the nearby chair. "Something you never do."

"I so have," I protested, taking a sip. "And I'm not getting drunk."

"Not hard liquor."

"Yes I have."

"Yeah, I know you've done it. But that's like...after the night you had to go to that car crash where the Kellian family was killed, right down to their two kids. Or when you had to respond to that call in the apartments, when you found out the dad had a bad trip and decided to kill his whole family."

I grimaced at the memories. Everyone in Fairlake did their best to push the town as a bright and happy place where everyone was content and safe. For the most part, that was true, but as eastern philosophers understood, there was darkness for every light. There was a nasty side to Fairlake, and it was my job to try to keep it as contained as possible. They didn't happen as often as in a larger town or city, but they still happened, and there were plenty of stories any of the officers down at the station could tell, though they probably wouldn't.

"Forgot I told you about those," I admitted, taking another heavier sip.

"And that's just the things you *have* told me," Isaiah said with a knowing smile. Then again, firefighters saw their own horrors and had to face their own nightmares. I knew a few of his stories as well, and just like me, I was sure he kept others to himself.

"Oh!" I grunted, setting my drink down. "How's Julian doing? I completely forgot to ask you about that."

"He's uh...well, I won't say fine, but he's not any worse off than before," Isaiah said, and my brow rose as I saw his cheeks color. "What?"

"That's what I was about to ask you," I said with a chuckle.

"No need to ask me. There's nothing to 'what' at me about," he said, even as his coloring cheeks continued to betray him.

"Methinks the lady doth protest too much." I smirked.

"Don't you start on me. Quit deflecting," he said, frowning at me.

"Or you're deflecting because, like those two hypocrites, you want to pry into my business and don't want yours pried into."

We stopped when Devin and Chase reappeared, Devin speaking first. "Is he still avoiding the subject?"

"Yes," Isaiah said with a roll of his eyes.

"I'm beginning not to like you very much," I told Devin, then glanced at Chase, brow raised.

Chase scowled, though I had the feeling there wasn't much heart behind it. "We're officially dating, are you happy?"

"For you both? Yeah," I said, beaming.

"Goody for us," Chase grumbled, but it didn't take an expert to see he was trying very hard to hide how happy he was.

Devin, however, wasn't bothering to hide how pleased he was as he sat on the arm of the chair next to Isaiah. "Now, I only kinda know what's been going on. You don't have to go into details—"

"Please don't," Chase interrupted. "I don't need to know the...bedroom stuff."

"He's about as hung as you and fucks like a champion," I said without hesitation.

"Goddammit," Chase groaned.

"Really?" Devin and Isaiah said, looking curious.

"Babe?" Chase asked, looking down at him in disbelief.

Devin smiled warmly up at him. "Idle curiosity. Your dick is the only one for me."

Absurdly, Chase smiled at him. "Thanks, I think."

"I'm beginning to realize how absurd this conversation is," Isaiah said with a frown.

"Just now?" Chase snorted.

"We've seen each other naked," Isaiah said, gesturing between us. "Devin and Bennett have both slept with you, and Bennett is the only one who knows what Adam looks like naked."

"Right, Bennett's a slut, we knew that," Chase said, but I could tell from the way he smirked that he was teasing.

"Brilliant deduction." I sighed. "And Isaiah has the hots for his grumpy co-worker."

"Hey!"

"Look, we know their business, and y'all are asking about mine. So, uh, yours is getting offered up."

"Oh! That cute redhead?" Devin asked.

"Cute?" Chase repeated with a frown.

"God, that's twice he's gotten jealous," I remarked. "What the hell kind of blowjobs do you give, Devin?"

"That's for me to know and for only Chase to find out," Devin replied, and I watched Chase once again soften.

"Deftly done," I said in admiration. "And yes, the cute

redhead. Nice to know you have a type for big, grumpy guys, though."

"You'd be surprised what kind of things you find when you dig under the grumpiness," Devin said, taking hold of Chase's hand. "Or well, considering you've been friends with this one for so long, and your best friend, maybe you wouldn't be all that surprised."

"Adam isn't grumpy," I said with a shrug. "Just very serious. An overthinker. And quiet."

"Very quiet," Isaiah added. "Now, summarize for us."

"Lovely," I grumbled, rubbing my face. However, there was no getting out of this, and I knew I'd have to get started before the three of them ganged up on me.

"Everyone here already knows I had a thing for him for years," I began with a wave of my hand. "So, we'll skip ahead to the jerk reappearing back in Fairlake and the night I took him to the bar."

"Glow Up," Isaiah added for the others.

"Right, there," I said, taking a deep breath and launching into the story.

I'd always heard people say that it was strange to tell what they thought was a long story only to find out how short it was. Yet as I went through the story, skipping the more intimate details as best I could, I found that there wasn't a whole lot to tell.

It seemed absurd that everything Adam and I had been through could be summarized so quickly. Everything about us had always felt so much larger than a handful of stumbling and awkward speeches. I had tried not to, but I'd genuinely believed something wonderful was coming our way. That despite all previous evidence, perhaps the dream of my youth would come to fruition.

And then Bri had come along and ruined everything. I couldn't even say I hated her, much as I wanted to. I couldn't fault her for how she'd handled things...for the most part. Personally, I thought once she decided she was going to keep the child, she should have found a way to tell him right away. Instead, she'd waited until the last minute, and now Adam was trapped.

"What a bitch," Chase added once I was done.

"From the sounds of it, they were both pretty ugly to each other," Devin said softly. "I don't think either of them has been thinking clearly about the other for a while. Breakups can be like that."

"Like I give a shit," Chase grunted. "It was a bitchy thing to do. The whole thing."

"Are you saying that because you think it was bitchy or because it meant Bennett got hurt?" Devin asked, smiling up at him.

Chase wrinkled his nose. "Look, I told this idiot this was going to crash and burn. I just wasn't expecting it to be Super Bitch that did it."

I laughed, not fooled. "Yeah, yeah, love you too, big guy."

"Fuck off," he grumbled, but it largely went ignored.

"So, what's he going to do?" Isaiah asked.

"I don't know," I admitted. "We haven't spoken. He's been preoccupied, and I can't blame him. And I'm...taking some time to get my head back on right."

"Your head hasn't ever been on right," Isaiah said with a smile.

"Yeah, fuck you too, Isaiah. How's wanting to suck your grumpy new roommate's dick working out for you?"

"Asshole."

"I mean, if that's what you wanna do, I'm sure you could—"

"Is he going to move back to Boston?" Devin asked.

"Again, I don't know," I said, trying to hide the uncomfortable squirm in my gut. "He hasn't said. We've only talked a little bit by text, but only him saying his mom asked after me or, like, random shit. Nothing serious."

"Is he getting back with Super Bitch?" Chase asked because, of course, he would be the one blunt enough to dive straight to the sorest part of the whole ordeal.

"Chase," Devin whispered with a wince.

"What?" Chase asked, looking around.

I smiled at Devin. "S'alright, I've been dealing with him long enough. He's a blunt asshole, but he doesn't always mean to be an asshole."

"What'd I do?" Chase asked with a frown, apparently feeling singled out.

"Just being yourself and asking the question no one else wanted to ask because it's the most sensitive part of the whole thing," I assured him. I knew he didn't mean any harm by it. That was just Chase for you. "And I don't know that either. I'm afraid to ask either thing right now. He doesn't need me freaking out on him when he's already dealing with a shit ton on his own."

"And you're not?" Isaiah asked.

"I don't have a surprise kid coming," I pointed out. "Or an ex who magically popped up and threw everything out of whack."

"Did he tell you to fuck off? He was done?" Chase asked, as blunt as ever.

"That's not Adam," Devin said, earning a look of surprise from Chase and me and curiosity from Isaiah. Devin wasn't blind, however, and had caught the looks and shrugged. "What? I remember him from high school. Kinda quiet, not a lot of friends, everyone liked him."

"He was one of the popular kids," Isaiah chuckled.

"The assholes you mean," Chase grumbled.

"Hey! I was part of that group…sometimes," I protested.

"I rest my case."

"Fuck you too, Chase."

Devin once more interrupted. "But he wasn't an asshole to anyone. Even told that dickhead James to leave me alone when he was giving me shit. Threatened to beat his ass. If he was willing to risk his status for some loser like me, I can't see him being an asshole to his best friend."

"You're not a loser," Chase growled.

"Kind of am," Devin said with a mirthless smile. "But it's alright. I'm getting better. I'll get there, and I've got you helping me, right?"

"Right," Chase said, looking conflicted at agreeing.

"I'm going to get a look that could kill," Isaiah began, grinning to show he didn't care in the slightest, "but these two are absolutely adorable."

"Fuck off," Chase grumbled, but I saw him squeeze Devin's hand.

"They are," I agreed.

"Fuck you too."

"Been there done—"

"Shut up."

Everyone laughed, and I felt the tension in my chest ease at the sound. It was the first time I'd laughed in a week, and it felt strangely cleansing. Everything I'd hoped for might have fallen apart, and my heart was cracked in two, but at least I still had friends, old and one new.

"You really need to talk to him," Devin said once we petered off. "And I don't mean about what he's going to do. From the sounds of it, this was a lot more than just friends with benefits."

I shrugged. "That's more or less what it was."

"That's what we had," Chase said with a frown, surprising me with his candor. We'd rarely talked about what we'd done, and here he was doing it in front of Devin. "It was good, we had fun, but we were always just friends. This wasn't friends."

"Agreed," Isaiah said, leaning forward. "And I don't think it was just friends for him either."

"He did try to chase you down before you left," Devin pointed out.

"Probably because he could tell I was upset," I said, picking up my drink and sipping it. "Thanks for making me a new drink by the way, Devin."

"Wasn't me," Devin said with a shrug, looking up at Chase.

Chase scowled. "You could have taken credit."

"Alright, well, thank you then, Chase," I said with a smirk. "Very thoughtful of you."

Devin waved Chase off when he growled at me. "How long are you planning on avoiding him? I mean, I know she's looked into some houses around here. What are you going to do if they move in together?"

"Wait, what?" I asked, snapping my head toward him. Then after a moment's hesitation, I looked up at Chase, who was doing a poor job of not looking guilty. "Christ, you really are this town's biggest source of gossip."

"It isn't even true," Chase said with a roll of his eyes. "I just overheard someone talking about it, is all. You know people like to make up shit based on something someone heard from others who got it wrong. And Devin? Quit telling people things I tell you. You're going to get Bennett riled up."

I snorted. "Fuck off, first of all. Second, she's not staying in Fairlake. I can promise you that. She's got a nice thing going on in Boston right now, and I don't see her staying here when she's got a damn good career. Thirdly, I don't plan on leaving Adam in the dark forever, guys, c'mon. Whatever happens, I'm still his best friend, and I'm going to help him."

"Which is why you're lying in your living room, day drinking," Chase said wryly.

"That you poured," I reminded him.

"Quit ignoring the point," he growled.

I rolled my eyes. "What? I'm not allowed to feel sorry for myself for a while?"

Pity parties weren't exactly my thing but damn it all, I had every right to feel bad for myself. I'd managed to avoid it when I'd realized Adam had drifted out of my life almost completely, but this was different. For just a little while, I'd tasted what it would be like to be with the only man I'd ever loved, so I was going to allow some time to feel sorry for myself.

"Well, of course you're allowed to feel like shit," Isaiah said, rubbing his hands together. "We're just worried."

"And you really should talk to Adam about this," Devin repeated. "If you're friends, he probably has a good idea what's going on."

"And is being a dumbass like you and letting you have your space instead of dealing with the issue," Chase said.

"And you would know this how?" I asked.

"Because he seems like the type. I just don't get why you're avoiding it. You never avoid shit. Like, it's annoying how much you won't leave shit alone," he informed me.

"Bless you for putting up with him," I told Devin, who only chuckled.

"You have to deal with it at some point," Isaiah told me.

"I'm aware, thank you, all of you," I said, glaring at them. "But I'm just...let me get these feelings dealt with, alright? I don't need to puke my feelings all over him while he's dealing with shit. Let me be in a better headspace before I take that final blow."

"Idiot," Chase muttered because he was an ass.

"Agreed," Isaiah intoned because he too was an ass.

"I think you're underestimating how much Adam wants to hear from you, even if it's about this. Or maybe you're just avoiding him because you're afraid of what that conversation will be like," Devin said because he was apparently a psychologist.

"Both," Chase grunted. "What are you going to do, Bennett? Wait until the kid is born?"

ADAM

Moving carefully, I held Bri's hand as I led her up my parents' front steps. They weren't the sturdiest things, and I'd repeatedly told my dad they needed to be replaced. He'd assured me it was 'on the list,' but so far, it seemed like everything else was taking priority. I was going to have to fix them myself without his approval.

"I can walk, Adam," Bri told me as we reached the top step, but I noticed she didn't pull her hand away. I had to give her credit. For the past couple of weeks, she'd done pretty well at holding the sharper edge of her tongue back.

I also noticed her wedding ring was back on her hand, which I tried to ignore.

"You can also fall, especially on these rickety things," I told her as I opened the door.

She rolled her eyes but didn't remark as she stepped into the house. My mom immediately called out in excitement, moving forward to help Bri into the living room. I wasn't surprised to see Bri let her without comment. She had always been pretty fond of both my parents. That and I wasn't sure there was anyone who had ever wanted to be rude to my mother, other than the one time I'd told her to shut up when I was fourteen.

A mistake I would not repeat for the rest of my life. That woman wielded guilt with the precision of a surgeon.

"Let me get you something to snack on," my mother told her once Bri was settled on the couch.

"Ugh, just saltines, please. Someone's decided that Mom isn't allowed to go through today without wanting to throw up at the slightest sniff of food," Bri told her with a grimace.

"Oh, don't I know all about that," my mom said, giving me a meaningful look.

"Don't look at me," I protested.

"Oh? Someone else was the one making me sick the whole pregnancy?"

"And then passed it down to his son," Bri said.

"Hey, if I did it, then that means either you or Dad did it first," I told my mother. "So it's not my fault."

"Passing the buck," my mom said as she walked out. "Erik!"

"What?" he barked from somewhere outside.

"You got that grill going yet?"

I snorted and drowned out their bickering as he complained back at her. My parents had always been like that, and I was sure by the time the sun was setting they would be sitting together in the backyard swing, hand in hand, to watch it.

"I see they haven't changed," Bri said, craning her neck to look up at me.

"They're never going to change," I chuckled

"That's kind of comforting," she said, drawing out her phone to check it as it beeped at her. "This whole town feels like that. Like you're in a little bubble where things don't change. Only the outside world does."

"I wouldn't go that far. It changes," I said. "I've noticed quite a few things that are different."

"Because you weren't here to see it happen. Otherwise, you wouldn't have thought twice about it. Think about it, in Boston, half a dozen things could change in a week, and that's just in the areas you visit all the time. You remember that deli you loved so much?"

"Oh, yeah. Don't tell me they closed."

"No. They moved two blocks over. I swear to god, they did it in the blink of an eye. Threw me off completely when I spotted them. No idea how they did it so fast."

"That's city life for you," I said, glancing out the window at the front yard. Despite what I'd told her, not a whole lot had changed in Fairlake while I'd been gone. A few minor things, but I could see what she meant. The town felt as though it were locked in a time bubble.

"It's quieter here," she said, following my gaze. "Being here for a couple of weeks has been an eye-opener."

"How so?"

"Oh. I can understand how you got to be the way you are."

"Uhhh—"

"I just meant I always wondered how you managed to be so damn calm all the time, why you were so patient and quiet. Then I come here and stay for more than a holiday and...I don't know. It's like wherever you went, you always carried a piece of this peaceful, quiet little town with you."

It was the first genuine compliment she'd given me in months, at least one that didn't involve our child, and I wasn't sure what to say in response. If anything, it made my eyes drift to the wedding ring on her hand before flitting away. From the slight smile on her face, I could tell she'd noticed.

The ring had made a reappearance without any fanfare or announcement, and I wondered just what it was she was trying to accomplish. I understood telling me about our son, but everything else confused me. It hadn't been on when she'd shown up at my house two weeks ago and had only been there for a couple of days. Was this her version of subtlety? Or was it her way of gently letting me know what she wanted?

Before either of us could say anything, I heard my mother. "Oh, go sit down then! Adam, get out here and do the grilling for us, would you? Your father hurt his back."

"I'm fine!" he protested, but as I walked through the kitchen, I could see the way he was hunching and trying not to. "You worry too damn much."

"And you don't worry enough," she huffed at him, waving him toward the living room. "Go keep your…Bri company. Adam is more than capable of getting some meat cooked over the grill."

"Thanks for the endorsement," I told my mom wryly.

"Enough out of you," she said with a point and then ushered my father into the living room.

Shaking my head, I grabbed my father's bottle of whiskey and poured myself a decent measure over ice before heading for the grill. I wasn't aiming to get drunk, but a nice buzz to help settle my thoughts was a welcome idea. Plus, it was some of my father's best whiskey, and the smooth taste was always appreciated.

The steaks were already seasoned and sitting on a plate beside the grill. Taking a moment to make sure the surface was hot enough, I piled the meat onto the grill with a sizzle. Almost immediately, the smell of cooking meat mingled with the smell of charcoal, and I smiled.

My momentary peace was broken by the sound of the back door closing, and I turned to find my mom. "Lord, that man. I know I've said it before, but please don't end up as stubborn as him. I don't know what I'd do with two of you."

"You're a little late on that one, Mom," I told her with a smirk. "Just ask B...anyone."

My stomach twisted, and I quickly turned back to the grill, pretending to busy myself with the steaks. It was hard to believe it had been two weeks since I'd last seen Bennett because it felt a hell of a lot longer. Not that Bennett had been ignoring me, but his text responses were pretty basic and had none of the energy and zeal I was used to seeing.

I knew he was dealing with this startling new revelation just as much as I was. Without knowing what she was doing, Bri had come blazing into our lives and completely upset the balance. Now I was facing fatherhood with barely any warning and left unsure what to do with my future.

In that, Bennett had been absolutely right. Only in the past couple of weeks had I realized how much my life was being tipped on its head. I couldn't very well expect to raise a child when I lived in Fairlake and Bri lived out in Boston. To split our son's time between our two homes would be unfair to him, and the only way he would live in the same place would be to fight over custody. In truth, I didn't want to separate him from his mother, just as Bri had chosen not to leave me out of his life.

"Still no Bennett?" my mother asked, and I realized she'd probably been waiting for a chance to get me alone. So far, I'd managed to dodge most of her questions, but I had a feeling that wouldn't work anymore.

"He's been pretty busy," I told her with a shrug, not turning around.

"Oh, I've noticed. He said the same thing, though he was pretty vague about what he was busy with," my mother said, and I could hear the knowing tone in her voice. "Too busy to stop by like he's done for years, and even more so since you came back."

"He does have a life, Mom," I pointed out.

"A life he suddenly found the minute your…is she ex-wife or wife?"

"Technically, wife. Never uh, sent the final paperwork in. I have time."

"So Bri reappears, and suddenly Bennett disappears?"

"Would you believe it's a coincidence?"

"About as much as I believed you and Bennett when you tried to tell me you had no idea how Bark ended up with paint on him."

"We were seven!" I protested, remembering the old hound dog I'd named as a three-year-old. "You have to start letting things go, Mom."

"Don't change the subject."

"I was complaining about something you said. That's on topic."

She stood beside the grill, making it nearly impossible to pretend I was avoiding her gaze. "What did you do?"

I looked up, eyes wide. "I didn't do anything! What the hell, Mom?"

"Well, he certainly wasn't avoiding every single one of us before," she told me, planting her hands on her hips. "And you haven't acted like a sad sack like this since he showed up here to drag you outta bed!"

"I am not acting like a—"

"Don't sass me," she cut across sharply. "Even your father noticed. *Your father*, Adam. Lord knows how obvious it has to be for him to take notice."

"I didn't do anything," I said because it was the truth and I knew lying outright to my mother while she was watching me was asking for trouble. "He left the morning Bri showed up, and he's been busy since, alright? And I'm not a sad sack."

Feeling off-balance, unsure of myself, and worried about everything that was going to happen? Yes. Feeling utterly lost and down because the one person I wanted to talk to had his own things to deal with? Yes.

But not a sad sack.

"Well, you're sure as shit a lot less happy than you were a couple of weeks ago," she said, glaring at me.

"Mom. Bri showed up out of the blue and dropped this bombshell without warning. How else am I supposed to act right now? I don't know what the hell I'm doing, so I'm trying to figure it out before my son arrives."

"I have bad news for you, bucko. Your personal life isn't going to suddenly pause or be smooth riding just because you've got a kid. So you need to start figuring out how to juggle a lot of plates at once, or you'll be in the shit."

"Aren't you always chiding me for bad language?" I complained, feeling seven years old all over again.

"You aren't leaving him alone while he's feeling like this? You can't be," she said, completely ignoring me.

"I'm not going to push him when he doesn't want to talk," I told her with a frown.

She threw up her hands. "That man already dealt with you leaving him alone once."

"Mom, that's not fair. We already dealt with—"

"And now he's having to deal with the fact that he might lose you again."

"That's not guaranteed, and we'll talk when he—"

"I'm sure his heart is just *breaking*. God knows how long he's been in love with—"

We both stopped at the same time, and I stared at her. Her hand flew to her mouth as she grimaced.

"Whoops," she managed, deflating quickly.

"You knew?" I asked, thinking I needed to tell Bennett he'd been right all along, but then had to remind myself that we apparently weren't speaking at the moment.

She pulled her hand from her mouth. "You know?"

We both jumped when my father's voice interrupted. "Of course he knows."

My mother and I both turned to find him closing the door behind him. "Dad?"

"That one," my dad said, pointing directly at me, "has been playing sucky face with Bennett for weeks now."

My eyes widened. "D-Dad?"

"You've been *what*?" my mother demanded, and I groaned at her tone.

I was in trouble. So, so much trouble.

"You've been having...relations with Bennett?" my mother demanded, thankfully keeping her voice low.

"God, that sounds so much worse when you say it like that," I complained.

"You've been screwing," my father added, helpful as ever.

"Never mind, go back to how Mom said it." I winced.

"How did I not know this?" my mother asked, turning to my father. "And how did *you* know?"

"Because our son is about as subtle as a shovel to the face," he huffed. "And I caught them getting handsy a couple of times."

"When?" I asked, head spinning at the revelation.

"Doesn't matter," he told me with a smirk. "I seen it. That's what matters."

"Oh god, no wonder he's been...I can't believe that you... and I didn't even—" my mother rambled and swatted me hard on the chest.

"Ow!" I yelped, stepping away from her to rub my chest. "What the hell?"

"Language," she hypocritically barked, then jammed a finger at me. "He's been *busy*, huh? Busy, my lily-white ass! He's been busy nursing a broken heart is what he's been busy doing!"

"Uh, Dad?" I asked weakly, hoping he would take pity.

"Oh no, I don't get to enjoy her starting in on someone else often," he said, with a sly grin that said he knew exactly what he'd done. "But you have this coming by a long way."

"I haven't done anything!" I protested again, knowing it was in vain.

"Don't play dumb with me," she said, swatting at me again. "That boy has been in love with you for ages, and you start messing with his head?"

"I didn't mess with anything," I said, dodging her next swat.

My father chuckled. "I'd bet you been messing with a few things."

"You, stay out of it. You and I are going to have words about keeping things from me," my mother told him. My reprieve was short-lived, however, as she rounded back on me. "Then, if you weren't messing with his head, just what were you doing? You couldn't have found some other person to get things out of your system?"

"That is *not* what I was doing with him," I retorted angrily.

"Then what were you doing?"

"Not that!"

"So, what then?"

"It's…complicated, Mom."

"Of course it is. You got your father's stubbornness, but you had to take my thinking too, didn't you? Lord have mercy, spare me from the idiots in my life," she said, throwing her hands skyward.

I glanced between them. "You, uh, guys really don't care that I was, you know, sort of with a guy?"

This time I earned a swat on the ass from the grill spatula. "Of course I don't care!"

"*Ow!* Mom, stop!"

"All we want is for you to be happy, doesn't matter what

bits they have between their legs," she snapped, raising the spatula again. "I can't believe you'd even ask that after having Bennett around so much, having him as a part of this family."

"Am I allowed to talk? Without getting hit again," I said, watching her warily.

"Depends on what kind of nonsense is about to leave that mouth of yours," she told me, narrowing her eyes.

"We never said what it was or wasn't. We were just"—I searched for an answer that would be appropriate for my parents—"figuring things out as they went, or just going with it. Ah! Mom, quit! It was his idea, I...Ow!"

"Alright, alright," my father grunted, stepping in and taking the utensil from her, then promptly checking the steaks. "Talk to the boy, Diane."

"It was his idea because he's always done what he's needed to in order to keep you around," she told me hotly. "Now, how long has this been going on?"

"Uh...a little bit?"

"Be specific."

"About...almost five months? Or would be around this time."

"Erik?"

"Yes, dear?"

"Give me that thing back."

"Mom, c'mon."

To my horror, my father held the spatula out to her. Yet when she grabbed it, he took her by the other shoulder and drew her close. I watched as he leaned in and began whispering in her ear. I couldn't make out a single word, but I watched what I thought was understanding enter her face, and her grip on the spatula eased.

"You and I are still going to talk about this," she told him as he eased away, but there was no real heat in her voice. "Adam?"

"Yeah?" I asked warily.

"Are you in love with Bennett?" She watched me carefully. "And don't you lie."

The question confused me, and I looked between them. "What did you say to her?"

"Answer the question," he said, and I realized they were teaming up on me now.

"Of course I love Bennett," I said, still looking between them. "When has that ever been in question?"

"I didn't ask about loving him. I asked if you were *in* love with him."

"I..." My voice dropped off, and I stared at them for several seconds, unable to summon the answer.

"Okay, let's try this. Are you in love with Bri?" she asked softly, glancing toward the glass door leading back into the house.

"I...no," I said, hesitating out of confusion.

"So you're not going to be dumb enough to get into a relationship with her just for the sake of your son?"

"What? No."

"Why's she wearing her ring then?"

"We...still have to talk about that."

"That's quite the growing list of things you have to talk about with people," my father said, brow stitching together. Crap, when he got serious and then frowned, that meant I was about to get it again.

"Things haven't exactly been giving me the room to talk to people about things," I said, annoyed now.

"And life isn't ever going to do that," my mother told me. "We went over that already, remember?"

"You didn't answer," my father said.

"What?" I asked.

"You didn't answer if you were in love with Bennett."

"Because it's—"

258

"You answered if you were with Bri. Had no problem answering that one."

"Dad."

"The way you been moping around, you miss him. And I know what a breaking heart looks like."

I stopped, swallowing hard as they both looked at me with an inexplicable amount of love and understanding. Without warning, I felt a sting in my eyes as I let the truth of their words sink in. Because I absolutely missed Bennett.

Every time something funny, weird, or annoying had cropped up in the past couple of weeks, I wanted to text him. I'd remind myself to tell him something in person or ask him later. In both cases, reality would come crashing into my thoughts like a wrecking ball.

It always left me feeling winded and dazed as I tried to wrap my head around this new reality. Where once there was the comfort and security of knowing Bennett would always be there, instead, there was a gaping absence. In the beginning, I might have thought sex and experimentation would complicate things, but against all logic, it felt like it had simplified them.

Then again, things had always been simpler with Bennett. The added affection and sex had followed the same path. If anything, it felt like a natural extension or an evolution of who we'd been before. Touching him had been easy and natural, whether it was innocent and affectionate or heated and loaded with desire. Unlike everyone I'd been with, things had just happened with Bennett without any second-guessing on my part, save for my own natural hesitation and anxiety.

"Did we break him?" my father asked, looking me over.

"He's thinking," she said softly. "And it's about time he started thinking in the right direction."

"Diane," my father said, squeezing her arm.

"I know, I know," she said, shaking her head. "But this whole situation is a mess, and I can't yell at Bennett right now, so he's getting it."

"Don't yell at Bennett," I said suddenly, scowling at her. "He hasn't done anything wrong, and he doesn't need you coming after him when he's dealing with enough right now."

"Nice to see you haven't lost *that*, at least," she grunted.

"Lost what?" I asked irritably.

"Lost your—"

"Uh, guys?" a shout came from within the house.

"Hell's bells," my father muttered and walked toward the house. He left the door open as he walked in, leaving my mother and me to awkwardly stand across from each other, afraid to speak about the topic anymore. Bad enough that they knew. I was *not* ready for Bri to hear any of this.

There was a thump, followed by my father's outraged shout. "Goddammit, not again! My couch!"

"Well, I can't help it!" I heard Bri protest.

"What the hell?" I began, walking toward the house as my mother inexplicably chuckled.

"Oh dear. I guess that child really is a member of this family if what I think happened actually happened," she said and, to my surprise, began rubbing my back. "Deep breaths."

"Mom?" I asked in confusion as we passed my father, who was muttering about wasted food and cleaning costs.

We stopped as we entered the living room to find Bri standing in a strange, almost half-squat. There was a huge wet stain on the front of her loose pants, and I could see it was all over the couch as well.

"Ohhhhh," I said with a sympathetic grimace. "Bri, I'm so sorry. C'mon, we'll get you cleaned up, don't worry about it. You already said he's been sitting on your bladder."

"Are you shitting me right now?" Bri demanded, staring at me like I'd grown another head.

"Sweetheart?" my mom said, taking me by the arm. "We need to get her to the hospital."

Alarm shot through me. "What? Why? Is she okay?"

"She didn't have an accident," my mom explained gently as she walked over to Bri, holding her up as I heard the back door shut and the sound of keys jingling. "Her water broke."

"What?" I asked dumbly, turning to find my father standing there, a towel in hand as well as his keys.

"Your son's coming," he told me.

"Oh…well, fuck."

ADAM

"Bri, just—"

"I swear by all that is holy and unholy on this fucking planet, Adam, if you tell me to breathe one more time, I will rip it off!"

I grimaced as a nearby nurse shot me a knowing look of warning, and I kept my mouth shut. Bri was sprawled in a bed on her back, sweat coating her face as she worked her chest heavily with each breath. I knew I wasn't helping, but all I could remember was that women giving birth were supposed to breathe. I had been so blown away by the very idea that I was going to be a father that I hadn't even considered what the birth would be like.

My parents weren't in the room with us, leaving just Bri and me there while she worked through each contraction. Occasionally someone would come in and check to see how far along she was, but apparently, birth was an extended process; it had been eight hours already, and they still weren't satisfied that she was ready.

"You sure you don't want that shot they offered?" I asked, the name escaping me.

"I'm not drugging our son," she snapped, but from her breathing, this contraction had passed already.

"Right, right," I said, looking around, unsure what to do with myself. Somehow the past eight hours had been the shortest and longest of my life. "Sorry, I uh…yeah, sorry."

"Probably should have thought about that before you stuck your dick in me," she ground out, laying back on the pillow.

I had the distinct feeling that pointing out she was the one who had initiated our little fling would probably get something thrown at me. Most of the time, her temper was sharp and focused, but at the moment she was like a wildcat. I couldn't predict if she would lash out at me like she used to or if she'd find the nearest hard object.

Instead, I checked my phone for the hundredth time. I'd texted Bennett to tell him she was giving birth. It had taken nearly twenty minutes, but he had responded.

Omg, seriously? Fuck, I'm so sorry, Adam, but I'm over in Fovel, helping contain people while they put out this HUGE fire. I'll be there as soon as I can. Promise.

I knew, no matter what was going on, Bennett wouldn't lie to me. That he sent a picture of him standing near a crowd, thick black smoke curling in the air behind him, had been added proof. My heart ached to see his face again, smeared with what I thought might be ash on one cheek but still managing to make a goofy face. I received three brief updates, and he ended each with the promise he'd be out soon. The last had been three hours earlier and—

The door banged open, and Bennett burst into the room, his eyes wide. The smell of smoke followed after him as he stood, still in uniform, looking between us. Almost immediately, I felt part of my worry die down.

"Christ, I'm so sorry," he said, first looking at me and then Bri. "It took *ages* to get out of there."

"Hell, what is that smell?" Bri demanded.

Bennett looked around and grimaced. "Sorry, that's me. Chief sent me to Fovel to help keep people corralled while a fire was being put out. Gas line thing, practically a whole block was lit up."

It was said lightly, but I caught the faintest shadow pass over his face. I was guessing it was more than just a few houses and cars that had been lost tonight. It was the first time I'd glimpsed just what sort of thing Bennett had to deal with in the course of his work.

He held up a plastic bag. "I'll change, don't worry. Can I use your bathroom?"

Unbelievably, Bri laughed. "God, yes, you smell like shit. I really don't want to puke right now."

"Gotcha," he said, eyes darting to me before disappearing into the adjoining bathroom.

"I have the feeling he came running here in the literal sense." Bri snorted. "Ethan texted. He said he'll be here in the morning. And informed me my parents are pretty pissed with me."

I wasn't surprised her brother was coming as soon as he could. He and Bri had always been close, even as adults. "Why are your parents pissed at you? Isn't that normally Ethan's job?"

Bri snorted. "My turn. They found out I quit the firm."

I froze. "You…what?"

"About four months back."

"W-why?"

"Because I was so goddamn sick of it. All the backstabbing and office politics. We were there to help people as a team, but everyone wanted to be number one. First among equals, and if you didn't try to be, you got the shittiest cases or none at all."

"You, uh, always seemed to enjoy that. I remember you giving me shit because I wasn't competitive."

"Oh, I'm still competitive as hell. The fire hasn't gone out of this girl, believe you me."

"Of that, I have no doubt."

That made her smile. "But I'd just got done bickering with Mosely, weaselly little bastard that he is, and I stood there for a minute, realizing I didn't feel any victory from winning that argument. Then someone kicked, and I realized I didn't want it anymore. Not that life, not that stress, especially not when I had a child on the way."

I cocked my head. "What are you going to do?"

"You'd be amazed what kind of work a lawyer specializing in real estate can get in the sticks," she said.

I blinked rapidly, trying to wrap my head around that for a minute. "Wait, you're…going to work out here? In Fairlake?"

"Or Fovel or any other town around here. Why not? I already told you I was falling in love with this place."

"Appreciating it isn't the same thing as living here. You realize how big an adjustment that would be?"

"Says the man who did the opposite sort of adjustment."

"I—"

"Of course," she began slowly, looking me over, "I'll have to figure out where I'm going to live before I start thinking about office space."

I froze, knowing full well what she was trying to ask me without really asking. I knew she had spotted the divorce paperwork sitting on my dining room table, but she hadn't said anything, and neither had I. While she'd stayed in Fairlake, I let her take my bed while I took the couch, which seemed better than letting her stay in the local motel. But now she was finally bringing to a head one of the very subjects I was hoping to avoid for a bit longer.

The bathroom door burst open, making me jerk in surprise. "Sorry, sorry. Tried washing my hair while I was in there. Christ, I don't know how smokers can stand smelling like that all the time."

"Practice," Bri said sourly and then hissed, hunching forward. "Ooh boy, that's a fucking good one."

"Shit," I fumbled, prepared to find a nurse to help.

"Sounds like a spicy one," Bennett said lightly, winding around to the other side of the bed. He reached into her cup of ice water and gently placed an ice cube onto her forehead, moving it in slow circles.

"Want us to breathe with you?" Bennett asked.

"So we can all be idiot fish out of water?" Bri snapped.

"I mean, you're the one giving birth right now. You have every right to look however you want," he said with a crooked smile. "If we did it, we'd just be the idiots."

Bri chuckled, closing her eyes as Bennett continued moving the ice cube around. "As much as it would please me to see Adam embarrass himself for my sake, I don't think that will make me feel better."

"Are you kidding? Watching Adam make an ass out of himself is one of life's greatest pleasures," Bennett protested, reaching to grab another ice cube.

I narrowed my eyes at him. "What are you doing?"

He grinned at me. "Bri, did you ever watch a cartoon called *Sailor Moon?*"

"Oh god, it's been years, but yeah, I remember that," she said, grimacing.

My eyes widened. "Bennett!"

"Do you remember how they had those transformation scenes for the girls when they would go into their powerful form?"

"Vaguely. It was always colorful and a lot of posing."

"Yep."

"Bennett!" I said, trying to reach his mouth to make him stop. I was unsuccessful, however, as it would require falling onto Bri in the process.

"Well, I used to watch it as a kid, loved the shit out of it. Still have the DVDs at home. So anyway, I got Adam here to watch it with me. Then, when we were like, eight, I convinced him to play it with me."

"Play...Sailor Moon?" Bri asked slowly, and I groaned at the curious disbelief in her voice.

"Yes indeed," Bennett crowed, all too pleased with himself. Personally, I was considering the best way to silence him forever and not be found out. "Up to and including those very, uh...flouncy transformation scenes. Which is bad enough, but then he ended up doing it while we were playing one time, and a whole barbecue's worth of adults happened to see him."

"Oh my god," I groaned, flopping my head down onto the bed. "Every single one of them stared at me like I'd lost my mind."

"What did you do?" Bri asked, even as I watched her lips thin.

"Nothing," I tried, but Bennett was quick.

"Burst into tears and ran to hide in his closet at home until his mom had to come and drag him out," Bennett told her.

"It was mortifying!" I protested with a scowl. "Just because you had no shame, even at that age!"

"Aww, that's adorable," Bri said, patting my hand. "I didn't know you were capable of it."

"Wanna hear about the time he had to wear a kilt at his cousin's wedding?" Bennett asked. "I didn't get the full view, but—"

"I'm out of here," I said, jumping up. "I'll go get some more ice."

"Was he wearing the kilt in the proper way?" Bri asked as I went for the door as fast as I could without running.

"Oh yeah," Bennett said. "Of course, no one knew that until—"

I closed the door, cutting off the sound of the god-awful story. I had ended up flashing my entire family. I didn't know if this was Bennett's form of revenge or if he was just finding the best way to keep Bri distracted while she went through this ordeal.

When I heard the two of them burst into laughter together, however, I realized I didn't care and walked away with a faint smile on my face.

* * *

I THOUGHT I was ready for what was to come.

I also thought wrong.

"Alright, we're almost there!" the doctor proclaimed as he hunched between Bri's legs, held up in stirrups as she bore down. "Keep pushing!"

"I am pushing, you brain-dead idiot!" she screamed, and I thought if her face got any redder, she might injure herself. "Maybe focus on that job you spent ten years working for and leave me the hell alone!"

I winced and sincerely hoped the doctor would decide to leave well enough alone, but then again, I was sure he'd probably dealt with just as bad, if not worse. The best I could do was hold her hand, while strangely enough, Bennett held the other. When it came time to get down to business, it had been Bri who insisted that Bennett stay with her along with me. I wasn't all that offended. He had spent the previous couple of hours keeping us entertained and calm despite the dark circles under his eyes.

"You're doing great," I told her, not even sure if that was

the case but damned if she wasn't fighting like hell to get through this.

"You, do not talk to me right now," she growled between clenched teeth.

"He's right," Bennett told her, even as the tips of his fingers in her iron grip turned paler and paler. "You're doing great. You're almost there, Bri. Just keep going. After this, I'll get you one of those cheap, sugary slushie drinks from the cafeteria."

"Sweet Jesus," she groaned, and I grimaced as she turned an even darker shade of red.

I tensed as the doctors and nurses flew into action. Bri made a noise that was somewhere between a yelp and a groan. Bennett's brow was raised behind his mask, but he continued holding her hand, staying right where he was on the other side of the screen blocking sight of anything happening between her legs.

"Dad?" one of the nurses said, and I shuffled forward without thinking. My eyes widened as I stared at the squirming mass they were bundling up.

Numb, I remained frozen as I watched them deal with what I distantly knew had to be my son while simultaneously working with some sort of fleshy tube. It was only when something was put in my hand that I realized what the tube was as I looked over the scissors.

"Is it...okay?" I asked as they guided my hand forward.

The nurse's eyes crinkled. "Go ahead. It'll be alright."

Feeling like I was going to make an absolute mess of things, I took her word for it and closed the scissors. For a moment everything was fine, but then the most horrible scream filled the air. Every alarm in my head went off as I jerked back, head darting around.

"What? What happened?" I asked in near panic.

The same nurse patted me. "Nothing."

"Hey," Bennett said, reaching over to grip my arm. "They just cleaned out his airways. They do a bit of crying after that. You just cut the umbilical cord, it's alright."

"Are you sure?" I babbled as they pulled the crying baby away, wiping at him and fussing with him.

"Believe it or not, this is the third birth I've been present at. At least this time, I wasn't the one delivering it." Bennett chuckled, then pulled me back toward the bed. "Now come check on Mom."

I spun around to find Bri collapsed back on the bed, blinking slowly as she heaved for breath. "Holy shit, Bri, I'm so sorry."

"S'alright, you were having a panic attack," she said with a snort. "I'm told that's pretty normal for first-time dads."

"Extremely," the nurse said, coming around with a squirming bundle of blankets. I reached out to help Bri so she could prop herself on the pillows. "Here you go."

"Oh," Bri breathed as the bundle was deposited gently in her arms. A tiny face peered out at her, squinting as he looked around the room slowly. He squirmed in the blanket, but it looked like he was calming down. "Look at you."

"What's his name?" Bennett asked, peering around me.

"Well, I never came up with any," Bri admitted, looking up at me. "We always agreed, any boys were named by you, any girls by me. So here we are."

"Seriously?" I asked in surprise.

"That's what we agreed on, isn't it?" she asked with a tired smile.

She looked exhausted, her blonde hair sticking to her forehead as she sat back. There was a glow about her, though, that made her absolutely beautiful, and for a moment I saw the woman I had first fallen in love with years ago.

"Colin," I finally said.

She nodded. "Middle name?"

"I think we should go with Erik or Jacob."

"So I get to choose between your dad's name or mine?"

"Uhhh—"

Bri smiled down at our son. "Colin Jacob Jensen it is. Almost alliterative. You were so close."

"We'll get you the official paperwork in a little while," the nurse said. "And when you two are ready, we'll take Colin here to get his checkup."

"Is something wrong?" I asked, pitch rising again.

Bri smirked up at me. "They have to measure him, weigh him, and make sure everything's fine. He's okay, Dad, see?"

Before I could react, I suddenly had the squirming mass of blankets in my arms. Panic shot through me as I suddenly worried about the position of my arms as though I'd never used them before. Then a hand reached out and steadied my fumbling, holding firm until I settled down before letting go.

I meant to thank Bennett, but then I peered down into the tiny face and the room and everyone in it disappeared. Against all odds, Colin had managed to get his mother's blue eyes, but unless it changed as it did with some babies, he had a dark patch of my hair on top of his head. He stared up at me, eyes searching my face in sudden quiet curiosity, and I stared down at him, absolutely dumbfounded. He was so unbelievably tiny, yet he felt so unbelievably solid and *real* in my arms.

"Hello, Colin," I whispered, eyes prickling. For the first time since childhood, I couldn't find it in me to hold it back as my eyes watered. "Look at you. Just look at you."

"I'd say we did pretty good," Bri said, and I could hear the smile in her voice.

I glanced over my shoulder at Bennett, turning Colin's face toward him. "Look at this. Look what we made."

Bennett ducked his head slightly, a small smile on his

face. "Bri's right. You guys did good. For an angry potato, he's pretty cute."

"He's not an angry potato," I said, turning to Bri. "Right?"

"Adam, all babies look like that." She chuckled. "We're just filled with so many hormones that we can't tell."

"Don't listen to them," I told Colin, heart skipping a beat when he yawned. "You're the sweetest thing in existence. They don't know what they're talking about."

"Oh god, I'm going to end up with a Daddy's Boy, aren't I?" Bri sighed. "How didn't I see this coming?"

"Already wrapped around that one little finger," Bennett chuckled.

I ignored them as I swayed while holding Colin. The little boy still hadn't reacted to what was happening around him, content to stare at me. In all fairness, I was more than happy to return the favor, returning his gaze before I realized I should probably hand him off.

"Sorry," I whispered, crouching to give him back to Bri.

"Thank you," she said just as softly.

"No," I said, wiping hair from her forehead. "Thank you. You really were great."

"Yeah, okay, Dad." She laughed. "Better go tell your parents. I think they're still waiting out there."

"Probably," I said, looking down at Colin. "You really wanna raise him here?"

"In this nice town, where he's significantly safer and surrounded by people who will love the shit out of him? Yeah, I'm pretty sure," she said. "And Mom could use the change of pace and a bit of quiet too."

"I should probably thank you for that too," I said, meaning it.

"If you're going to get sappy on me, then we should... Woah, where'd Bennett go?"

"What?" I straightened, looking around and finding us alone. "What the hell?"

"How did he come in here so loudly and then leave like a ninja?" Bri wondered aloud.

"He can do that," I said, trying not to grit my teeth. "I'm going to go get everyone else. I'll be back in a little bit."

"Sure," she said with a wispy smile.

I barely made it down the hallway before I saw my parents walking toward me. My father wore a sour expression, which I realized stemmed from the wrap I could see tightly cinched at his waist. Apparently, my mother had decided to get him checked out while they'd been waiting.

"Boy, of course, Colin Jacob Jensen, he's the sweetest fucking thing in existence, and I cried a little," I told them, coming to an abrupt stop.

"Oh, that's okay, honey. Your father bawled like a baby when he held you," my mother said, pulling me into a hug.

"Damn right I did," my father grumped. "Stupidest thing I ever did, lookit you."

"Love you too, Dad," I chuckled. "You see Bennett?"

"We did, but he didn't see us," she said, frowning. "What happened?"

"Nothing," I told them. "Go be grandparents. I'll be there soon."

My father grabbed my arm, meeting my eyes. "Whatever you're going to do or say, make sure you mean it, son."

"I know," I said, pulling away.

After that, I began jogging as fast as I could without outright running. Unless Bennett was sprinting, I'd probably find him in the parking lot. I had let him drive away from me once before, but not this time.

BENNETT

Wiping my face, I dropped the mask into the trash can outside the front lobby. I supposed when I got home, I could probably squeeze in a few hours sleep and not risk screwing up my sleep schedule too badly. Chief Price had insisted I take today off after the long day I'd had yesterday, and as much as crashing and not waking up for twenty hours sounded great, I knew it was a bad idea.

Ignoring the swelling ache in my chest at the memory of watching the two proud parents with one another, I tried to remember where I'd parked my car. I'd known coming here to support Adam would be hard. Sure, it had started easily enough when I just had to sit there and entertain the three of us, if only to keep Adam from losing his shit.

The sight of Adam staring down at his son had threatened to undo me on the spot. It had been the sweetest thing I had ever seen, and that memory at least would be something I could treasure. Watching his dark eyes well with tears from the sheer happiness as he stared down at the tiny baby he cradled in his big arms.

Just so long as I stopped it there and didn't replay the

moment he gently wiped hair from Bri's face, then it would be a good memory.

"BENNETT!"

I jerked, stumbling as I went to walk over the curb near the parking lot. I caught myself, successfully sparing myself from a nasty spill, even if it meant I hit my head on a pole in the process.

"Fuck my life," I groaned, holding my hand to my forehead.

"Shit," Adam called as he jogged toward me. "You okay?"

"I was until you scared the shit out of me," I complained, rubbing my head. "What the hell are you screaming at me like that for?"

"I called you several times," he explained. Sweat had broken out on his face, and he was breathing pretty hard. "But you didn't respond. Figured I had to get through somehow."

"See? You should have joined me on my runs. Then you wouldn't be gasping like a wounded buffalo."

"Fuck off." Adam laughed. Almost immediately, his expression shifted to grave concern. "What are you doing?"

"Getting a concussion, apparently," I told him and knew immediately it wouldn't work.

"Nice try," he grumbled. "Now try again."

"I'm going home," I said with a sigh. "Unless you're going to have another almost meltdown, I'm pretty sure you're all set here without me."

"Like hell," he said, stepping around me as if cutting off my retreat. "I haven't been 'all set' for weeks now."

"Well," I drew out, "you've been getting your head around your wife returning and your son arriving."

"Ex-wife."

"Pretty sure you're married still."

"Not for long."

I stopped, peering up at him. "What?"

Adam shook his head. "Did you really think just because she showed up pregnant I was going to, what, forget everything that brought me back to Fairlake in the first place?"

"How was I supposed to know?" I grumbled, suddenly feeling stupid.

"Well, talking to me about it would have been a good start," Adam said with a scowl. "Then again, I probably should have pinned you down before today to tell you that. I should have admitted to myself that you were avoiding me, not taking time."

"Hey," I protested, jutting my chin forward. "I was—"

"Avoiding me. Avoiding talking to me. Now look me in the eye and say that wasn't what you were doing."

"Dick," I muttered, looking away. It was clearly the answer to his question, but I wasn't ready to admit it. "That doesn't change anything."

"It changes a lot, I'd bet," he said dryly. "I'm not in love with her."

"Alright," I said, shoving my hands into my jeans. As much as the news made me feel a little better, I knew that wasn't everything, not even close.

"I'm in love with *you*."

I froze, swallowing hard as the words sank into my consciousness. Slowly, I looked up to meet his intense gaze and barely croaked, "What?"

"I can't tell you when it started. Maybe it was pretty much from that first kiss, or maybe it was later. Maybe there's no point when it really started, and it's just always been that way," he said with a shrug while I stared at him in utter shock. "And it's on me for not realizing it sooner. It shouldn't have taken so long for me to figure it out, especially not after you were gone, and then to have my mom and dad scold me over it."

"You're...you're serious?" I asked softly.

"Yes, I'm serious," he said, frowning. "This isn't something I'd joke about, Bennett. I'm sorry it took me so long. I know you were always there, always dealing with it the whole way, and I should have stepped up and figured it out on my own."

"I could've said something instead of running," I muttered, still trying to get my head around everything. Was this really happening? Had I been knocked out when I hit that pole and instead was dreaming all this in some vain attempt to make myself feel better about the terminal crash my life was becoming?

"Maybe, but I can't exactly hold that against you. I did far worse than that."

"Adam, I told you we were past that."

"Yeah, I get that. I still feel like shit about it, and I probably won't with time. But I'd feel a thousand times worse if I hadn't finally found the sense to hunt you down and tell you. I love you, Bennett, so please, don't run away from me."

I floundered for a response as I stood there staring at him in helpless confusion. How the hell had everything been so absolutely horrible only moments before, and now one of my lifelong dreams was literally playing out right in front of me? The moment felt unreal, even as the joy inside me swelled to breaking point.

Launching myself at him, I wrapped my arms around his neck and held him tight. I buried my face in his neck and realized I gave a faint sob as I did. In the cool morning air, I could feel the heat radiating off him, and god, he was so solid and strong. He was right there, holding me tight in response, muttering that he loved me while I fought to gain some semblance of control.

"I'm sorry," I finally managed to get out. "I shouldn't have run off...both times. This was supposed to be your day, a wonderful day. And now you're out here in the cold, chasing me down so I can sob in your—"

"Shut up," he said, gripping my face and kissing me.

It was by far the best kiss I had ever shared with him, and I whimpered as I gripped his shoulders as tightly as I could. It was only then I realized this was really happening, that Adam was here with me, he had really said all those things, and this wasn't a concussion-induced dream. My best friend had just proclaimed his love for me, and I could barely stand how wonderful the entire thing was.

"Sorry for the snot and tears," I said with a watery chuckle.

"You puked in my lap at the state fair when we were fourteen. I've dealt with worse," Adam said with a chuckle, still holding my face. "Do you get it now? Because I do, and I'm—"

"I love you," I whispered. "I've wanted to say that to you for years and years, Adam. I love you. I'm *in* love with you."

"I'm in love with you too, dork. But maybe from here on out, we can shorten it to just I love you. Now that we've both got the whole 'in' part out in the open." He chuckled, kissing me gently again.

"Right, sure, yeah, of course," I babbled, pulling away to wipe my face with my sleeve. "God, are you sure?"

"Absolutely," he said with a patient smile on his face.

"I'm having…this still kinda feels like a dream."

"If it is, it's one we're sharing. And when we wake up, I'll find your ass and tell you again."

"Fucking hell, that was the corniest thing I've ever heard you say." I laughed, pulling him closer by his shirt and kissing him fiercely.

Adam bumped our foreheads together gently once we broke apart. His eyes were closed, and he breathed deeply. "I can't believe I waited so long to get around to saying it."

"C'mon, we both know how you are. You said it, right?"

"That's the thing. It was the easiest thing in the world to say. I've always struggled saying shit like that before, but with you? No problem. It's never been a problem when it was you and me, Bennett. And that's how I want the rest of our lives to be, just you and me, like we were before just, you know, as adults, with adult things."

"Like bills, responsibility, sex, and alcohol?"

"And a kid."

"Oh shit," I said, backing up with wide eyes. "Adam, wait. But—"

He shook his head. "Bri decided to drop it on me at the last minute. She's staying in Fairlake."

I'm pretty sure my eyes bulged from my head. "*What?*"

He rolled his eyes. "While you were changing out of your uniform. Which you left in the bathroom, by the way."

"Oh shit," I said, glancing toward the building.

"I guess she fell in love with the place while she was here. Wants to stay and raise Colin here."

"Uh, was that before you told her you were still going through with the divorce?"

"Yeah, um, we uh—"

I sighed. "Another thing you have to talk to someone about?"

He grimaced. "I'm batting zero at this point, I know. Come with?"

"You…want to do it now?"

"Look, I did this, right? I might as well get it out of my system. If I don't, I'll keep putting it off, telling myself it's not a good time."

I could see several holes in that logic, but it wasn't like Adam to be so immediately determined to do something that popped into his head. It probably wouldn't go well, but at the very least, he could live with himself afterward.

"Alright," I said, reaching out and taking his hand. "I'll go. But if she throws things, I'm using you as a human shield."

"Fair enough," he chuckled, and we began walking back toward the building.

"Fuck," I grunted as we entered the lobby and toward the elevator. "It just hit me."

"What's that?" he asked, pressing the button for the right floor.

I glanced at him. "If she really does stay here. And there are no major custody issues. And if we stay together."

"Uh-huh," he said with a wry twist of his brow.

"I'm going to be a—"

"Stepdad?"

"Yeah."

"It's okay. Bri mentioned making you a godparent, so clearly she doesn't mind you being a part of Colin's life," Adam said as we stepped out of the elevator.

"Really?"

"Really."

"And uh…the whole two guys together thing?"

"Dunno how she'll feel about that, but her brother came out when he was fourteen, and she adores Ethan. So that aspect should be pretty safe."

"Oh," I said and stopped when we reached the door. "Uh, are you sure about this?"

He let go and pushed into the room. "Nope, but here we go."

Not at all reassured, I followed him into the room to find his parents standing near the bed. Diane was holding little Colin, cooing down at him while Erik beamed beside her. Bri smiled at the two of us as we entered, holding a hand up and wiggling her fingers at me.

"Hey, you, wondered where you got to," she said to me, looking pleased.

"Hey," I said, suddenly feeling like a thief.

"Bennett! Here," Diane said, and my eyes widened as she approached.

"Oh god, shouldn't Bri hold him?" I said, almost taking a step back. I did not want to hold her son while Adam talked to her.

"Oh, hold him," Bri said with a smile. "He needs to see his uncle."

"But," I managed to spit out before the baby was dropped in my arms. I would never understand why people liked to do that sort of forceful handoff with nervous people.

A wrinkly face stared up at me, and I saw they had cleaned him better since the last time I'd seen him. His eyes were wider as he looked at me, a little arm wriggling free from the confines of his warm blankets to smack my chin lightly.

"Well, hello there," I said with a little smile. "I was right. You are pretty cute for an angry potato."

"He is not," Erik protested, even as Diane and Bri chuckled.

"Quit it," Adam told me, then looked at his parents. "Can you give us a minute?"

Diane looked between Adam and me, eyes narrowing. "Adam—"

"Please?" Adam requested politely.

Erik's brow raised at his son, but he silently put a hand on Diane's lower back, leading her out of the room. She was the only one to look over her shoulder, shooting Adam a suspicious look before the door closed behind them.

"What's this about?" Bri asked, the sleepiness gone from her face as she looked at us warily.

"Oh boy," I muttered to Colin, who was still trying to grab hold of something on my face. I just hoped it was enough to distract him from the tension that was about to fill the whole room.

"I'll admit this is a shit time for this," Adam began, grimacing. "But I think it's time I get it out in the open. I've been avoiding a few things, and I'm not going to do it any longer."

Bri watched him, her face devoid of expression. "Okay."

"I'm going to send the final paperwork to Roy sometime this week."

She blinked twice. "Your lawyer."

"Yes."

"You're finalizing the divorce."

"Yes. I don't know if I misinterpreted things, but I had the feeling you were thinking of rekindling things," Adam told her, and I saw his shoulders go back, bracing himself.

"It had crossed my mind," Bri said slowly, and I watched her eyes dart to me before returning to Adam. "I was testing the waters to see how you felt about it."

"Do you still plan to stay in Fairlake, knowing that?"

Bri's nostrils flared. "I wasn't telling you that to convince you to stay married to me, Adam. What kind of manipulative bitch do you think I am?"

"All things considered, I probably shouldn't answer that."

"Adam," I hissed as Bri bristled.

Adam closed his eyes, shaking his head. "You're right. I'm sorry, that was unfair. We've both been…rough these past couple of years. I can't keep beating you up if I'm not willing to beat myself up too."

If I had thought it was a manipulative statement rather than a genuine one, I would have begrudgingly given him points for skill. Especially when I watched Bri slowly deflate, then look down at her lap.

"I suppose we have been pretty awful, haven't we?" she

asked softly. "I wonder how long it would have taken before we did it again."

"I'd hope never again, but—"

"But you're not willing to find out."

"I love you, Bri, but we both fell out of love with one another a long time ago."

To my dismay, I saw her eyes go glassy as she nodded silently. I think it was the first time either of them had spoken so candidly to one another in a very long time. If it weren't for the fact that I was holding their kid and had promised Adam I'd stay here with him, I would have left them both with their privacy.

"And I've been dating Bennett in all but name the past five months," Adam stated.

"Holy shit," I muttered to Colin, glad he wasn't of the age where I had to worry about him picking the language up.

"I...excuse me?" Bri asked, and I didn't have to look up to know there was a look of pure shock on her face.

"The whole thing is more complicated than it should have been, which is my fault, but yes."

"Son of a bitch," Bri muttered through gritted teeth. "I wondered, goddammit, I wondered. But no, I told myself, no, Adam isn't like that. Adam is completely straight. So what, you're bi?"

"Well, for one person at least," Adam said with a glance.

Bri looked up, and I gave a weak smile in response. "That's why you took off when I showed up and haven't been back, and that's why you took off today."

"God, she's good," I muttered, having a hard time meeting her gaze.

"Reading people is half my job, though apparently being in denial is half of my life lately," she muttered with an angry snort. "And you didn't think to say anything? I mean, Adam I get since he's as emotionally aware as a brick—"

"Hey. Fair, but hey."

"But you? You played nice to my face?"

"First off," I said, ruffling at the unspoken accusation of falsehood. "It wasn't my ex-wife. That wasn't on me to say anything. Secondly, I distanced myself because I thought, well, I thought what you'd been tempted to try."

"So, I thought he might give it a try with me again, and you thought that's what he was going to do."

"Yes."

"So I was left wondering, and you were left afraid because he didn't say anything?"

Adam looked around in horror. "What is happening right now?"

"Don't you talk. I'm *so* mad at you right now."

"But—"

"I've forgiven him...for the most part. And I know that sounds easy coming from me," I said with a light shrug to make sure not to jostle Colin too much. "And I can't speak for what sort of things happened between the two of you, but I've known him pretty much my whole life. I know how badly he can screw up and how much he doesn't mean to hurt anyone."

"I wouldn't be so sure about that. I remember a few intentional barbs."

"People are different with different people. He is who he is, and I love and forgive him for that."

Bri stared at me for several heartbeats before sighing. "I'm not happy. I'm angry and...hurt, but at the same time, I should have said something before this. This is both our faults."

"I accept my part in this," Adam said, frowning at his shoes.

"Good. Maybe we can move past this on a personal level...and everything else sometime later. But right now, I want to focus on our son," Bri said, smiling at Colin in my arms. I didn't hesitate to step forward and give him back. "We can talk about custody arrangements soon and get the paperwork in shortly after that."

"You want to take this to court?" Adam asked with a frown.

Bri chuckled. "I'm not doing it for a dispute. It's an agreement that the courts uphold. That way, if either of us gets any bright ideas to be petty to the other through him, the courts will step in."

"You and your safety nets," Adam said in a way I almost thought was fond.

"You know it," she said. "Now go get your mom so she can hold him a bit more. Maybe we can convince your dad to do it too."

We stepped out of the room, and I wasn't surprised to find his parents waiting only a few yards away. His mother advanced, glancing between us. "So?"

"All out in the open," Adam said, and I could see how much of a toll the past few hours had taken on him. "She's not nearly as pissed as I thought she'd be."

"And you two?"

I opened my mouth to reply, but Adam grabbed me, pulling me closer. Thankfully the kiss was brief and didn't deepen in the slightest. There was no mistaking the intent behind it, however, and I pulled away with a cough, feeling my cheeks warm.

"Huh, to the point. I can respect that," Erik said with a grunt.

"That should have been stranger to see than it was," Diane said, cocking her head slightly. "Now I'm wondering why this didn't happen sooner?"

I jammed a thumb at Adam. "He ran away to Boston for a decade and left us behind."

"Ah yes, thank you, sweetheart," she said, kissing my cheek. "And don't think you and I aren't going to talk about you disappearing without a word for two weeks."

"Oh," I groaned, frowning when they walked past me, Erik chuckling as he patted my shoulder. "I haven't been yelled at by your mom in ages."

Adam tugged at my shirt, drawing me closer. "You kind of deserve it. Avoiding me is one thing, but my parents?"

"True," I admitted. "Doesn't make me look forward to it any more."

"Sucks to be you," he chuckled, kissing me. "Thanks for sticking with me through that. And good job dealing with Bri. She can be kinda scary if you're not used to it."

"She's just upset, and I don't blame her. I know what it's like to be so disappointed it hurts," I said with a shrug.

Adam frowned. "I'm sorry."

"No," I said, kissing him back. "We're going to work past all that, alright? We've got plenty of time, and we've got more than enough good things to look forward to."

"Hmm, speaking of," Adam said, reaching out to grab the handle, "there is one more thing we need to discuss."

"Oh?"

"Yeah, when am I moving in with you?"

EPILOGUE

Three Years Later

I woke to the feeling of a warm body pressing against me, and even in my hazy state I knew Bennett was being a giant bed hog again. It honestly wouldn't matter what size bed we got, he would inevitably find his way to my side. He liked to claim he was simply seeking me out in his sleep for cuddles, but I called bullshit every time I woke up and he was a goofy-looking starfish while I had three inches of space.

Grunting, I flopped my arm over him, finding his waist and giving a tug to straighten him out. It was the only way to ensure he didn't maneuver his way horizontally to take up more space. The fact that it also allowed me to cuddle him properly was just a bonus.

"Mmph," he grunted, scooting backward into me. "Morning to you, ya brute."

"Shush," I told him, pressing my face into his hair and

breathing in his smell. It wasn't quite the fascinating, almost earthy smell that followed him after a good run, but it was still him all the same. "Sleeping."

"Doesn't feel like you're sleeping," he said with mischief. This was accompanied by him backing his ass into my groin and rubbing against it.

"That's called morning wood. It happens."

"Really? So I should stop?"

"Didn't say that," I said with a chuckle, sliding my hand under the band of his sleep pants. Considering what I'd just said, I wasn't surprised to find him hard, but that didn't diminish my delight. "Now you can say good morning."

"Keep doing that, and it's going to get a lot better."

"What do you think I'm trying to do?"

He gave that low chuckle I knew and loved, which always signaled, no matter what was happening around us, that his mind was thinking all sorts of inappropriate things. He rolled over and immediately caught my lips with his. While he busied himself kissing me, I shoved the fronts of our pants down so I could wrap my hand around our cocks, stroking us.

Ever the expressive one, Bennett groaned into the kiss. "Fuck, why is it always so much more sensitive in the morning?"

"Because you're a horndog who has sex dreams."

"You are the sex dream."

"You're so corny," I told him with a snort, bending my head to nip at his neck.

"Horny," he corrected, thrusting up into my hand.

As if it wasn't obvious, but no one would hear a complaint from me. Sex might not happen as frequently as it had years ago, but it still came easily to us. He had even finally introduced me to the world of bottoming, and despite not knowing what the hell to do with the initial weird sensations, I had to admit Bennett had converted me enough to add it to our repertoire.

Gone were the days when I was awkward and nervous about anything I did. If I felt up to it, I'd bend him over the counter to fuck him or use my refined skills with my mouth while he played video games. In the same vein, he was just as willing to ride me while we watched TV in bed or, if he was in the mood, start showing enough attention to my ass that I knew just what he was after.

"We should probably get to it," Bennett muttered against my mouth. "It's already—"

A wail broke through his words, and we both sighed as one. A thump quickly followed, and we could hear shuffling footsteps speeding down the hallway toward us.

"Incoming," I said, and Bennett slid off me. It was only a few seconds before the door opened, but we were well and truly wilted by that point.

Colin burst through the door, his lip jutting forward as his new sister wailed in the next room. Neither Bennett nor I were surprised when he clambered onto the bed and immediately buried his face in my stomach.

"Hey, buddy," I soothed, rubbing his back. "Did Amber scare you again?"

He nodded with a hearty sniffle.

"Don't worry. Bennett's gonna go get her," I said as I watched Bennett slip out of the room. I wasn't surprised in the slightest when her wail went from louder than ever as he opened the door, to almost silent sniffles when she caught sight of him. "Your sister's just not used to it here yet. She'll get used to it."

"Don't like her," he muttered against me.

"It's okay, I know it scared you, but she didn't mean it," I said, reaching to pick him up and hold him against me. I swore every time I looked away from him he managed to grow. "But she's pretty scared too when she wakes up. She thinks she's alone, and that's what makes her cry."

An understatement, but he was too young to understand that Amber had come from an abusive and neglectful family. Barely taken care of, she was usually left sitting in her crib and then room without anyone around to take care of her. We had adopted her a couple of months before, but the little girl was still adjusting to the idea that she wasn't being left alone. Which usually meant our mornings were met with a screaming eighteen-month-old as she panicked.

"See?" Bennett cooed as he entered the room, bobbing Amber up and down on his hip. "We're all right here."

"Aww, baby girl." I sighed at her snotty, tear-streaked face. "We're here. See Colin? She's okay now she knows we didn't leave her."

He turned to peer at her warily and I chuckled. Colin was still adjusting to no longer being an only child, and I supposed it was good practice. In another few months, he would have another sibling when Bri gave birth to his half-brother. She and her boyfriend Keith were thrilled, but I knew she would be even more thrilled after the boy was born, as I'd helped Keith pick out the engagement ring.

"C'mon," I said with a groan. "Let's get you in the bathroom while Bennett changes your sister. Then, maybe start some breakfast."

"Waff!" he crowed.

"Waffles it is," I chuckled, stopping to kiss Bennett as I passed.

"Let's get you nice and dry, sweetheart," I heard Bennett say as I walked down the hallway.

I dropped Colin in the bathroom but stayed nearby. He was generally very good about taking care of things, but wiping was still a struggle, so we always tried to stay on hand just in case.

I peered out the bathroom window and spotted my mom across the street, already in her front garden patch. She'd been thrilled to bits when Bennett and I decided to sell his house and move into the one across the street from them. It meant more room for the three of us, and Bennett and I had been talking even then about possibly adopting or surrogacy.

"Done?" I asked after he'd finished peeing.

"Yeah."

"You sure? No more?"

"No more."

Christ, he was so solemn when he said it I couldn't help but believe him. He had his mother's eyes, but he reminded me so much of my father in his face that I was sure that meant he looked like me. Sometimes I wondered if I really did look as serious as my son.

"Alright, wash your hands, then waffles."

Solemnity gave way to the joy only a child can manage, and I left him to his cleaning. I opened blinds and curtains as I went, letting in the warm light of the morning. I spotted Chase backing out of his driveway while Devin waved him off as they did every morning Chase worked at the shop. It turned out Chase was less of a dick than I'd originally thought, though Bennett swore up and down that was Devin's influence.

"Waff!" Colin announced as he barreled through the house.

"I've gotta make them first, bud," I told him. "You wanna play or watch something while I do that?"

He squinted, thinking hard before saying, "Play. With Ambuh."

"If she wants to play, be my guest," I told him. "Just be nice."

"Yeah!"

Chuckling, I busied myself pulling out the waffle iron and ingredients. Bennett insisted some things just had to be homemade, no matter how busy we got. Waffles happened to be one of those things, and since my son's latest food obsession just so happened to be waffles, I had become proficient at making them.

And when Daddy Bennett wasn't looking, there was a box of Eggos hidden in the back of the freezer.

Bennett emerged with Amber, smiling when Colin called out to her and depositing the little girl on the floor with him. She played shyly, wary at first, but I'd seen this before. It would be two minutes tops before she warmed up and babbled louder than he was. I suspected that if she ever managed to get past the damage done to her, she would end up bolder than Colin would ever be.

"I do love seeing a man cook," Bennett said, stepping up to kiss the back of my neck.

I chuckled. "Set it on the counter. I know I forgot."

"You always do, might wanna wait till you're not playing with batter, though," he said, slapping a perfect twin of the ring on his left hand, albeit bigger, onto the counter where the kids couldn't reach it. "And Christ, I thought living with my parents was the biggest cockblock, but no, no, no, no, it's kids. They're so much worse."

"We'll just have to wait till nap time," I said with a smile.

"Can't," he said, flopping down into a dining room chair. "I'm supposed to meet up with Isaiah and Julian."

"For your chief's surprise birthday party, right?"

"Yep, they're getting the firefighters involved. The chief is gonna shit a brick when he comes back from Guatemala with your former brother-in-law."

"I really wish you'd stop calling him that."

"If you stop wincing every time, I'll consider it."

I rolled my eyes. "Did you talk to Ethan first? That way, he's on board."

"Duh," he said as if it was the most obvious thing in the world. "And since Grant is back from meeting his husband's family, he's able to make us a bomb-ass cake."

"I can't imagine marrying into a famous family." I snorted and eyed my husband. "When you say bomb—"

"Edible glitter bomb," he said with a grin. "Chief is gonna love it."

"I really don't want to be a widower because your boss killed you," I groaned as I poured the batter into the iron.

"You worry too much. Don't worry. I'll be back for dinner."

"You're always home more when it's our week to have Colin," I said with a smile.

It was an arrangement that worked perfectly for both Bri and me. One week on, one week off, rinse and repeat. Since we lived in the same town, literally two blocks from one another, we shared holidays and birthdays. Since Keith didn't have a family of his own, it made it easy. My mother, of course, was delighted at having her family suddenly bloom in just a few years.

"Babababa," Amber piped up from the living room.

Bennett stood up so she could see him over the counter separating the kitchen from the dining and living room. "Right here, baby girl."

"BA!"

"Right on!"

"BA BA BA!"

"Hell yeah!"

"Bennett," I sighed. "Little ears."

"Er, heck yeah!"

Sometimes he really was like a big kid, and other times he was this grown man with whom I had fallen hopelessly in love. There had been arguments, including the near melt-downs we'd both had when Amber first came into the house and we didn't know what to do with her. I think our stupidest argument had been over whether to have carpeting or hardwood in the house. Bri had shown up to yell at us after my mother complained to her about how stubborn we were.

In hindsight, two grown men giving each other the cold shoulder over flooring was pretty ridiculous.

"Where are *you* going?" I asked, hooking my arm around his waist and pulling him close.

"Children," he warned though he didn't move.

"Child appropriate," I said, kissing him.

It was a routine for us, but somehow, that made it all the more wonderful. I could kiss him whenever I wanted. I could touch him whenever the mood struck me. I could always reliably trust that he would be in bed next to me unless he worked a late shift, and even then, he was a phone call away if I needed him.

No relationship was as easy and straightforward as the one we shared. Sometimes I forgot that, like when we got on one another's nerves, but nothing could beat the decades of friendship and love between us. Now it was something that was equal parts both of us and something so much more than the two combined could hope to be.

"I love you," I told him.

"I love you too," he whispered, picking his arms up to wrap around my neck.

Only to stop when an unhappy shriek was met with crying.

"I got it," he grumbled. "You're burning the waffle."

"What?" I yelped, turning to smell the burning waffle and cursing as I fumbled with the iron.

Suddenly the air was filled with the smell of burned

batter, a screaming toddler, and Bennett scolding Colin for being rude. One moment I was enjoying a sweet moment with my impossible and wonderful husband, and the next, everything had gone to hell.

Honestly? I wouldn't have it any other way.

ABOUT THE AUTHOR

Romeo Alexander lives in Michigan, USA, with his dog and two cats. As a certified night owl, coffee and a wicked sense of humor keep him going most days, as does playing with flavors in the kitchen.

As a gay man, he believes in writing about what you know whenever possible; his stories come from the heart and with a dose of humor thrown in. His characters grapple with relationships, emotions, and real-world issues, good and bad, using their hearts as a guiding compass to get their all-important happy ever after.

Connect with Romeo on Social Media
www.romeoalexander.com
alex@booksunitepeople.com